MARTIN MACINTYRE is an accla[...]
worked across these genres fo[...]
works of fiction and three colle[...]
In 2003 his short-stories in Gaelic and English, [...] (*[...]tance*), won The Saltire Society First Book Award. His novels *Gymnippers Diciadain (Wednesday Gymnippers)* and *An Latha As Fhaide (The Longest Day)* were in contention for their Book of The Year awards in 2005 and 2008, while his second story collection *Cala Bendita 's a Bheannachdan (Cala Bendita and its Blessings)* was shortlisted for both The Donald Meek Award and The Saltire Literary Book of The Year in 2014. In 2018 his novel *Samhradh '78 (The Summer of '78)* was long-listed for the Saltire Fiction Book of the Year and *Ath-Aithne* was published in French as *Un passe-temps pour l'été (A Summer Past-time)* – a first for Gaelic fiction!

Martin has written two novels for younger people *Tuath Air A Bhealach* and *'A' Challaig Seo Challò'* the latter of which one The Donald Meek Award in 2013.

Martin's bilingual poetry collection *Dannsam Led Fhaileas / Let Me Dance With Your Shadow* was published in 2006 and in 2007 he was crowned 'Bàrd' by An Comunn Gàidhealach. Since 2010 Martin has been an Edinburgh 'Shore Poet' and was a Poetry Ambassador at The Scottish Poetry Library 2021–23.

A new collection of poems – *A' Ruith Eadar Dà Dhràgon / Running Between Two Dragons* – inspired by Catalonia and Wales, which won The Gaelic Literature Award 2021 for an unpublished manuscript, was published in April 2024 by Francis Boutle Publications in Gaelic, Catalan, Welsh and English – a first for Scottish poetry.

Another new collection, *Poems, Chiefly in The English Dialect* was published in July 2024 by Drunk Muse Press and launched at the Belladrum Music Festival.

Martin has been a guest at Stanza and The Edinburgh International Book Festival. He appeared at Scotland Week in New York, IFOA Toronto and was a regular contributor to The Ullapool Book Festival. He often performs at The Scottish International Storytelling Festival.

Martin was Co-ordinator of the major digitisation sound archives' project, *Tobar an Dualchais / Kist o Riches*, from 1998 to 2003 and founded Edinburgh's Gaelic community social and Arts' club, Bothan, also in 2003. He was The University of Edinburgh's first Gaelic Writer in Residence 2022–24. Martin is currently completing a collection of *Celtic Myths* for children which will be translated into many languages and published by Dorling Kindersley (DK).

A Summer Like No Other

MARTIN MACINTYRE

Luath Press Limited
EDINBURGH
www.luath.co.uk

First published 2018 in Gaelic as *Samradh '78*
First published 2025 in English

ISBN: 978-1-80425-174-4

The author's right to be identified as author of this book under the Copyright, Designs and Patents Act 1988 has been asserted.

FSC® C018072
MIX
Paper | Supporting responsible forestry

Printed and bound by
Clays Ltd., Bungay

Typeset in 11 point Sabon by
Main Point Books, Edinburgh

© Martin MacIntyre, 2025

*In honour of my uncle Dr Fergus Byrne
and his late wife, my aunt, Shonna Byrne*

Chapter 1

Bha uair ann reimhid ma-thà... once, a long time ago, when the Gàidhealtachd of Scotland and Ireland were one, there was a band of warriors, the Fèinn, who were duty-bound to protect its lands and shores from any possible invaders. Among them was a young man by the name of Oisean, Oisean mac Fhinn ac Cumhail – Oisean the son of Finn MacCool.

THE JOURNEY FROM Greenock to Glasgow Central, then north from Queen Street, was all too familiar though I'd never travelled it alone. The West Highland Line had been the usual route to Oban, twice, sometimes three times a year until my father purchased our first modest family car near the end of primary school. This wasn't an advancement I announced with pride to my wealthier classmates. It would have been like saying, guess what lads we've finally decided to switch from porridge to Rice Krispies. 'Wow, really Col!?'

God's own island, specifically the crofting township of Eoligarry, had looked forward to *Màiri Iagain Iain Mhòir's*[1] return home with her brood since first she showed off her new baby, James, in the summer of 1955. I followed in '58 and then my twin sisters, Celia and Flora, a year into the swinging decade.

My dad, Tom (or Tam) Quinn was also made most welcome, but a bus-driver's limited holidays couldn't always mean Barra. 'Blackpool, Mary? Whit aboot Scarborough this year, doll?'

---
[1] Mary, daughter of Big John

For Mum, time with her parents and sisters was crucial – and demanded. She couldn't really see why anyone would choose to go elsewhere and pay good money for the privilege. Respectful daughter did though press notes into her mother's fists on departure – '*Dìreach son a' bhìdh, a ghràidh.*'[1,2] None of us had ever ventured across the sound to Uist, nor indeed to any of the other Western Isles.

This year the *Claymore* would call briefly at Colonsay before heading further into the Minch, four hours west, to Castlebay – Barra's 'bustling' capital. For the first time ever, I would not disembark here but sail a further two hours to a more languid Lochboisedale.

The thought of spending a fortnight in South Uist with my mum's brother did not thrill me. It just wasn't the right time, I protested – for him or me. Ruairidh was a nice enough fellow and always an interested uncle and generous with birthdays. He was also a stickler for application. Dr R J Gillies swore by hours spent sitting on one's *tòn*[3] and the by-product. His 'kind' suggestion I join him for the second half of his month's locum on the island was as good as an order in his younger sister's view.

'*Dè eile a tha thu a' dol a dhèanamh?*'[4] her musical North Barra Gaelic demanded. 'Certainly no exams stopping you for now, Colin, or...'

'A job?' I enquired faux-cheerily. This sentence was one I'd completed often in the preceding few weeks, since opting not to take second-year finals. Forced good humour once again stopped my yelling in her wan face.

She was of course correct. The 'for now' indicated that while, by mutual consent, my advisor of studies – Big Ron – and I had lost hope of summer success, given some harsh-reality, Ruairidh Gillies-style effort, I might still try in

---

2 Just for the shopping, my dear
3 backside
4 What else are you going to do?

August. Passes in Psychology, English Literature and Modern European History would offer a scraped place in Junior Honours? 'We'll see Mum,' I said.

Academic Year 1977/78 was a most sociable one at Glasgow Uni and sudden release from formal assessment had helped boost its potential greatly. With a full grant, a large, shared flat in the West End and cheapish tastes in food, alcohol and clothes, there was no desperation. As one of less than ten percent of Scottish twenty-year-olds in Higher Education – Father Cairns liked to remind us – I was well off, except that now I was on the verge of failure. So why wasn't I scared?

Ruairidh had enjoyed none of these luxuries in the St Andrews of the '30s and '40s and had 'just got on with it'. His questions would be uncomfortable. My parents, neither of whom stayed on beyond fifteen, (nor James his sixteenth birthday), had pinned considerable academic hopes on their second child. 'Our Colin might well try Law in the end, though he's still considering teaching.' Really? The Colin Quinn I knew had no wish to lose hours of real life mugging the minutiae of dead tomes or babysitting bored kids with writing for which he felt scant passion.

'And it's not' – my mother's other refrain – 'that you wouldn't make a good doctor, if that's what you chose to do.'

Like her husband Ruairidh, Aunt Emily – an elegant, refined lass from Perth, had chosen and indeed succeeded in medicine; her painful death eighteen months previously being the cruellest of Christmas presents.

This then was my uncle's first locum on the island since his darling's grave was closed. Until that point, over a period of some twenty-six years, he'd become a regular feature on the visiting professional Gael landscape; quite a small, discreet group of men. His usual routine entailed a week at home in Barra – with and at the family – then a further week's 'holiday' on Uist relieving one of the local GPs; he and Dr Marr had been housemen together in Dumfries. Eric Adams, a tough Yorkshire lad, would remain on-call for all surgical emergencies. Ruairidh could cope with the rest, including most childbirth scenarios, and crucially he also had anaesthetic skills.

This year, having wrested himself from partnership in Duns, he could give the fine chaps a whole month; they would each get their first proper holiday in fifteen years. And my proposed role? To walk, fish, chat and presumably not quaff too much if Ruairidh was on-call round the clock.

So, I agreed to go; an initial commitment of a week that could be extended if all was cordial.

My 'passage' proved uneventful – the extra time on board the vessel a challenge to fill, and no compelling book to help achieve this. The sea was its usual grey, rolling, choppy self, but not nearly as turbulent as I had experienced it. A greasy pie and beans slid down in The Sound of Mull and behaved themselves thereafter. If any of those travelling knew me, none took the additional step of saying hello.

There was, though, a table of drunks in the bar – still high from the previous day's cattle-sale – who were continuously hassling a guitar duo who denied knowledge of any popular Gaelic numbers. The young singer had a sweet voice and his rendition of 'Yesterday' was well-practised and supported with care by his friend. The boys soon tired of the facile jibes, returned their instruments to the luggage rack and donned duffle coats to escape outside. I passed them on deck near Mingulay – a first romantic visit there was still pending since delighted Catrìona MacNeil raved about the deserted island's cliffs, between kisses, on my seventeenth birthday.

Uncle Ruairidh was on Lochboisedale pier as promised and undaunted by the hour – around 2.00am. 'Almost had to send a stand-in,' he joked, 'but wee Anna cracked on and now has her fifth boy to carefully place in front of the TV to shout for Scotland.'

'We're on the march with Ally's army!' – another song the ferry pair refused to play – had been recorded weeks previously by comedian Andy Cameron. He gallusly assured us that football manager, Ally MacLeod, would lead Scotland to World Cup victory in Argentina. Our opening game, against Peru, was still over a week away.

'*Do bheatha dhan dùthaich!*'[5] My uncle's more formal greeting, as he opened the neat but adequate boot of his silver MG. 'A new acquisition, Colin,' he added, half apologetically. 'Always fancied one, but with a family it was never a practical consideration. Suspension's much better than you'd think – it can handle the worst of the roads here. I see the hair's not got any shorter!' he then said with a funny little smile, which I answered by hooking a few strands behind my ears. 'Just like a wee lassie', my dad would grunt on a bad day. 'Anyway,' said Ruairidh, 'how's everyone?'

We exchanged family news as he drove, firstly to Daliburgh Cross, then right onto the main island artery. Both my older cousins were now down south I learned: Claire had recently moved – 'with our first precious grandchild' – to London for her husband's job. Much of Ruairidh's 'our' must still have belonged to Aunt Emily, but he made no mention of his late wife that night and nor did I.

'Bill has sorted me a rather interesting house this year, Colin. In Eòrasdail. Bit further from Cnoc Fraoich Surgery but nothing is too far away in this machine.' I again stated my ignorance of South Uist, much as I had when he phoned to confirm travel plans.

'Yes, yes,' he said, 'I'd only been here once myself before starting locums all those years ago. Now I know the place, the South End anyway, like the back of my hand – probably better than I know Barra these days. Did you ever visit Eòrasdail in Vatersay?'

---

5 Welcome to the land/country!

'Nope,' I admitted.

'A lovely spot, Colin. I was at a wedding there once, all ghosts now. Look at that sky, there is not a star hasn't come out for you, lad.' He was right and The Northern Cross dazzled more on Uist's vast celestial canvas than I'd ever previously seen it.

An island GP, Ruairidh went on to explain – with many older people still without cars – was expected to make many more home visits than their mainland counterparts, even in a semi-rural Borders towns like Duns. These houses were often located at a distance from the main road and could be challenging to find, especially in the dark. Overall, though, the *Uibhistich*[6] were a stoic lot, and would only call out a doctor when absolutely necessary – too often a tad too late.

'And what are you up to, Colin?' he enquired. 'General Arts degree, is it? Then what?'

'Not sure.'

"*N d'rinn thu sgath Gàidhlig?*"[7] he probed. I shook my head. 'Understand it all, just not used to speaking it that much and I couldn't take it at school.'

'No, the Jesuits don't indulge such leanings; all proud Roman and erotic Greek ones with them!' My uncle changed down gear and then roared past a pensive van in a passing-place with a vantage point over the Atlantic that promised daytime delights.

'Got some Latin, though?'

'An O' Level, then...'

'It might be worth your meeting John Boyd. He's an old Fort Augustus pal – though his dad was a *Barrach*[8], from Bruairnis! The Celtic lot are always on the lookout for students that are a bit different. Seonaidh's now Departmental

---

6 Uist folk

7 Done any Gaelic?

8 Someone from Barra

Head. We've been corresponding about my recording work, with which you are very welcome to help. This island boasts the very finest traditional singers!'

I looked at my uncle as we turned west into the village of Eòrasdail. What practical assistance could I possibly offer in the field of folklore research? Under pressure, I would just about manage to render our genealogies back a couple of generations, but beyond that you might as well plonk me on a Chopper Bike and point me down a steep brae.

My uncle, though, was on a roll. 'And, do you know, Colin, there are still some truly remarkable storytellers here, though you always have to coax them.'

'Really Ruairidh?' I said, failing to stifle a yawn. 'That's great.'

The cloud-filled sky was bat-dark but I could see, by the lights of the little sports car, that our accommodation, Taigh Eòrasdail, was a fair size: an old square, two-storey, farmhouse at the end of the village. Ruairidh explained it had been the manager's family home until 1909, when many of Lady Cathcart's remaining farms or tacks were divided into crofts. Some of these original dwellings fell into ruin or were subsequently demolished – the stone transferred to more modern homes. This one had survived but was in need of modernisation.

My downstairs sleeping-quarters was more like the lounge in our West End flat, with its high-ceiling and coving, and far more spacious than my cramped brown bedroom in Greenock. It had a not altogether unpleasant mustiness about it, with brown-paper lined drawers and a camphor-wafting solid wardrobe. Both windows pulled up easily and could be secured on rusty clips. The firm double bed was pre-warmed with bricks wrapped in a worsted blanket and deliciously cosy. Four digestives with cheese and a glass of milk sat on a small bedside table. These nibbles invited me to partake without worrying about tooth-brushing, but guilt or habit, and a need to further empty my bladder, had me groping the walls around 4.00am.

The bathroom was located to the rear of the house in a corrugated-iron roofed porch. It had been added, I reckoned, within the previous twenty years, at a point, perhaps, when it was no longer convenient to empty boiled pans into a tub in front of the range, or squat to the inquisitive lowing of much less constipated cows in the byre.

That night, the light switch – neither fixed at shoulder height nor as an easily found cord – frustrated and eluded me. A brief crack in the sky let rays through the curtain-less frosted glass and beyond towards the cistern. I sat quickly for safety and an ice-bolt shot up my spine.

The deep ceramic sink offered only one built-in tap, but I could now see the thin hot-water pipe emerging from a small tank suspended above the basin. That luxury could wait until later in the morning. The cold tap was stiff, growled and burped for a good thirty seconds before delivering peaty liquid onto lathered hands. I'd stupidly left my toothpaste in the bedroom and if Ruairidh had any use for this stuff there was none lying around. A brief washout would have to do. I was merrily gurgling, when I felt the fuzzy sensation on my chilly toes – the tickle of whiskers advancing in the direction of my bony ankle, the accompanying scratchy sound on the slippery lino. My scream, Ruairidh confirmed at breakfast, could be heard in the hills of Harris.

There would definitely be mice, he said, large ones and rats in old farmhouses like these. Entry points were plentiful. He would throw down some gin-traps – lace them with that quality Wensleydale from the deli in Melrose. This, though, would mean an end to bare-footed roaming or sleepwalking, else I'd be returning home not just a little nibbled but maimed in half my lower leg.

The clang of cutlery had woken me. Through still-closed eyes, I pictured teaspoons being placed just so on saucers beside white china cups, then plain-loaf toast transferred onto a larger plate and centred on the round table. These images – of definite Greenock and Barra origin – were juicily brought to my Uist bedroom by the sizzling of bacon and fresh eggs.

A lightly sung Gaelic refrain confirmed my hunch that these culinary skills were not Ruairidh's – any male's in fact.

'You got up, then!' accused a woman, perhaps in her fifties, wearing an apron-covered, plain cotton top and brown skirt. She seemed a wiry, energetic, pleasant-smiling sort.

'Yes!' I admitted. I had done more than that. I'd got up and thrown some clothes on.

'I'm Ealasaid,' her reply, as she wiped her right hand on her pinny, before extending it formally. 'Colin, or Cailean *'n e?*'[9]
'Yea,*'s e.*'[10] I shook her hand. What now? A kiss on each cheek? A bear hug? Perhaps not.

'Uncle's long gone,' Ealasaid enthused. 'Up with the lark to visit the sick and the infirm. 'Eat!' she commanded, flipping four slices of bacon and two fried eggs onto my daisy-trimmed plate.

Anna, who'd 'cracked on' so well, had begun bleeding at 5.30am; just after I'd fallen asleep, cocooned in my starched sheets and scratchy blanket, safe from further rodent intrusion.

Ealasaid Iain Alasdair[11] (her full patronymic) was accustomed to feeding men. 'Plenty brothers I have and always hungry, the lot of them!' For the last three years or so, she'd also been employed on an official basis to look after Dr Marr and Mr Adam's locums – especially the single ones. Being on-call for a week, or weeks on end, required sustenance; Ealasaid knew lots about sustenance.

---

9 is it?
10 it is
11 Elizabeth the daughter of John of Alasdair

'They're all working – mostly fishing,' she explained. 'Back at the prawns this last two month. Got them over and done with first, then I drove down here. Years and years since I was visiting in this house – could do with some maintenance mind you, inside and out. The Old Post Office was much more suitable. And what work will you do here now, *a Chailein*[12]?'

There it was, another reference to my assumed idle state; abject too, it seemed, in this woman's presence, observing and savouring her industry; imagining her well-fed men out in small bouncy boats on the Atlantic. Learning of my uncle's return to duty mere hours after he had got to bed also induced panic. So, what was I going to do *now* in South Uist *and* in the future? Ealasaid's straight talking, and the traditional, practical, feel of Taigh Eòrasdail, demanded I address this issue immediately. People worked hard here – very hard. What 'work' then was Colin or Cailean Quinn going to do?

'Don't know,' I answered. 'Not sure yet. I'll try and help somehow, I could...'

The door opened and Ruairidh Gillies entered, Gladstone bag in hand, a russet Winston-knot half-visible at his flecked collar above the shallow V of his bottle-green sweater.

'This boy's here to work!' Ealasaid informed him. 'But first of all, your breakfast. And Anna's fine, is she?'

Ruairidh's assurance about the woman's haemorrhage was helpful and discreet. Ealasaid was a cousin of Anna's husband's and the first to hear of her complication – being so closely tied to the doctors. It was she who had convinced the tired mum to phone immediately and not leave a thing like blood-loss a minute longer. Her kind heart and Mini Clubman would head straight over there after galley-duties were completed in Eòrasdail.

Perhaps a little ahead of its time, there was no longer a

---
[12] 'Colin,' when being addressed.

scheduled Saturday surgery in Lochboisedale – a stipulation of Bill Marr's when he arrived from Broughty Ferry in 1970.

'Nonsense!' he'd rebuffed those who thought such a service mandatory. 'If they are genuinely ill, they'll soon find us and us them.' Mr Adams agreed.

By way of compensation, Cnoc Fraoich Medical Centre was happy to see patients until 7.00pm on a Friday evening. Ruairidh, who'd had a busier than normal week and who had worked every second Saturday morning of his post-graduate life, could have seen that late clinic far enough.

Consulting, he said, had commenced with the usual round of coughs, sniffles and sore throats, but then a woman in her early sixties appeared. Her pallor was of chalk, the only hue on her hands the dirty yellow of nicotine. She sat flanked by two younger females – daughters, he presumed – whom she banned from entering the room with her.

My uncle didn't divulge any clinical details, but I inferred from his head shaking and our early return visit that what he'd found had concerned him.

'What else are you going to do all day long, Colin, if you don't come round the houses with me?' his swift reply to my earlier enquiry. 'You'll enjoy it and so will I. This soul hadn't seen a doctor in thirty years. Not once. Not even a Blood Pressure. Dear, dear. I wish she had.'

Perhaps if Ruairidh had spent a month in Uist a few years back this might have happened. People, I soon discovered, would reveal things to new doctors and new priests and new nephews that they had stored up unexplored for months or years.

The patient lived two villages south, down a narrow road very near the sea but the little sports car coped admirably. Hers was a drab pre-war croft-house, whose walls and roof needed significant attention. Perhaps as she had been flanked the previous evening in Cnoc Fraoich, two modern homes sat either side of the original family dwelling.

A range of rusted farm implements and one old wheel-less Hillman Imp, raised on breezeblocks, adorned the overgrown forecourt. As the brake screeched up, doors of both new houses flew open and two be-scarfed women emerged and darted across.

Since the weather was dry, I chose to stay back at the car, fending off remonstrations regarding cups of tea or a little something to eat that would be 'no trouble at all'. Two collies – perhaps banished to keep me company – begged, with hungry eyes and a burst leather ball, for a game. I obliged and, using the flatter side-panel of the Imp, threw and kicked their gnawed toy at a range of deft, exhilarating, angles.

Much later, when my uncle emerged, Bob and Glen leapt on him demanding he resume the fun I had so wantonly abandoned. Ruairidh petted and talked to the dogs like old friends, but he didn't play.

A smell of whisky from his breath and a prolonged silence on the way home in the teeming rain stirred a feeling of disquiet. What were the norms here? Where were the professional boundaries?

Our attendance at poor woman Norma's funeral the next week allayed some of those fears.

Chapter 2

Oisean was a likeable lad and got on well with his father, Fionn – the mighty leader of the Fèinn – and his uncle, Diarmad, their skilful swordsman. However, if these two, and many others among the band, were keen on fighting and killing, Oisean had a very different type of character.

'RIGHT, COLIN,' RUAIRIDH said the first Monday heading out to post-surgery house calls. 'The normal rules of confidentiality just aren't going to work here if you've to get to know the Uist people. Coming out with me will also give you a bit of an insight into what's involved in this job; you wouldn't be the first to switch between Arts and Medicine.' Aha, I thought, so was this Ruairidh's – or indeed his crafty little sister's – plan from the start? It would have been nice had either of them consulted me about it. Perhaps it slipped their minds.

I gave my uncle a non-committal nod, then clocked a speckled cow lift its tail and splatter an enormous steaming *cac*[13] in the middle of the village road. The heavily pregnant black one which followed, stood on it and almost skited headfirst into the ditch.

'Of course, Colin,' my uncle continued, 'I'll ask everyone's permission first, just as I do with the medical students, and if there's anything sensitive, well you can play with the dogs,' he smiled. 'Or the kids? But the people here are fine. Very little bothers them.'

A crofter in his forties had caught his leg in a bailer and was lucky not to have lost it. Fortunately, he'd suffered only

---

[13] shit

an uncomplicated fracture, which Eric Adams had set and plastered ten weeks previously. There was now some concern regarding a possible infection of the newly healed skin.

This patient might reasonably have been expected to attend the surgery – as his femur had fused – but the fact he lived over a mile up a rough track (a couple of miles north of the official practice boundary) and didn't drive made it difficult. Calum hadn't called requesting a visit; there was no phone in the house, and he would happily have sat watching his leg fester rather than bother a doctor or bother himself to prioritise his health.

Ruairidh judged the limb to be infection-free – 'a mild inflammation only' – and discharged him from the repeat-call list.

The fellow's face was particularly whiskery and his few days' growth much greyer than his thick black hair and lamb chop sideburns. A faded image of Elvis Presley in Las Vegas sat incongruously on a neatly arranged ornament-filled dresser. I doubted his mother – a rotund soul with electric eyes – was the main fan: *'Love me tender, RIP'* slanted in deliberate ink across the poster's bottom edge. 'These'll give Ealasaid something to do,' Calum said, handing over a sack with two skinned rabbits in it. 'By the way, mac Sheumais Bhig[14] and Joan very much enjoyed your *cèilidh*[15] the other night.' This was a reference to a recent visit – folkloric, not medicinal – in Kilphedar. Ruairidh had recorded two stories and a few songs with his large Uher reel-to-reel machine. I had stayed back at the house to read and think, though Ealasaid hampered much of that.

Ruairidh agreed. Iain and Joan MacDonald were very nice people indeed. 'Iain was saying his father was full of stories and that he remembers only a fraction of them. I thought he was very good. Is that man 85 yet, Calum?'

---

14 The son of Small James
15 social visit

'Soon will be, Doctor; the day Holland thrashes Scotland. Not a patch on big brother though.'

'Sorry?'

'Alasdair.'

'His big brother, you said?'

'Yes, by age.' Our reluctant patient was now enjoying showing off his inside knowledge. 'Alasdair's now quite a bit shorter than Iain, but sharp as a tack.'

'*Seadh*,'[16] Ruairidh checked. 'Alasdair Sheumais Bhig, is it?'

'Alasdair **mac** Sheumais Bhig is what we call him.'

'And where does he stay?' I could see my uncle was excited – like a little boy at the prospect of a treat.

'You'll have heard of Fionn MacCumhail?' the man continued, ignoring Ruairidh's directness. 'He's got a good few of those stories they say. Seumas Beag, his father, had them all and fine ghost stories. Frighten the life out of you, they would!' To this, he added a large chesty laugh.

'So is Alasdair in Kilphedar too, Calum?' Ruairidh pushed. 'Colin and I could just call in – ask after his health.'

'You could,' he replied with a knowing nod. 'But you won't get near him. Nor will he tell you a single thing. And he doesn't speak to his brother, so don't bother trying Iain. If Ealasaid gets these rabbits cooked tonight, they'll feed the both of you over the weekend.'

With that, Calum retreated to raise his weak leg and listen to the news. There was no TV set in evidence or a curtain in the living-area behind which one could be resting nor had I noticed an aerial bound to the chimney. Newspapers galore though – the house was full of them with a sturdy old Bakelite wireless strategically placed in the window.

'What do you know about Finn McCool, Colin?' Ruairidh asked, as we drove from the rocky gravel section back onto the tarred, still narrow, road through the village. The curved concrete

---

16 Uh-huh

shelter to our right was missing its Virgin Mary, but contained flowers, candlesticks and a white prayer book. Ruairidh saw me peering. 'A wild northerly must be due,' he said, 'Or else Our Lady's gone *cèilidh*-ing. Do you still willingly go to Mass, Colin?'

I had accompanied my uncle to St Mary's in Bornish the day before and would be in Garrynamonie for the chalk-white woman's requiem, but the answer was no. 'Anyway,' he said, moving on. 'Fionn MacCumhail, or Finn McCool, was a legendary Celtic warrior, both here and in Ireland. He and his troop, the *Fèinn* or the *Fiantaichean* got themselves into lots of interesting scrapes against the *Lochlannaich* – the Vikings. And of course, Fionn was the leader of the gang – bit like Gary Glitter, but in a more medieval macho way.'

I laughed. That singer was a fat joke. I'd never liked glam-rock and was glad his star had lost much of its brash lustre. At the time, bands like Queen and the mighty Led Zeppelin were still my thing; 'Whole Lotta Love' had been the *Top of the Pops* theme tune for years.

'Mum never mentioned Mr McCool,' I said. 'She's a good storyteller in her own way – family tragedies and all that.'

'*Tha i sin!*'[17] her older brother agreed. 'Lots of these Fingalian legends were gone in Barra, even in our time! Màiri did well though speaking Gaelic to you four in Greenock. You should use it more.' He glanced across – for quite some time, I felt, for someone driving on a narrow road. I met his stare then looked away. 'I didn't even consider it, Colin, when the girls were small. Claire's keen, but as a new mum in England it won't...'

'Be easy,' I supplied. 'Or for us – you – to get anything Fingalian from Iain *mac* Sheumais Bhig's big brother.'

'We'll see about that,' he answered. 'But first we've got to find him.'

We were in the heart of the middle district and after a third

---

[17] Sure is!

cattlegrid my uncle suddenly pulled up at a well-maintained, white-washed, house with a perfectly built peat-stack at its west-side and equally orderly chickens beyond. Not for the first time since I'd arrived, did I witness Ruairidh's use of the art of his healing craft.

He started with a good warm chat about family – bit of teasing of the woman of the house about her having retained her good looks, whatever was her secret! Interest was then expressed and sustained on aspects of crofting: the animals in particular, what were they now sowing for them on the machair? Was silage going to help matters or be a hassle and how would that then affect feeding costs?

Husband and wife sat there placidly – *daoine uasal*[18] – their drowned son squinting out of a square silver frame on the mantelpiece with a single un-bent Lenten palm trapped behind him. The other round wooden frames presented two beaming brides and two bashful grooms. The small woman sang at the end of the consultation – which did not include an examination, but did confirm that the new tablets were helping her sleep and dream less.

Ruairidh asked if she'd also like to try '*Cumha Sheathain*',[19] and the simple, unadorned, rendition of this elegy moved me suddenly and unexpectedly – a feeling which lingered for the rest of that day.

'And did you ever hear of an Alasdair mac Sheumais Bhig?' Ruairidh of course asked them, just at the right moment, before rising to leave.

Sure, they'd heard of old Alasdair – knew him well – and cautioned unequivocally against visiting him.

---

18 decent people
19 A Lament for Seathan, King of Ireland

Chapter 3

There was nothing that Oisean liked more than to recite his poems and sing his songs. Oisean was famous throughout the land as the bard of the Fèinn; a bard who never killed a man.

IT WAS NOW my sixth day and Uncle Ruairidh couldn't settle. There was a ten-year-old boy in South Boisedale with abdominal pain whom he'd seen twice in Cnoc Fraoich. Though the lad hadn't become significantly worse, he wasn't that much better five days later. Now he'd vomited and had a little diarrhoea: likely to be a virus – though as time went on the exclusion of something serious became crucial. Ruairidh knew several families in Uist who'd had near misses with late-diagnosed septic conditions and one who'd lost their daughter from a perforation – described by old Dr Grim as trapped wind until she collapsed.

A likely appendicitis in a child might require an Air Ambulance to Glasgow, if there were one available and it could get in through that thickening mist.

We turned abruptly south and made an impromptu visit on our way back from Uist House – the home for the elderly. Ruairidh was delighted to find the young lad up and about and with much-improved appetite and energy and obsessing, as were all the boys of his age, with Scotland's football fortunes against Peru.

'*Bheir sinn dearg dhroinneadh orra!*'[20] he pronounced in quaintly idiomatic Gaelic. 'Specially if Derek Johnstone gets a game,' he added in English, presumably for my benefit and to confirm that his Old Firm allegiance was to Rangers.

His mother was delighted by her son's renewed vigour

---

20 We'll thoroughly drub them!

and Ruairidh's obvious concern. Iseabail reckoned she would be returning to teaching the following day. She also showed awareness of Ruairidh's interest in Uist lore and mentioned some potential informants who had been missed when 'The Scottish Archive people' forayed west in the '50s and '60s. Alasdair mac Sheumais Bhig was not on her list.

'You see, *a Dhotair Ruairidh*,' she explained. 'These people were still quite young then and far too busy to sit yacking into a microphone. Is it a book you're writing, *ma-thà?*'

'Perhaps in time, Iseabail. For the moment, I'm just collecting what's still out there. I'll deposit the lot with The Archive, but I'd like a copy to remain in Uist.'

'Why never Barra?' I asked, as we neared Àsgarnais.

'Too close for comfort, Colin,' he replied, 'Nor nearly the same access. Did you see the wee fellow guzzling those scones, I hope he doesn't spew tonight from all that!'

After a while in silence, bar my uncle's slightly annoying humming, we turned towards the village of Ormacleit and followed a long, narrow road down, then up, past Clanranald's sad ruin; the decaying walls looked as if the buttercups in the field below had spray-painted their colour on them to tart them up a bit. *'Thig an dà latha air mòran, tha fhios'*[21] – Ruairidh's take on the castle's condition. 'Their best days here were short-lived anyway. Fixing this place would make a good Job Creation project if anyone were interested. There'll be two hundred in the Southern Isles working at the scheme, Colin. That's a lot of people with unemployment at twenty percent. And it's to end in December!'

Shortly after this, and having passed some industrious looking crofts, he asked me to open the gate to a field with a caravan in it, displaying equally modern damp and neglect. A complementary rust-pocked, off-grey, Bedford Van sat parked outside.

---

[21] Many experience a (negative) reversal in their fortunes.

'This isn't one for you, Colin,' he said, 'I won't take long!' He didn't and his sighing afterwards and references to the destruction wrought by alcohol in these places told enough.

'They'll promise you the moon and the stars,' he added, 'But then who feeds the kids? Especially in that midden? Over half the houses here are considered "intolerable", *a Chailein*. Inverness couldn't give a damn, and these places will bear the legacy for years to come despite the new Council's best efforts. Right, time to organise a little pleasure.'

We continued through the next village, then back to the machair and west past the church out to Rubha Àrd Mhaoile and its broch, Dùn Mhulan. 'This gave Bornish its name,' my uncle said, on reaching a stone circle full of little pink flowers, 'and that wasn't yesterday. Iron age, *a Chailein*, with no shortage of pork on the table either! I hear it's a hog-roast for the Ìochdar barbeque on Friday – if the heavens don't open again.'

We returned to the main road, past the memorial to the fallen of The Great War, and back in through the next township, Kildonan – a most active township by all appearances including the amount of newish agricultural machinery throughout. Ruairidh then began winding his way south on a rough road by the sea – a squawk of warring birds on the rocks below us – which soon became a much bumpier machair track; the sand ridges rhythmically skelping my low-lying bum, before we turned up towards the neighbouring village. On entering Milton, we passed a farm dwelling on our left not dissimilar to Taigh Eòrasdail, except that it was larger and looked permanently occupied. Ruairidh pulled up at a small house on the opposite side with a zinc roof and a neat, felt-covered, byre.

Retired postman Teàrlach Toilichte[22] appeared flattered by Ruairidh's interest and was not in the least reticent regarding his storytelling abilities. 'Well, I'd have a few, right enough, if I could remember them.'

---

22 Happy Charlie

That afternoon, he had overdue painting to do for a neighbour and would be in another's the following evening for the opening game of the tournament – his house contained a colour TV and a tolerant wife. Friday would be perfect – no plans whatsoever. Of course, Teàrlach had a phone! Ruairidh would call if anything were going to delay him. Likewise, he could be contacted there in an emergency – both Ealasaid and the hospital would be given the number.

The old postie saw us to the gate and commented on my resemblance to Uncle Ruairidh but also to another Gillies brother whom he'd seen only once in his life, sitting in the saloon of The Lochearn; in 1959.

'Yes, yes,' Ruairidh confirmed. 'Poor Eòin. He died the following summer – fell off a roof while building Easterhouse. Is that' he enquired, pointing half a mile across the field, 'Alasdair mac Sheumais Bhig's house?'

'The very one, *a Ruairidh*,' confirmed Teàrlach. 'But that snazzy wee machine won't take you there. Leave it at the end of the path or you'll never get it out! If you see a blue van…' he began, then stopped, and allowed us to return to the MG.

'Do we give it a go?' I enquired.

'Why not?' Ruairidh answered. 'I reckon it's our lucky day.'

The parking spot at the path-end was empty, but there was clear evidence of a vehicle's recent presence in the muddy verge. We left plenty of room and headed south on a rough footpath towards a tufted hillock.

Beyond the hillock was another smaller one – covered in the yellow of blooming *cuiseagan*.[23] A scraggy sheep greeted us with her toothy smile, before darting off, as if we'd fired a gun, down and out of sight. A thin line of smoke rose ahead of us from an attractive tall clay chimney pot.

This mac Sheumais Bhig's house was a meticulously and newly thatched two-roomed cottage. Immediately adjacent

---

23 tansy / ragwort

stood a similarly roofed but much smaller, hive-like, byre and behind it a felted barn – *an àth*.

The whitewash on the walls of the house wasn't this year's, though I could see that the exterior surface of the deeply set windows had been spruced more recently.

The low door had a muted brown hue but was clean, showing no flaking paint. Ruairidh knocked, and without waiting turned the handle and entered the *bodach*'s[24] dwelling. Although it was still a relatively bright day outside, Alasdair had lit one of his Tilley lamps – its glow leaking out through a sooty frame to warm the 'living room' whose stove was struggling to get going.

'Anyone in?' Ruairidh cried, as if half-expecting the old fellow to appear by magic in his empty armchair or, as his cat did, dart out from under the bench.

'One minute,' was the muffled response dispatched from behind the wallpapered partition. The door then opened, allowing the briefest of glimpses through to the old man's sleeping-quarters. A colour-tinted photograph – presumably his parents – sat centre-stage in a large wooden frame above his bed. To its immediate right hung a much darker, smaller, crucifix. In the corner I spotted – on an upended flour-chest (I reckoned) – a cruisie lamp and beside that a large enamel jug. Familiar mustiness mixed momentarily with the strong peat smell of his *rùm*.[25]

'How are you today, Doctor? he asked Ruairidh. '*Suidhibh*!' he commanded us both as he might a sheepdog. 'Sit!'

Ruairidh replied that we were in good form. 'This is my sister's son, Cailean,' he clarified and then added. 'Do you think he'd make a doctor?'

I smiled nervously. This old boy gave a penetrating stare from small sea-green eyes. A stare, I felt, that could see that

---
24 old man
25 main room

my entering this field would be far from straightforward. I half-coughed a '*Ciamar a tha sibh?*'[26]

'Thought we'd call,' Ruairidh continued for me. 'See how you were.'

'She keeps me very well. Very well indeed,' Alasdair's reply. 'You'll not want to visit too often? I'll drop one day and that'll be that! What else, at my age?'

No tea was offered. No biscuits hurried onto a plate. The two large kettles atop the Modern Mistress sat quietly, patiently. Alasdair did though open the door of his range and add more peat.

'I could have a wee listen to your chest or your heart?' Ruairidh suggested. 'Have you had your pressure taken this last while, *ma-thà?*'

'Bit late for all that now,' his lost patient's rebuttal. 'When it's all borrowed, who wants to know when it has to be given back?'

'Young Cailean was wondering,' Ruairidh then tried. Why this approach, I wasn't sure. 'If you might have any of the old stories? *Làn chinn a Ghàidhlig aige,*'[27] he then added, by way of endorsement, though we hadn't spoken a word of English since entering the house.

'Ach, well...' Alasdair began.

'Has a doctor not got more to do than harass old men?' barked a youngish, plumpish, short woman as she dashed in. 'Not even had time to get dressed properly, eh?' she scolded, and immediately advanced to Alasdair's chair, secured two loops of his button-braces and then tucked his shirt into his dungarees before pulling down his fresh-looking fawn sweater. 'Did you not finish that?' she demanded, lifting an encrusted plate off a narrow wax-clothed table and emptying what she could of the contents into a large soup bowl on the floor.

---

26 How are you?
27 He's full of Gaelic

'Sceòlan,' she hissed and a lean, black and white collie-mix, rushed in and began guzzling. 'Soup again, I'm afraid,' she then said, taking a lidded pot from a plastic bag before placing it on the stove. 'But it's hoch this time – your favourite. *Dia, Dia, bidh sibh seo gu sìorraidh a' feitheamh!*'[28] With that she thrust some more peat and sticks in through the top of the range.

All this, she did without acknowledging our presence further or including us in any way. I could feel Ruairidh's awkwardness.

'Hi,' I tried, in English, 'I'm Colin.'

'Are you really?' she answered, 'That's amazing! I've asked herself to come tonight,' she continued to Alasdair. 'Twins have got that stupid concert thing at the school. I don't want to keep you up. But I'll see you in the morning. *Seo,*' she handed him two newspapers, then turned round to face us. 'Goodbye, Doctor Ruairidh.'

My uncle rose and nudged me to do likewise. 'Thanks, Alasdair,' he said, turning back towards the old man. 'See you soon.'

'And thank you, very much, indeed, to the both of you for coming,' replied the *bodach*.

'Look after yourself, Jane,' my uncle then murmured not making eye contact with the woman. 'Give my regards to Ìomhair.'

'Dash,' he said as we walked over the hill. 'Dash, dash. How bloody addled do I have to get, Colin. Fucking Jane and Ìomhair.'

I shot a glance at him: my grimace made obvious the distaste of his expletive.

'We're all human, Colin. Jane MacDonald would do well to remember that. And of course, they've all been trying to warn me off the old boy, but I'm so bloody thick I couldn't see why.'

'She might let him speak to me,' I said.

'Why?'

---

[28] God, you'll be forever waiting!

'Because I'm not you?'

'Really? You think she took a bit of a fancy to you, do you, eh?'

This was getting weird. Why was my uncle behaving so unpleasantly?

'Hardly,' I parried. 'Just thought there might be a way through. And after all,' I grinned. 'I'm not a doctor yet.'

'Nor do you want to be,' he said, as we arrived at Taigh Eòrasdail, 'with the Jane and Ìomhair MacDonalds of this world ever poised to put the boot in! Your mother always…' my uncle began, but chose not to add any more and I respected his silence, early days.

The smell of Ealasaid's lamb stew and her warm, authoritative, smile cheered him sufficiently to throw his coat – successfully – onto the sturdy mahogany stand. This produced two verses of a plaintive song – '*An Eala Air A' Chuan*'[29] I learned later, as my interest grew.

'Heard Nan Eòghainn singing it the other day, Ealasaid. Do you know it?'

She shook her head. 'Give me another couple of lines.'

'Sorry, I can't,' Ruairidh replied. He did, though, la-la the tune.

'No, *a Dhotair*, but very nice. That woman has more songs than safety pins.'

An odd expression, I thought. Positive? Negative? Neutral? Hard to say. But certainly, Nan Eòghainn, whom my uncle hoped to visit often that summer, was over-endowed with verses – many of them waulking songs from her mother and grandmother.

The telephone croaked just as Ruairidh tossed a pinch of salt over his left shoulder; a stunt surely for Ealasaid's benefit. I'd never once seen him perform it in Duns when Aunt Emily would fold her slim, slacked, legs under the oak dining-table.

---

[29] 'The Swan on the Sea'

Ruairidh sighed and the *Ban-Uibhisteach*[30] obliged. Her retreat to the hall was swift and purposeful.

'Yes, yes,' her words. 'Of course, Doctor. Well, well, well.' We then heard the heavy clang of the large, old-fashioned, receiver being replaced.

Ealasaid didn't re-enter the dining room. Uncle Ruairidh took a first small mouthful of stew and helped himself to three of her brother's flowery machair potatoes from a deep bowl.

'Nothing serious, I take it?' he called. Silence. 'I presume it wasn't...' he began in a louder more urgent tone. The response to this was the wrenching upwards of the kitchen hatch, which I'd thought permanently seized. A modest boat-shaped ashet of cauliflower with a steaming cheese sauce was thrust through.

'Lift that, *a Chailein!*' she ordered. 'The plate's safe. It was only going to spoil.'

'No major emergency, then?' Ruairidh enquired.

'I said you'd speak to Dr Adams, when you'd finished your supper. They eat so very early in that house. Almost as bad as *mac A' Chìobair*;[31] but he went to bed at eight, then died – about thirty years ago.'

'I'm very sorry to hear that, Eric.' I heard my uncle say on the phone after tea, still dabbing at stray custard with a folded handkerchief. 'Consider it the only solution! Just you tell Bill to do whatever he has to, and no need to bother calling me.'

This rather protective, older to younger man, concern didn't quite fit my image – gleaned from Ruairidh and some unsubtle patients' comments – of the stern, infallible surgeon, Mr Eric Adams.

'Bill Marr's mother has gone doolally!' Ruairidh confirmed, when Ealasaid had left. 'She thinks Churchill wants to send her to the Somme on a bicycle.'

---

30 *Uist woman*
31 the son of The Shepherd

'Oh, dear.' I stifled a chortle. 'Easier ways to get there.'

'Indeed,' he grinned. 'You'd need to start a good twenty-five years earlier – and with another commander. However, Bill's an only child and the old woman's now in sunny Taunton. So, it looks like we're here a bit longer, Colin. I take it you're happy to stay on?'

What could I say? I knew Ruairidh was enjoying having someone else around – another male to buffer Ealasaid's best intentions and travel about the island with him! While he'd yet to admit it, I also knew that my uncle was pinning some hopes on my getting to Alasdair mac Sheumais Bhig, whether by charming his grand-niece and husband or otherwise.

If I did stay, though, I'd need to get my mother to send up some books – or else, perhaps take them to Barra? Yes, that would work. Time was passing at a much more useful pace here – hours lasting at least sixty minutes. In that context, three one-chance exams were do-able. I could succeed. Summer evenings in South Uist would provide the necessary quiet and space. My own involvement with Alasdair might end up being minimal: Jane refuses to pull up the shutters or, on my having snuck through the tiniest of gaps, the old boy begins acting his age – which was 88 – and becomes difficult or forgetful?

Ruairidh's la-la'd refrain of the swan swimming on the sea steadily pursued me later – the bard's lover gone forever, and the weather there and here miserable.

I spent the rest of that evening in my bedroom. Though early summer, a brisk wind had spurred me to light the fire, which took well. Having scanned a two-day-old *Scotsman* – full of pre-match brio and gauche tartanry – I began reading a poor, partisan, article on next year's vote on a Scottish Parliament and fell asleep. The toxic pong of newsprint, stuck with drool to my lips, soon choked me to my senses.

Ruairidh had been called out, or gone out, and had charitably left me to my dreams. He had though passed-on a copy of the local bulletin, *Am Pàipear*, in which I learned that a crowd from across the football spectrum: South End, North End, Benbecula, North Uist, had travelled to join 30,000 others at Hampden, in cheering the national squad off on their long journey to a scorching country in the grip of a '*Junta Violente Terrible!*' – as thought many commentariats at home and abroad.

According to the Uist lads, The Tartan Army would be on its best behaviour this time – in complete contrast to the thugs who ripped up Wembley last year. In the same piece it was confirmed that manager, Ally MacLeod, had no Lewis or Skye connections. Quite how this genetic glitch might affect the Scottish team's fortunes was left unstated. Were I back home in Greenock or Glasgow, World Cup fervour would have demanded I got 'involved' to some extent. But here in South Uist, having missed the early games – my uncle had refused the offer of a TV – I felt pleasantly removed from the whole matter. It might not really be happening, especially if I crumpled the back pages of the newspaper and flamed them with an easy throw. In saying that, Ruairidh and I had received invitations to two houses the following evening to watch the match.

Ealasaid Iain Alasdair had been insistent and would surely win. Tormod Mòraig, an ex-merchant seaman, two doors down, had taken a much more relaxed approach. 'I'll be here anyway. So, you can just do as you please.'

Beside an advert for a Stornoway garage and a schoolboy's request for war medals in *Am Pàipear*, I'd also noticed a forthcoming event – *Turas nam Filidh*: two Irish poets and a musician would perform with local artists in Creagorry Hotel on Tuesday.

I had never heard Gaeilge being spoken – far less recited – and was intrigued. I had though witnessed Sean Daley's superb button-box playing, one night by chance in Glasgow's Park Bar, and was keen to hear more. Ruairidh was forever extolling the virtues of the Irish and their respect and determination to retain their culture. 'If it wasn't for their efforts, few voices would have been recorded in Scotland, with the exception of Fear Cholla's work obviously.'

The moon suddenly broke through the murky sky and spilled through my back window. I had a look out, wondering too whether to have a last cup of tea and slice of toast – both from newish appliances – but the illumined fields held my attention. Their sepia wash conjured daytime vigour gone-by rather than today's empty waiting evening.

Then a thud against the loose wooden frame threw me back a few feet. 'What the...?' My first thought was of a dead body unloaded and allowed to fall under my very nose, but the preceding silence pointed against this. A gormless, toothless, goat-grin pushed my humour more than it should have.

'*Thalla!*'[32] I screeched, lifting the windowpane. The billy darted backwards then forwards again, as if mimicking a dog. It wanted me to play – perhaps throw a ball like that poor woman's collies. Unusual for Ruairidh to leave the gate open. My cool enquiries outside confirmed he hadn't. The wily beast had slipped through a barbed gap in the fence. It did though exit through the gate. I made sure of that. But who kept goats in Eòrasdail?

While 1971, the year of my thirteenth birthday, will forever be linked to Creamola Foam – mostly orange – 1978 was the summer of lemon curd. I had tasted the stuff before, but it wasn't something my mother ever purchased. Ruairidh had got it in for me on Ealasaid's recommendation. This surprised me a little, as the homemade jams at Duns had been so varied and plentiful; but, of course, while much lauded by Ruairidh, these really had been the 'preserve' of Aunt Emily.

I remember laughing at this unexpected, unintentional, pun

---

[32] Scram!

and wondered if I might slip it casually into conversation with my uncle. Given our earlier encounter with Jane MacDonald, perhaps it was better I didn't prod memories of his late wife's prowess, or risk offending him, when I was greatly enjoying lathering my toast with Co-op bought goo.

A bit strange, I thought back in the sitting room, that someone as able as Emily never returned to work after she'd had Iona, the elder of my cousins. Had running everything connected to hearth and home provided as much satisfaction as a busy hospital job? Neither daughter had chosen medicine. I wondered whether this was a consequence of their mother's decision or more from having lived with Ruairidh.

In the living room, I'd stretched up to turn on the radio for the headlines when the front porch door opened. While swivelling the aerial, I learnt that a previous despot's life had just been 'ended' in Comoros. Where exactly was this troubled country, I wondered, as muffled sounds slunk through Taigh Eòrasdail's passageway?

And what might be the impact of the other news: that Labour, and not the SNP, would now represent Hamilton in Parliament – even though the bi-election was brought forward to accommodate the World Cup? No, none of my uncle's usual brisk movements or a hummed or whistled tune were in evidence.

The programme finished, the pips played out in full signalling 11.00pm, and we were well beyond Rockall in the Shipping Forecast, before I heard a hand on the opposite side of the door. At first it failed to open – that worn brass handle could slide a little, even without the help of errant butter or lemon curd.

'Ruairidh?' I shouted, leaping to release the latch from my side. My uncle half-stumbled, half-fell, through, still in his coat and hat. Tears filled his normally lively, now-dulled, eyes.

'He was almost gone, Colin.'

'Alasdair mac Sheumais Bhig? O dear...'
'No! Stuff him and his poisoned-dwarf minder. The wee fellow. Anna Morrison's new baby.'

Ruairidh suspected a near cot death, the child being blue when his frantic father ran into Daliburgh Hospital at 9.00pm. He had fed well, exclusively on the breast – despite the pressures – and had shown no change in character all that day. Plenty wet nappies. No unusual or prolonged crying. No signs of a cold or fever. Nothing. Anna had placed him on his tummy like all his brothers and he'd slept contentedly without a fight.

'They'll have to do further tests in Glasgow's Yorkhill, look for some sort of underlying condition. Having a child die on you is horrible, *a Chailein!*' My uncle's last sentence in Gaelic: *mìchiatach*, the descriptor. 'By the grace of God, or some sixth sense, I popped in on my way home from an old dear in Kenneth Drive. Of course, Eric Adams rushed down and stayed. His wife arrived later with soup and a new shawl, a lovely gesture. The family were in total shock. You still on the lemon curd? Well done, *a laochain.*'[33]

How might it have been for Uncle Ruairidh, I considered, while tossing and turning on the pillow, to have come back to an empty house after such an incident, especially if the baby had died? To sit there where I had been sitting – a widower alone with his mortality and the bleak unyielding rhythm of the Shipping Forecast? Ruairidh needed me now, no matter what happened with the bold Jane. He might though ban me from trying.

My late dream that night contained the image of a young footballer in a blue top, ceaselessly scoring the same goal, but on turning to receive adulation from his fellow players is reminded that he is dead. '*Tha sibh mìchiatach!*'[34] he screams and tries again.

---

33 lad
34 You're all horrible!

Chapter 4

Crowds would gather to hear Oisean perform, and one day, in the middle of a particularly long lay, a beautiful woman on a white horse approached the group. She dismounted and sat among them. Oisean, who had stopped singing, went back to the start and never sang it better.

As half-expected, Ealasaid would not manage down next morning. There were still plenty eggs, she promised, in the pantry. Porridge and bread sufficed and, for the first time since arriving in South Uist, I shared a cup of coffee with my uncle.

'I was eighteen before I tasted coffee,' Ruairidh said, perhaps to say something. Our 'Continental' breakfast having been thus far in silence. 'Last day at Fort Augustus.' He filled my cup. 'Nancy had called a handful of remaining sixth formers into his study. The unfamiliar drink, I must say, I found less taxing than the Head's awkward rendering of our Christian names. "Milk, Angus? Sugar for you, eh, Roderick?" I'll have to call in on the Morrison family after morning surgery, Colin.'

I made this my cue. I would stay back at Taigh Eòrasdail, tidy up a bit, my room at least, as Ealasaid had left little else to do. Ruairidh seemed satisfied with this plan and promised to stop in if calls took him back north.

'No, *a Ruairidh*,' I insisted. 'I'm fine. Just you do what you need to do.' I heard myself now appropriating his words of reassurance to Mr Adams but was careful not to imbue them with the same tone; that would have been rude.

'*Tapadh leat*,'[35] his grateful answer. 'I'll run you to Ealasaid's later for the football, or were you thinking of Tormod's?'

'Best not offend the boss.'

'No. Indeed,' he agreed.

It was nice to have the house to myself on a bright June morning and I was soon humming reasonably melodically to a song my uncle had heard in his youth but was yet to collect in Uist. My arrival less than two weeks previously, rather than help the recording process, had coincided with – not caused, I hoped – a falling off in activity.

Ruairidh's reference to my possibly switching to medicine had managed to trick my interest – make me consider what I might need to do before applying. Physics had been straightforward enough; I just preferred History and my teacher – one of the more personable priests left at St Al's. Most said Biology was a crashable Higher, so would that not be enough when I already had Maths and Chemistry? Ruairidh's near-tragic encounter with Baby Morrison had, though, sobered this logic with a double-dose of reality.

I removed the wireless from its mantelpiece perch and, on failing to find any other socket in my bedroom, decided to swap its prongs with those of my bedside lamp. I wondered, fifteen minutes later and sweating profusely, if anyone had ever tried this before.

The signal, however, was much better and Radio 1's anodyne Dave Lee Travis was soon followed by Simon Bates's 'Our Tune' – a pilot piece he told us.

That day a wistful Charlotte had chosen Rod Stewart's classic song 'Sailing' for her 'Mike of old'. The DJ's linking of our own national, gyrating, pop star's love of football to Scotland's opening game was well done and generous.

A second successive World Cup with Scottish but no English

---

35 Thanks

representation, I mused, while working a wire-brush into the corners of the ceramic fireplace. Must hurt a bit, a lot even?

Big Andy Cameron or Wee Ally MacLeod might have crooned 'Ally's Tartan Army' to them, perhaps as a comfort? 'Reached number six in the UK charts in March,' Simon smoothly reminded us – without playing the actual song – 'And now that great track those likely lads were snuggling up to: "I Can't Stand the Rain" by Eruption.'

Charlotte had first met Mike (all names changed, the DJ assured us), when he was stationed with the Royal Navy in Portsmouth. They both knew it oughtn't to have happened and that it couldn't last, but still they had their memories and their special song. Apart from lovely Catrìona MacNeil, I had few romantic experiences to draw on then, leaving an unshared musical journey of my late-teens pretty impotent.

Listening to this twee tale, through the crackles of Hebridean VHF, midst the must, dust and stoor of yesterday, induced a pang of nostalgia. I yearned for our own home in Greenock; my wee bedroom with its 'long-haired poster posers'; Mum's voice – which I hadn't heard since the day after arriving and Dad's warm Glaswegian humour. I couldn't just jump on the boat home. No, but I could possibly go to Barra.

In the meantime, with the house tidy and the radio silenced and returned to watch over the living room, I grabbed an apple from the crystal bowl on the sideboard, fastened my coat, and jogged towards the shore.

Tormod Mòraig met me shortly after I'd re-secured the heavy blue rope around the wide fencepost. This gate separated the village proper from the common grazing – a half mile stretch of sandy arable, shared by the crofters for planting crops and vegetables. Neat, low, rows of hay billowed seawards in the unimpeded east wind like youngish dancers.

Tormod sat astride his Massey-Ferguson, just as John Wayne had trotted on the back of Rex the night before I left for Oban, and waved appreciation of my running back to open the gate. Perhaps this clearing of the path for his shuddering tractor, or his need to press on, let him continue on through, without stopping for a chat, and then with a more enthusiastic wave, shift up a gear.

I wandered on past flowing green fields and then through a vast plane of flower-rich meadow. I identified pansies, poppies and heaps of clover, but little else, though the machair contained much more in a profusion of colours. Some cows were clustered at one end, munching vigorously.

Having climbed a little rise, I found myself on a bouncy sand dune facing the foaming sea. I leapt from it, screaming 'Geronimo!' and roly-pollied onto the soft powdery sand below.

I hadn't heard a single footstep or a breath, but then, suddenly, became aware of a presence. The boots, standing directly in line with my vision, were familiar. This was the traditional footwear worn by the older crofting fraternity; they did not suit Jane MacDonald except in their stiff unyielding design.

'Playing yourself?' she accused.

'Yes,' I matched her Gaelic. 'Fancy a go?'

'Ha,' she scoffed. 'Not a wee girl anymore.'

'No,' I agreed. She wouldn't be that much older than me. 'Shame,' I offered. 'It's fun.'

Jane, I remember thinking, must have left fun behind many years before. Did a Gaelic expression exist for the carefree, careless, 'fun' I'd just experienced diving down the sand dune at the age of twenty? Both s*pòrs* and *dibhearsan* seemed a tad tame – unfree. To what extent had Jane's upbringing imposed that world-weary *drèin*[36] on her pale face? Or had she been keen enough to adopt it? There was, though, something more immediate in evidence – an agitation.

'Lost something?' I enquired.

---

36 unhappy, angry look

'What do you think?'

I held up my hands. She'd certainly lost some civility. I remained silent. Let her take the lead.

'Stupid beast's always roaming. Find her in bloody Lochmaddy next time!'

One of Jane's cows had strayed further than normal, causing a march in old men's boots – with grim face and stiff stick – north along the machair/shore boundary.

'Certainly not met anything or anybody who meets that description this last half-hour,' I tried. 'No new prints in the sand either.' She nodded assent as the vast Atlantic crashed.

'*Aithnichear bò gun fheum air a ceum cearbach,*'[37] she then voiced, naturally, like a woman three times her age. I was suddenly aware that Jane's anorak was a deep blue colour and thin, dirty and frayed. She gave a shudder – like a lost cold cow in a foreign paddock.

'Daft slut will be looking for Seumas Mòr's bull,' she then said, rather shockingly.

'Better let you go,' I said, taking a few steps back, as if she were the one in search of coarse gratification at a time when she either was or wasn't in heat.

She made another remark – which I didn't catch in full – about the frustrations of cattle. Somehow, though, this strange formulaic exchange, plus the chance to show off, had reduced the hostility in her tone. Still, I could detect little obvious warmth.

'Didn't you listen well!' I applauded, now aware of the darkness of the sky above and the imminence of heavy rain. Our waterproofs would be inadequate, though I judged Jane might continue for hours; until she was soaked to her downy skin.

'Alasdair's been expecting you, but no one ever came,' she then said in English, deliberately ambiguously; as Gaelic

---

[37] A useless cow is recognised by its awkward gait.

would not have been regarding the plurality, or otherwise, of the '*you*'. I could easily have tried to clarify but recognised that code-speak was best met with similar to make progress. Her oval eyes sought and found mine.

'Ruairidh's been busy these last few days,' I began, and was interrupted by 'Shameless beast!' and with that she took off remarkably swiftly across the strand, wielding her walking stick like a scorned Samurai warrior.

Jane MacDonald had, though, invited me – not Ruairidh – to come and record her great-uncle. Was I up to the task? Was I equipped for her and her tricks, which could be plentiful?

A first meeting that evening with her husband, Ìomhair Dubh,[38] shone some light on her prickliness.

By 8.45pm, a living room of males was gathered at Ealasaid's to watch Scotland's first game against Peru on the largest screen for miles around: a London cousin and someone else's promotion had contributed to its being in Àsgarnais.

'Daft darkies!' Ìomhair yelled at two players seen limbering up in the penalty area as the teams waited permission to start. 'Back you go to your jungle-huts!' he then added; a more specifically crass comment on an island almost devoid of trees, and from someone who'd lived, Ealasaid told me later, in one of the sparsest dwellings in Carinish. His violent father, who was 'never right from the war', had left it to rack and ruin. No one refuted Ìomhair's assertion; no one declared any more developed knowledge of Peru's ethnic mix. Of course, I didn't challenge him either, but answered a younger lad's question to confirm that, yes, like Argentina the official language of Peru was Spanish.

'But compared to Argentina,' I continued, 'The native Indian languages – their Gaelic if you like – are much more widely spoken.'

---

38 Black-haired Ivor

'Who are you calling an Indian?' was Ìomhair's take on my over-inclusiveness – trying to get to know them all a bit. 'You're the Indian, pal. We're the cowboys! Aren't I jolly well right, Mr David Coleman?' he spat in a fatuous accent at the TV – BBC Scotland's line was down, but not the one through London, yet.

Had my uncle stayed with us, Ìomhair would not have dared try this or his crude ill-informed comments on the Peruvians.

Ruairidh, however, had favoured a gouty old soldier with a heap of tales on *Mac 'ic Ailein*[39] – chief of South Uist and Benbecula until 19th-century decadence consumed the dynasty. Some in Uist believed *Calum a' Bhalaich* to be descended from these Clanranald gentry. If true, he had inherited none of their original wealth or status but still retained a huge interest in their lore.

Jo Jordan's tight-angled opening goal, after a quarter of an hour's play, eased the atmosphere around the large hot box in Ealasaid's sitting room, raising cans and glasses and the expectation of much more to come. 'He did it for us in '74 and now he's done it again!' one of her brothers shouted with glee and a burp. The excited conversation which followed, for the most part in Gaelic, led to more liberal use of first names. Thus, I learned that the boor in the corner was Ìomhair, but not until I'd told Ruairidh my sad tale in the car home, which particular Ìomhair. Also present were a John, Murdo and David – an apprentice at the Rocket Range whom Ìomhair reckoned was destined for the moon. 'Along with half those useless fools', the Scotland team (not us!) who, having gifted Peru their equaliser on half-time, had just missed a penalty; Quiroga the goalkeeper had made a most competent save from a powerless Masson slice.

'I've seen,' said John, 'Raghnall Eàirdsidh Màiri give his cat a better kick than that!'

---

39 The Son of the son of Allan

Another of Ealasaid's brothers – 'the surrogate male host' – was also there, but made little comment and didn't appear under any obligation to introduce me to the rest. It was as if he assumed I'd know people and if not, I'd just grill someone – Ruairidh perhaps or Ealasaid – at a later stage; help pass the time as I got over the 3–1 defeat.

'Poor was it, Colin?' my uncle asked as we reversed into a tight passing-place.

'Disappointing,' my view. 'Scotland played well for the most part. But they were good; too good for us and let's face it Cordoba's far closer to Peru than it is Scotland. It's like us playing at Anfield again.'

'Against this year's South American champions!' Ruairidh added, looking across. 'Ally should have taken a proper history.'

My uncle had done this with Calum a' Bhalaich and eased the man's burning pain with a small amount of codeine. Obvious interest in Mac 'ic Ailein's fate at the Battle of Sherrifmuir let the old fellow award himself a generous tot in an opaque glass. He was apparently in great form afterwards and sang a fragment of a Clann Mhuirich composition.

I still hadn't told Ruairidh about meeting Jane earlier or her invitation, to me at least, to visit Alasdair mac Sheumais Bhig. Ìomhair's performance – intended to disconcert me – had achieved the desired effect. Now was time to think how best to play this one, both with Jane and my uncle. Highland sensitivities and deference protocols were all too familiar.

'Tell me, *ma-thà*,' I asked, 'About these Fèinn stories. What are the key elements?'

That night in bed I had a disturbing dream involving a rutting bull and a grim-faced milkmaid, but Don Masson's poor penalty dominated where it hadn't while watching the game. Ìomhair was nowhere to be found – his offensive taunts and their impact dissolved well beyond the imagined duvet.

Chapter 5

When Oisean had finished his recital, those who had gathered departed, except the beautiful woman. 'I very much enjoyed your poems and your songs,' she said and Oisean thanked her. 'Can I return tomorrow and listen to some more?' 'You can return,' Oisean replied, 'Any day you wish!'

WE WERE ON 'deep-south' house calls the following day, mostly routine stuff, but last of all a thin, sad-looking, woman, who was being treated for a chest infection or an early pneumonia.

'What's the difference?' I asked my uncle.

'Well with pneumonia the infection goes deeper, Colin, materially changing the lung. Patients tend to be more unwell with it too. If it were twenty years ago, I'd have put a wee sum of Bill's kind stipend on TB. I still did the tests, but the chest x-ray looked like a straightforward acute infection.

'And it can't be both?'

'Now you're talking, lad – of course it can. You could make a sharp doctor or a detective or…'

Or what? A probability spinner? A professor of applied conjecture? Or else…?

The woman, Theresa, seemed improved physically, Ruairidh reckoned, but much less cheerful about her fate. Her conversation was limited. Also her house showed signs of recent rather than long-term neglect.

Gentle probing revealed nothing very useful. Her medical card showed little, save the births of two children – without incident – in 1974 and 1976. 'And an in-growing toenail successfully dealt with three years ago,' my uncle said, heading for the car. 'Not been seen since. That cough is a new thing. She'll be fine.'

'Who put the call in?' I asked, when we'd returned to the main road – a neat carpet of primroses smothering the hillock to our right as we headed north.

'Her mother, I think.' Ruairidh acknowledged a one-finger wave.

'So not herself or her husband?'

'No. Be exhausted, too, running after those children. Neither of them school age yet.'

'And where were they – the children?'

'Out playing, probably, or... children here...'

'Could she be depressed, Ruairidh?' I asked. 'She never once looked us in the eye. Prolonged undiagnosed baby blues?'

'Been doing some reading, Colin, have you? Well, yes, and thus less interested in her health and house?'

'And children? Who someone else currently has; her mother?'

'Possibly. We'll keep an eye on her, check back when the course of Penicillin has finished. Appearing unannounced often gives you a better picture than the pre-arranged call. Though clearly little was done about Theresa's house to honour our visit today.'

He slowed for a recalcitrant, heavy-fleeced, sheep. 'You'll be taking over my job next, *a Chailein*,' he said turning to face me. 'In need of a fank here too, it would appear. Though many have been built these last few years, and fences – like that nice one over there, look how... *oh, come on my darling off you trot!*'

Now wasn't really the time, but the approach of Jane's blue van forced the issue. She stopped, rolled down the window, flicked a cigarette to the ground, and then took forever to clear her lungs.

'Good morning,' Ruairidh eventually offered, to confirm, I judged, that her stopping beside us was intentional – we were now interacting. Ruairidh's choice of language – aimed to maintain distance – was only partly professional.

'He's a sore chest since last night,' she stated, making undefined, clear, reference to Alasdair mac Sheumais Bhig.

'Will I call in now, Jane?' Ruairidh asked generously, patients would soon be gathering in Cnoc Fraoich.

'*Cha ruig thu a-leas,*'[40] her rude retort: my uncle was forty years her senior and not a close acquaintance.

'If you are quite sure?' Ruairidh had withdrawn to professional neutrality. He revved the engine – a metaphor, I felt, for getting out of his car, in the pouring rain and giving Jane a stern talking to!

'My cures is working fine,' she expanded. Was this woman for real? 'Got him to near 90, didn't I?' Then she addressed me. 'Better leave your visit until Wednesday. He'll expect you after seven. Start with Fionn and Diarmad. Is that what you want from him? Is that what turns you on?'

With that, she turned on her own engine, lit another cigarette and rammed the gearstick into second.

Ruairidh was silent en route south. I desperately wanted to comment on Jane's behaviour but felt on shaky ground; so easy to say the wrong thing. Instead, I followed my uncle into the surgery and, once we'd thrown back a cup of tea, he asked me for the first time to join him in the consulting room. 'The best way to get a feel of this doctoring business, Colin,' he enthused, 'is to see it in action – in its various forms, wouldn't you say? Plank your behind on that chair there and try not to fall off!' I obliged; Ruairidh was not the easiest man to challenge – never had been.

'You probably will have to go to Milton,' he said flatly, as we awaited Ealasaid's ministrations later that day. 'The *bodach* will be fine with you.' I nodded understanding.

---

[40] You [familiar] don't need to bother

Our drive home had been a safe mix of general chat on crofting rhythms – what people were busy with at this time of the year: I'd never been to Barra quite so early and felt my knowledge a bit lacking.

This was a transitional period, Ruairidh explained; most spring tasks completed weeks ago – especially with the good weather. There would be, though, repairs pending and preparations to be made before sheep shearing and the bringing home of peats.

His last patient of the day was a tetchy electrician with far too much work on to have hay fever or, as Ruairidh pointed out, 'worsening asthma, Donald!' – which would soon need steroids, hospital admission even. His poor wife got hell as she reversed awkwardly out the car park; such that she screeched up the hand-break, abandoned the wheel, and made 'Mr Perfectly Well' drive them home.

'Wed-nes-day,' I repeated back in Taigh Eòrasdail – copying Jane's cadence – this got a laugh and softened somewhat Ruairidh's preoccupied manner.

After a deadly bread and butter pudding, Ealasaid made her excuses for not delaying her departure. Ruairidh demanded she go 'right now'.

'Cailean's an expert at washing dishes,' he informed her. '*Thalla*, take the rest of this wonderful dessert to Anna Morrison's family. They'll be missing Mum's cooking since she left with the baby.'

'A real Christian you are, *a Dhotair!*' she said. 'My cousin's doing his best, but his best is quite basic. But what do you expect from a youngest son?'

'I'd intended to visit the family again today,' he told me, a seabirds' dish-towel comedically perched on his left shoulder, 'But Wee Jane interrupted my good intentions.'

'She is quite aggressive,' I said, 'Like Ìomhair Dubh.'

'Yes, 'Ruairidh agreed, 'Angry people. She might actually

be worse – more dangerous – she's got a brain. Ìomhair's more predictable, I think.

'Friends of old?'

'Not that old. Jane was sixteen, about to return to Fort William for Highers. Her mother was a nice soul – now also angry, and down on the world – the odd time those of us in the world see her. He's originally from North Uist. The boys were up here for a football game. Ìomhair scored two; got his hat trick after the dance with Jane. The rest is history.'

'Oh, dear me,' I said. 'Actually, I was meaning between you and them?'

'You could say we had a brief, eh, challenging, encounter a few years back, Colin. Should all be well over by now – but with the MacDonalds, things fester and swell.'

'Then smell?'

'Do you know the word foetid?'

'So why should I go to Milton and record the old boy?' I pushed.

'Because if you don't it will be worse. And if he's as good as they say he is you'll enjoy the experience or at least learn something. She'll not bother you much. She has another child now – will be about five and her twins are ten.

'What?'

'Yip. Worth, eh, noting, *a laochain*. Anyway were you not keen on hearing these Irish poets?'

I'd forgotten all about them.

'We could pop along briefly – see what's doing. They'll easily get me at Creagorry. I'll just give Sister the number of the payphone in the public bar.' My uncle made a goofy, gummy smile.

I laughed; glad his humour was returning. This Benbecula hostelry's fame as a hard-drinking den was legendary, including Guinness Book of Records recognition for whisky sales on one splendid cattle-sale day. The 'Bar' was probably socially out of bounds for Ruairidh – a pity, his boozy nephew felt as the tame, tawny, Lounge held much less appeal.

'Actually Colin,' he chided himself, 'the concert's now in the school. The hotel was going to host it, but then, yes, some local dancers muscled in on the act so...'

'So?'

'Let's visit *Bean Lawrence*.'[41]

We abandoned the dishes and jumped in the car. 'One of her daughters,' Ruairidh said – as a large white swan washed its wings in Loch Bì – 'lives in another village, Greenwich Village in New York. And the mother's first name is... for goodness' sake... totally addled. It's horrible getting old, and being a widower. Though this poor woman – Mòrag, that's it! – knows all about that.'

Mòrag, now in her seventies, had lost her husband soon after giving birth to their fifth child and had soldiered on regardless. Her second oldest spent her first month's pay having the phone installed in her mother's zinc-roofed porch. Little did she realise that within a few years they'd be chatting together on Sunday evenings across the Atlantic. If she had, she might have got it put in the warmer living room.

My uncle's assertion that, no, he hadn't brought 'that machine' with him, and nor could he stay for tea, helped Mòrag reward us with a simply beautiful rendition of '*Fàgail Bhornais*'[42] – the bard's plaintive reflection on his friend reaching the cruel forests of Canada.

'I had a great *cèilidh* with her last time,' Ruairidh said, as we drove to the school. 'Song after song after song. She seemed less bright tonight. With this 'clientele' you've got to strike NOW, while the iron's white-hot. "*Ge b' e nach gabh nuair a gheibh, chan fhaigh nuair as àill!*"[43] Alasdair

---

[41] Lawrence's wife
[42] 'Leaving Bornish'
[43] He who doesn't take his chance when he has it won't get it later when he desires it

mac Sheumais Bhig might not be here next week never mind next year. I wonder if many will be at your thing, tonight, Colin. Look though, cars here already.' There were a good few, and a half-full hall of mostly women.

The two Irish poets contrasted in looks and delivery. One was a young, flamboyant, blond, long-haired guy – looked Australian – who addressed us mostly in English and whose poetry broached contemporary themes: *Na Triblóid*[44] in Belfast; the modern emigrant meeting the culture-seeking tourist and a recent night of passion with an open-ended denouement.

The other man was perhaps twenty years older with bushy grey hair and a weather-painted complexion. He would not have stood out from the crowd at all, had any males of his vintage chosen to attend.

The Donegal bard was buttoned into a tight three-piece suit, an extra one perhaps narrowing the gap between his lips. Were it not for the Xeroxed booklet, with all poems given also in translation, I wouldn't have followed a thing. 'Himself' used only Irish.

Despite their difference in approach and the immediate accessibility of the younger man, I'd find myself re-reading Tomás O' Leary's deeper, existential, work as I sat patiently at the breakfast table waiting for Ruairidh to join me – another aspect of the ageing process, he assured me, in addition to his morning prayers.

Sean, the melodeon player was truly exuberant and very funny with it. His close accompaniment of the young Uist dancers added verve to their well-practised routine.

Towards the end of the event the MC, a city teacher home on holiday, asked one of South Uist's own poets if he might give a taste of his work.

Iain Nill Dhòmhnaill's verses were not included in the booklet, but beautifully rhythmical images reverberated in

---

44 The Troubles

my mind for days after. Further enquiry confirmed that his second and longer piece was one he started mid-ww2 but did not complete until his return from France's 'hell of madness.' By all accounts, Iain narrowly missed winning the Bardic Crown at the 1950 National Mòd and never tried again.

It was during the long applause and gestured cajoling of a stout woman to end the night with a song, that I spotted Ìomhair standing at the back. Could he perhaps be a closet poetry fan on the cusp of coming out? Unlikely, but someone had asked him to give the bard a lift home as they lived in neighbouring villages. While Ìomhair Dubh knew plenty of people in Ìochdar he had continued to Creagorry Hotel and picked a fight there with a barman who refused him a 'double'.

'Not with the car, Ivor!' the brave young chap asserted.

'I'll leave the fuckin car,' he had blurted, as one of the nurses' husbands sipped his pint. 'And how will you and Iain Nìll Dhòmhnaill get home, then?' the lad asked him, but the *peasan*[45] had slammed the door shut. 'Time to grow up and be a proper husband and father!' someone else called, in a voice that the enraged, 'improper', Ìomhair could never have heard.

'You're back at the *bodach's* on Wednesday,' he accused, walking past me in the school hall, the stench of whisky revolting on a young man's breath.

'That's right,' I said.

'We'll miss your know-all points of information at the game. What's the other language of Iran? The one the plebs use?' Ìomhair's cheeks bloated at the pleasure of this phrase.

'Their main language being?' I asked.

'Lewis Gaelic!' he spat, saving me the affront of failing to find a quick riposte if he'd said Iranian. A rush of cold sweat ran down my back.

---

45 pest

What language did they speak there? Persian? Or was that the Iraqis? Baghdad – Persia, yes? I certainly had lots to learn and how best to deal with Ìomhair MacDonald wasn't high on the agenda.

'Enjoy the match,' I offered with a smile. So would I, I hoped, but not where Ìomhair would be – Ealasaid's house again? If so, it seemed a little strange not to get a second invite, any possible reasons?

I'd ask Tormod Mòraig if I could watch it there. The visit to Alasdair mac Sheumais Bhig would just have to be postponed to another time. There was no way round it.

My uncle was not at all impressed. Nor did he put the kettle on on our return to the house. Alasdair was an old man; he'd have made some preparation for my visit. 'Yes, Ruairidh,' I repeated, 'but the World Cup happens once every four years. When will Scotland next qualify?'

'Time people were sleeping,' his forced diplomatic reply. 'Bloody football!' I then heard as he banged his bedroom door shut.

Chapter 6

So, the beautiful woman did return, day after day, and her joy at Oisean's words and music was plain for all to see. And every time the crowd dispersed; she stayed behind to spend longer with this gentle bard.

BREAKFAST NEXT MORNING was a checklist – Ealasaid's inventory of those in attendance at the school the night before.

'And you didn't see Effie and Dùghall, Doctor?'

'*Chan fhaca.*'[46]

'They were there, *ma-thà*. She has a limp on the left – you'd hardly notice it if you weren't looking for it. Bad, bad arthritis all the way through her. The mother was a cripple in the end.'

'I'd have to confess...' Ruairidh began to confess.

'And Seòras and Eilidh were there; at that?'

'In the flesh, Ealasaid.'

'Always so skinny, he was, but what an awful weight that's gone on him these last two years. He doesn't suit being a fatty.'

'They were just a few rows behind us. Seòras smiled over in recognition.'

'Yes, he would do that, all right. He's a good smiler, Seòras. There's some that never smile, even when they're ecstatic.' I laughed aloud, then apologised immediately.

'Glad you're enjoying yourself, Colin,' she shouted. 'Getting out and about and taking that old uncle with you. A man can't work all the time, you know.'

---

[46] Nope

Ruairidh grunted. Would he be happy, I wondered, to be described, by Ealasaid, as my old uncle? Why, though, was he doing this locum at this stage in his career? Surely, he could have afforded just to come to Uist and work on the folklore without the considerable burden of being the only on-call GP in town.

'Colin's going to be busy with some of my other work too, Ealasaid,' Ruairidh then said with obvious pride.

'The song gathering?'

'Stories too.'

'All fine if you've got the time! You're lucky, *a Chailein*. Though to be honest, I wouldn't have the patience to sit there listening or recording or whatever it is you do. Who are you after now?'

'Alasdair mac Sheumais Bhig,' Ruairidh confirmed triumphantly.

'*Dia gam shàbhaladh!*[47] Now, that is wasting your time. He did hear a lot, I'm sure, out there in the back of beyond, but she's got him so well protected he's weird.'

I wanted to laugh again. 'Ecstatic', 'weird' – these words were injected with an indefinable hilarity in Ealasaid's mouth; but I didn't.

'An old man now, too. What a shame for people to be harassing him.'

She was beginning to sound a bit Jane-like. Were Ealasaid and the poisoned-dwarf chimney somehow in cahoots against folklore collection? Or, more likely, were they related?

'So, I'm not the only one?' Ruairidh enquired, squaring knife and fork before moving his plate to one side.

'No, no!' Ealasaid fully understood what Ruairidh was saying. 'Not at all. There's plenty people gets sent packing from that house!'

'Anyway,' he said, 'Colin's planning to head over there

---

[47] God save me!

tonight,' and then, as my parents might do – like too many of an older generation in my family – he added, 'At Jane's invitation.'

'Watch that one, boy! She's trouble,' Ealasaid proclaimed, looking immediately at Ruairidh before clearly, but non-verbally, completing her sentence: Your uncle knows all about that!

'As I said last night, Ruairidh,' I asserted. This was my chance. 'I can't go to Milton tonight. The Iran match is on...'

'Who ever are they playing?' Ealasaid was on an emotional roll.

'Scotland?'

'Yes, yes, what am I saying? Dòmhagan Òg's will be the place to be, but you can come to me, just the same, Colin. I'll make pancakes unless...'

'No, no... please, no bother,' I protested, blushing. 'I'll just...'

'You'll just keep the promise you made to Alasdair mac Sheumais Bhig,' my uncle insisted, *in loco parentis*, and unused to being challenged. 'Iran will hardly give them a game.'

Here was another trick parents played from time to time – one, I despised, especially since leaving home. Ruairidh had no right to give an order in the presence of someone so removed from the matter, or the family, that my challenging it would cause only personal embarrassment.

Bizarrely, my saviour in distress was my own father – on the phone at 8.10am!

'Is Mum sick?' I immediately asked, as Ealasaid passed the receiver. She was fine, Dad assured me, but now en route to Barra (with requested books!) leaving a slightly lost Tam Quinn to fend for himself for at least a week.

'A couldnae get the days son,' he informed me in refreshingly straightforward Glaswegian. 'Couldnae even swap ma backshift the day. I'll catch the second holf, but you'll hiv to watch the first wan fir us, Colin – all right pal? I'll phone you again ra morra – bit in the evenin – cause it's too dear at this time of the day. Right son, am awae oot a message afore ma work.'

I wondered was Dad heading for the bookies to place a wee, unsupervised, bet. Ealasaid and Ruairidh were back to the night before in Ìochdar School.

'And then,' my uncle said, 'Iain Nill Dhòmhnaill read two of his own poems.'

'That one's Gaelic is deep, deep for me, *a Ruairidh,* and long, but he's a lovely man – always very nice to us as children and a wizard with horses. Why don't you visit him, instead, Colin – you'll have a far better...'

'Perhaps *I* will,' my uncle asserted. 'Once I've dropped this football fan off at Alasdair's.'

Ealasaid looked across sympathetically. 'And your poor father's working tonight, Colin. Was he ever in Uist?'

'Nope.'

'I'll tell mac Sheumais Bhig for you on my way south,' she stated, looking at Ruairidh. 'Haven't been in that house since before Dòmhnall died. The two brothers lived there so long together. But that's going back a few years now.'

I was most grateful. My uncle was silent.

'So,' Ealasaid continued with slight self-deprecation, 'if Colin's at Iran tonight in Argentina, will it be Milton tomorrow or Friday?'

'Either,' I assured her, though I wouldn't have minded catching the World Cup Round-up on the Thursday – so many games and teams I'd missed.

'I'll let you know this afternoon, Colin.'

'*Tha mi duilich 'ille,*'[48] Ruairidh said when Ealasaid had gone.

---

48 Sorry, lad

'*Carson?*'[49] I replied.

'For pushing you – putting pressure on you – on my agenda. You've plenty of time to do lots of different things. And why shouldn't Alasdair mac Sheumais Bhig outlive us all – the old bugger!'

Morning surgery was busy, patients taken as they came and just one doctor and his 'able' assistant waiting to greet them.

'They're all just getting checked out before the big game,' I joked with Kirsty, the stand-in receptionist for Mrs Marr. 'Wouldn't want that interrupted by any sudden drop in health.' Her blank expression drew an 'Iran?' from me. I almost added Ealasaid's witty 'in Argentina' and was glad I hadn't.

'Would you call that a big game?' she said, 'I'd have thought the Holland one was far bigger!'

'Yeah, you're probably right, *ma-thà*,' my contrite assurance.

It had struck me, that while accompanying Ruairidh on house calls might be reasonable enough – i.e. what else does a lonely, drifting, nephew do all day bar studying for his finals – was my presence in Cnoc Fraoich Surgery on such firm ethical ground?

Of course, the patients were told who I was, what I was supposedly considering as a career option and asked if they minded my being there to garner knowledge.

Not a single person requested I leave the room. But really would they have, and did that in any way reflect how they actually felt about my listening ear?

For his part, Ruairidh seemed to have forgotten the hurdles ahead were I to try switching courses. When in full flow, he now treated me as if I were a senior medical student or at least one with some knowledge of the broad disciplines involved.

---

[49] Why?

Having pointed out finger clubbing in a wheezy *cailleach*,[50] he listed some of its more common causes once she'd closed the door behind her. 'Imperative, Colin,' he intoned. 'That we rule out a neoplasm.' My blank expression brought a loud whispered 'Cancer. Because, as you so rightly intuited with Theresa, two conditions can co-exist: one common, the other less so. Ina's long-standing bronchial problems could be consistent with those chubby, squishy, fingertips but so is a malignant tumour of the lung.'

'And both caused by the same demon?'

'Which is?'

'The fags of course.'

'Often, yes, Colin. But not in poor Ina's case. She has a genetic predisposition, and her house is extremely damp.'

I rose to open the window, but then remembered Ruairidh had already done so before hailing the woman in.

'What points against cancer, currently, Colin?' he later asked, turning sharp left past The Royal Bank.

I shook my head. 'That she doesn't smoke?'

'Well, yes. But she inhales plenty of her brother's Bogey-roll.'

'Pass.'

'Her girth, which continues to increase year on year: lack of aerobic exercise, despite hard domestic slavery. No, Colin, cancer in older people often takes its time to become manifest, but when you peer down your retrospectoscope, or switch on your hindsight properly, early and sustained weight loss are usually there. Hold on we ought to say hello to *Maighstir Pàdraig*.'

My uncle pulled in opposite the school by the Lasgair turn-off – '*School Board of South Uist 1909*' still legible above the entrance – leaving ample space for the black Volvo Estate to join us.

Dr Ruairidh Gillies and Father Pàdraig MacLean shook

---

[50] old woman

hands manly and warmly; as two Barramen on Uist should. Lochboisedale's pupils were all indoors it seemed; or had they abandoned the classroom for a distant nature topic?

'I heard you'd come, *a Ruairidh*,' the priest applauded. 'I was in Lourdes. We just returned on Saturday. A young doctor with you?' he added, not in the least fooled, I felt, but accepting my support role.

'Well, he's thinking about it,' Ruairidh replied. 'Meet Colin – my sister Màiri, in Greenock's, son.'

I smiled a 'hello', squirmed out of the car, blushing again – this was worse than adolescence – and made my way round to the driver's side to shake hands with the sweaty priest.

'Never met your mother,' he informed me, 'but I did meet your father once – on a bus in Hope Street. He tried to let me off with my fare, but I insisted.'

'He would have paid it for you,' I returned, defending Dad's generosity rather than his willingness to diddle the Corporation. I then wanted to retract my statement – laced with the suggestion that priests were what: spongers or artful chancers in their own right?

'He's up for folk work too,' Ruairidh's helpful intervention. I did wish, though, that my uncle would stop telling people this and just let me get on with it – in my own way, in my own time. 'Colin's...' he began and then left it, thankfully and the priest didn't probe further before entering the school.

'Some of the clergy are quite protective of the old people,' he said, as we moved off. 'Understandable., I suppose. Many got used and abused in the past. But Mgr Pàdraig's not too bad in that respect – if you don't encroach on his territory.'

'Which is?'

'*Orthachan*: incantations; pre-Roman prayers; local religious customs and beliefs. He really has little interest in secular stuff.'

'Other than football.'

'Loves his football, Pàdraig. It'll have traumatised him to have been tossing about in the Minch while Scotland played Peru.'

'Are we going to accept for Sunday?' I asked. Mgr Pàdraig had invited us to supper and to watch Scotland's final group game against Holland.

'We'll see, Colin. We'll have to go at some point. He understands my on-call situation. Many don't. The Parish House is close to the hospital too with a reliable phone, and a housekeeper who could challenge Ealasaid in the kitchen – but not at stew; Ealasaid's stew is the best in the Western world!'

I soon dozed off as we drove south from Daliburgh, when suddenly Ealasaid, a tiny Chinese woman and a large, beaming, brightly clad Bangladeshi were going head-to-head in the World Stew Championships. Poor Ealasaid Iain Alasdair was in tears. '*Seall na th' acasan de dh'ingredients,*' she was saying, '*is gun agam fhìn ach Bisto is uinneanan.*'[51]

My uncle rapped my window with his loyal, gold-band of wedlock. Having located the house in Smercleit and on finding the poorly patient absent – presumed to be shopping – he had made straight for Anna Morrison's. The Sick Children's Hospital investigations had shown nothing untoward, and mum and baby had flown home the day previously; now the wee one was thriving.

We were now parked outside the house of the woman with the chest infection and the flat demeanour – Theresa.

'Her antibiotics won't be finished yet, will they?' I asked, rubbing my eyes.

'No,' Ruairidh replied.

'Did you get the TB results?'

'No, but I saw the house in darkness with not a single curtain drawn.'

'Also shopping?' I suggested.

'Let's hope so.'

It seemed that Ruairidh would appreciate some support

---

[51] Look at the ingredients they have… and me with only Bisto and onions

should any discovery in the dim interior of the house distress him, but surely my uncle would have had to cope with adverse events, all his professional life. Was this also partly the reason for my being with him in Uist?

I was going to suggest he enter first and then, if appropriate, call me in, but the front door opened and a burly man in a thick-knitted sweater and wellingtons appeared with a toddler at his side.

'Hello, *ma-thà,* Angus,' Ruairidh's opening gambit. 'It's not a bad day.'

'Not at all,' the fellow agreed. 'I'm Iain. Angus is my brother.'

'Yes, yes,' agreed Ruairidh. 'I thought I'd call on Theresa, see if she was any better?'

'She's doing very well, but you'll have to return another day. I'll say to her you came by.'

And with that, Iain did an odd thing, he took a long key out of his pocket and locked the door. He then eased a heavy-framed bicycle off the harled wall and carefully placed the toddler on the saddle in front of him. Images from Vietnam leapt to mind and despite the warm Uist light this scenario was equally black and white in its essence.

'That was her husband's brother, Iain, with their child,' my uncle said grimly while putting the car into reverse.

'And where was she?' I asked. 'Or Angus? Both in there too? And now locked in? Elsewhere, surely? So, who was looking after the little boy before Iain cycled over?'

'Lots of questions, Colin, and no straightforward way of broaching them.'

'Police?' I suggested.

'What!' his reply. 'You've been watching too much telly, *a bhalaich.*[52] I'll have a word with Mgr Pàdraig.'

Tormod Mòraig's house described a clean, frugal, bachelor:

---

[52] boyo

one who'd been to sea and had mastered more than the basics of domestic maintenance. He welcomed me, unannounced, at the door at 8.30pm and without any fuss or frantic palaver, produced a couple of bottles of MacEwan's Export, some crisps and peanuts. We sat down pleasantly, un-stressfully, to watch Scotland's second match against Iran.

As if presuming an easy win, the focus of the commentators' early discussion was on former Rangers star, Willie Johnston's, humiliating return home two days previously for failing a drugs test. Tormod Mòraig had hoped Graeme Souness might have started the game. As had commentator, Archie Macpherson, his dulcet tones pulsing tonight unfailingly all the way from Cordoba to Eòrasdail. 'Surely now,' he said, 'Scotland can relax into a competent rhythm and score effectively.'

Tormod and I watched calmly, often in silence, as a disinterested, lacklustre, national team limped to a 1–1 draw; a slapstick own-goal giving Scotland its meagre point against 'a bunch of bloody amateurs'. Allan Rough's shaggy, blond, mop flaunted the spite of a hair-stylist's prank, as he stared into his net after Iran's tragicomic equaliser. Ally MacLeod's fast-thinning hair and stinging scalp, he grabbed in varicose, beleaguered hands.

I could imagine Ìomhair's loutish taunts and curses at Dòmhagan Òg's house in Kilbride and was so glad I was a good few miles away.

Tormod Mòraig was a man who'd found solutions to a number of challenges over years with practical acumen, but more importantly with a calm assurance. A poor game of football in South America (that few bothered attending) was a mere minor irritation to such a survivor. 'I'm telling you, Colin, our North End would have been far stronger than that lot; and have played as a team; and scored goals! They've got some excellent players right now, *a Chailein*! No one here's getting near them.'

We drank a second bottle. I was enjoying spending some

time beyond the company of my uncle, his responsibilities and focused agenda.

Ruairidh perhaps also respected my need for space and while he suggested joining us for the second half, the MG stayed put at Taigh Eòrasdail. He'd caught part of the match on the radio, he said, when I woke him up slumped in the chair at 11.00pm.

'Nice fellow, Tormod Mòraig.'

'Very nice,' I agreed. 'Very relaxed – but organised too.'

'You'll have enjoyed that Colin, despite the score.'

'Could have been worse, their number eight ran forty yards to nearly grab a second. That really would have scuppered our chances.'

I had run nowhere but fatigue again overcame me in Uist. I excused myself abruptly, fell on my bed, started, and just managed two lines of *The Thorn Birds*, before falling into the deepest of slumbers.

Chapter 7

It wasn't long before Oisean had fallen in love with this beautiful woman and she with him. One day they were strolling, and he asked her a question. 'What is your name?' 'My name is Niamh,' she replied. 'And where is your home, Niamh?' 'I belong,' she said, 'to Tìr nan Òg.'

RUAIRIDH AND I had talked about the origins of the Fèinn: They were a band of mythical warriors, raised by the High King from among the tallest and strongest in Ireland. In time they rebelled and chose their own leader, Cumhal. The enraged monarch plotted to have this upstart killed. He hired Arca Dubh who gladly ran him through – with Cumhal's own sword! – as Cumhal and his bride lay on their wedding night.

Years later, Fionn, the son conceived of this union (a tad before the sword-bit), but reared in secret, avenged his father's death and returned home. He proved his identity by his dog, Bran's, stag-hounding skills and in his own expert clanging of *An Dòrd Fiantaich*.[53] He was hailed as his father's heir and Fionn MacCumhail, the new fair-haired leader of the Fèinn, soon gathered his men around him.

'This is fiddlier than it looks, *a Ruairidh*,' I said, still trying to wind and thread the thick tape through the heads of my uncle's large recording machine. It was hard to believe professionals didn't use cassettes like the ones we all had to grab the charts or copy pals' albums.

'You'll get used to the thing,' he assured me. 'Make sure the tape is nicely threaded through the guides, so its full

---
53 A loud percussive instrument

width sits in the driver-head assembly, otherwise you'll come home with the wailing of a ghost, but not much else. Also don't go near that speed-switch, it let me down badly once when I shouldn't have been so mean with my tape. *Ceart, a laochain*,[54] a demo. Ask me some questions!' Thus began my recording career.

COLIN	I'm sitting here in Eòrasdail House with Dr Ruairidh Gillies.
RUAIRIDH	Ask me your questions in Gaelic – is that not what you'll be speaking to Alasdair?
COLIN	Suppose so. Ruairidh, where are you from?'
RUAIRIDH	Eoligarry, on the Isle of Barra.
COLIN	What do they call you there, *ma-thà*?
RUAIRIDH	*Mac Iagain Mhòir Chaluim*. From Bruairnis my grandfather, but he got a croft in Eoligarry when the tack was divided in 1919.
COLIN	And there were eight of you in the family?
RUAIRIDH	Keep your questions open, Colin – how many were there in your family? They might mention someone or something unexpected.
COLIN	*Seadh, ma-thà*, tell me about your family?
RUAIRIDH	Well, Anndra's the eldest, then it's myself, then Raghnaid, followed three years later by poor Eòin and after that came your mum…
COLIN	But you're the only one of them that continued in education. Why was that?
RUAIRIDH	Good question, *a Chailein*, a little personal but still a good question. I'm sure I'd have followed a similar path to the others – who did receive further education, just not of a formal type, but…
COLIN	And wasn't it the eldest who inherited the croft, who had to…?

---

54 Right, lad

RUAIRIDH Don't interrupt your informants so early or so abruptly – let the natural pauses dictate when to move them in the direction you want.

And as I was saying to you, my father was quite a pragmatic man. He saw I wasn't much use on the land – nor interested – and how capable Anndra was; and I was doing well at school.

He had a sister living near Glenfinnan who was a widow – a wealthy one too – well, my father wrote to her, and it was herself, my auntie Jessie, who put me through – firstly to Fort Augustus, then afterwards to St Andrews. She was dead by the time the rest could have gone on.

But believe me, *a Chailein*, your mother was the brightest of us all. The Head, Nugent, and the priest, Maighstir Iain were always on at my father to let her stay on at school – that they would help somehow. But he refused. While he'd let his sister who'd done well – due to her man – pay back her 'share', he wouldn't accept 'charity' from strangers. So, I got the chance the others didn't...

COLIN And is that why you're still working – making yourself keep going?

RUAIRIDH It could have something to do with it, I'm sure... and...

COLIN *Seadh, ma-thà...*

RUAIRIDH You're getting too good at this, Colin – I'd almost say you are a 'natural'. But don't be quite so personal with mac Sheumais Bhig. Or he might clam up and then you won't get a single story out of him.

I jammed on the STOP button and then responding to his eager nod, rewound the tape. We listened back in silence to our efforts. My uncle's voice was imbued with considerable gravitas – a combination of his more measured thoughts and the bass distortion of the Uher. He seemed satisfied both by the quality of the recording and its content.

'We could do a bit more?' I suggested.

'What?'

'I could interview you too, in the quiet periods, when old Alasdair's dried up – just for fun, posterity – if you'd like.'

'We'll see. The first task is to get that old fellow talking uninterrupted by fear of reprisal from the grand-niece. She'll be there of course.'

I knew she would and felt strangely fearless. Jane had asked me to do this, so she'd have to support its achievement somehow.

'They wouldn't mind if you accompanied me, Ruairidh,' I said, as we sat at the path-end in Milton – the blue van this time in residence.

'Are you daft, Colin,' he asked, 'or getting cold feet?'

It was quite the opposite but what should one admit?

'What, then, are the key aspects of the Fèinn again?' My uncle's eyes were piercing.

'That Fionn MacCumhail likes Fish Fingers whereas Diarmad prefers a Vesta Curry.'

'*Thalla, a ghloidhc!*'[55] His warm endorsement and I headed east over the tufted hillock.

Jane had Alasdair very presentable – washed and shaved within the last few hours wearing a newer, darker, jersey in the same pattern as the fawn one and with a full but unlit pipe of tobacco.

She was sitting on his throne to the right of the stove having placed Alasdair in the corner of the bench nearest to the heat. Plenty of space had been cleared, so that I could sit

---

55 Away you go you idiot!

there too and strategically position any equipment or papers between us. The light from the two small-paned windows was far better than it had been the afternoon Ruairidh and I visited. Yes, it was a clear night, but where was the sun in relation to the house? Perhaps also the windows had been cleaned and the net-curtains pulled back?

Jane was sporting a Cheshire cat grin, which didn't suit her. Was she nervous about how this recording was going to work out? What if it all failed, I proved an inept fieldworker, or Alasdair – albeit knowledgeable – was unable, in his advanced years, to perform in front of a microphone or to a stranger? What then for Jane and her needs for this old boy?

'Tea now or afterwards?' she asked. 'After maybe, eh?' she answered herself eagerly, and lit a cigarette with tremulous haste, then her great-uncle's pipe.

This gave me the opportunity to remove the recorder from its case and slot the microphone into its side. The machine was a new model Ruairidh had purchased prior to coming up to Uist; ahead technologically, he maintained, than the BBC were using. 'They'll soon catch on,' he smiled. 'Buying a few score of these would cost a bit. The secret with the mic, Colin, especially for these old folks, is to hold it about 70:30 in favour of the contributor and a little below the mouths of both of you.'

The Uher's continuous recording time could be up to six hours, from five large round batteries. While some people now powered toasters and tumble-driers, in addition to a colour TV (or two!) in their traditional cottages, Alasdair had no electricity. Our trialling at Taigh Eòrasdail had all been on the mains, so I was supremely confident.

Jane evinced no interest in the kit – it had a job to do, that's all. She did, though, let out a rather bizarre whoop when I played back our faltering introductory remarks – to make sure all was well with the tape and the recording levels as good as Ruairidh assured me they would be. The sound was lovely – tonally – better, it seemed, than earlier in the day with Ruairidh.

'*Mi seo an taigh Alasdair mhic Sheumais Bhig am Milton*,'[56] I began.

'*Geàrraidh Bhailteas*,' he corrected, 'is the Gaelic.'

Jane coughed loudly and stubbed out her cigarette.

'Sorry, yes, in Geàrraidh Bhailteas. And what did you think of last night's game?'

I regretted my trite question the minute it left my lips. He looked over to Jane for help.

'Football,' shouted Jane. 'He's talking about football. Remember I said Ìomhair would be in Kill...'

'I thought he'd come about old things – stories and that?'

'You're right,' she assured him. 'He's just...'

'Making a start, 'I supplied, and followed that with. 'What did you have for breakfast this morning?'

'God save me,' he replied. 'That's a long time ago! Weetabix,' he then said. 'I stop the porridge on Easter Sunday and then I don't go back to it again until the end of August. That way I don't scunner myself – that's what this one says anyway, isn't it?'

'Aye,' her reply.

A minor adjustment on the recording volume and a slight shift in my body in Alasdair's direction was all that was required thereafter.

'I told him you were full of made-up stuff!' Jane shouted, removing another cigarette, but not offering to relight Alasdair's pipe.

'Some say that's what they are,' his soft-voiced reply. 'But others know that parts of it really happened.'

'Who did you hear tell your stories?' I probed, fairly gently I hoped.

---

56 Here I am in Alasdair mac Sheumais Bhig's house in Milton

'Who else but my own father! Full of tales and legends was Seumas Beag – some he picked up from the old people growing up. Two old men who lived out in Loch Sgioport for many years, and with nothing else to do but practise their storytelling to pass the long winter nights.'

'And I wonder if you can remember any of those today, Alasdair? Could you try and tell me one of them now?'

'Och, well, I don't know.'

Jane gave her uncle an intense stare but said nothing, she drew heavily on her cigarette and let the smoke escape through her nostrils – like a hardy little dragon. We shared another longish pause, not altogether uncomfortable. Alasdair broke this with a sigh.

'I used to tell her them all the time when she was small. She was the only one who bothered with Donald, my brother, since she was very young. He was slow and that wee girl would be looking out for him. I have another brother who lives on this island, but you'd think he...'

'*Istibh!*'[57] Jane hissed. 'They had their own problems. So does everyone.'

'Not at the start,' his rebuttal. 'I was the one that got the job of caring for Donald, whether I wanted it or not.'

'What sort of stories do you have?' I asked, to push through this family issue.

'The usual ones,' his certain reply. 'Events that happened, some that people were hiding – ghosts and legends, that sort of thing.'

'Did you ever hear tell of a Fionn MacCumhail?'

'Plenty times. If I could remember.'

'Was he ever in Uist?'

'I'm sure he was; of course, he was! However, it was on Tiree that he got married – near Tràigh Bhì. We have a Loch

---

[57] Quiet!

Bì here – '*Gul na h-eala air Loch Bì*'[58] goes the sad song. Well, there is a beach there and though I've never seen it with my own two eyes, it's there all right, in Tiree. But just a little while after the wedding, she and Diarmad go off together and hide in the big cave in Ceann a' Bharra.'

'And who is *she*?' demanded Jane helpfully.

'Gràinne. Who else?' Alasdair replied. 'And everyone who was anyone came to see her and Fionn MacCumhail get married. From throughout Scotland and Ireland and far, far beyond. And they had a celebration on Tiree that they'd never seen the likes of before; there or anywhere else.

'Anyway, Fionn was married before. But his first wife had died, and he now wanted a new, younger, woman. And Gràinne was much younger than he was. And he took a liking to her – *Gràinne Nighean Charmaig A' Chuilein.*'[59]

Alasdair's eyes were ablaze. His speech rhythms now in gear. A quizzical expression formed on his heavily lined face – as if he might be telling or hearing this story for the first time; unsure how it might go, which moral or character trait might prevail in the face of adversity. He then hacked up some dark-stained saliva in a small bowl I hadn't noticed – which held a good *steall*[60] of the same – snatched his pipe and began shakily to light and suck it at the same time.

'I'll light you,' Jane exclaimed, and I thought she might just do that – light her great-uncle. She pulled out a silver, masculine, device – perhaps Alasdair's own – and crossed the room.

'Suck!' she commanded, and a waft of sweet-smelling smoke escaped between the few front teeth, which held the pipe in their wobbly grip.

'Steady it with your hand!' she then urged and we were swiftly back to Tiree.

---

58 The wail of the swan on Loch Bee
59 Grainne the daughter of Cormack of The Hound
60 quantity of liquid

Though my eyes were smarting and my chest a little tight, I knew my allergy of old was gone and would not return.

'But after a while, did Gràinne not grow tired of the *bodach*, Fionn. Because he really was a *bodach* by this time. A hero, but an old man. And well a young wife, she'll want what Fionn couldn't give her, being up in years, you understand.'

'We understand very well!' barked Ìomhair Dubh, opening the door. 'Get a move on,' he threw at Jane, and she rose immediately. 'Your children are waiting – or maybe you'd forgotten all about them?'

'But Alasdair's still...' she protested.

'Don't you worry dear,' the old man assured, 'Many's the time I made my own way to that bedroom.'

'I should head off,' I suggested, and no one tried to stop me.

'Ìomhair will take you to the road-end,' Jane offered warmly, too obviously warmly. She didn't want me frightened off; her husband was okay – could be obliging, in his own way, once you got to know him. I had little desire to complete the induction process!

'No, no,' I insisted, 'It's nice out for a walk. Sure to meet Ruairidh at some point.' My uncle though wouldn't be passing for another hour, presuming no late calls.

My saying goodbye to Alasdair contained a promise of an early return to finish our story. 'Yes, yes!' he agreed, 'There's lots more to come! I'm here all the time, so you can just please yourself.' I felt I should confirm my attendance the following evening but was reluctant to do so in front of Ìomhair or, indeed, organise anything independent of Jane.

A beautiful, cloudless, night welcomed my release from awkwardness and the summer sun was just showing signs of how it might set. The air was warm, in a natural sense, and smelled healthy – peat now sweet from a subtle distance when not intensely inhaled with cigarette and pipe smoke.

It was a welcome change to be stretching the legs. I hadn't

realised just how much my muscles had tensed while sitting on Alasdair's bench. Despite Ìomhair's rude interruption, I did feel I'd got off to a good start. The *bodach* liked me. Although Jane's approval was crucial, he would talk more. I was looking forward to re-playing what I'd 'caught' on tape to Ruairidh before Ìomhair's crude commands; Jane's behaviour had been quite different to her open aggression with my uncle – all that anger and impudence were a question of focus. Ruairidh provided the focus, it seemed.

'Lovely evening,' a tall but stooped man, wielding a scythe, hailed me. 'Weeds and weeds,' he added, pointing with it at the roofless ruin. 'The nettles are the worst of them all. In and out.'

His tanned, cured, hands had no interest in gloves, which might reduce dexterity for the sake of the odd sting.

'*Daoine a bhuineadh dhuibh a bha a' fuireach ann?*'[61] I suspected the answer to be 'yes' but was delighted to ask properly and thus not pry.

The fellow's eyes lit up. This wasn't a stranger abroad, but someone who understood not only the physical, but also the emotional, toll in attacking the overgrowth and the reasons for its existence.

''*S e, a bhalaich*,' his poignant reply, its intimacy unspoken and untranslatable. 'Myself and my parents before me, if I still belong to them or them to me these days? Where in Barra are you from?' he asked generously.

'My mother's from Eoligarry.'

'Big seamen, the Barraich.'

I nodded.

'Here in Uist we're,' he said, rubbing sweat with his forearm from above his eye, 'too tethered to the land. Hardly worth it. It just consumes you in the end.'

I didn't feel at all uncomfortable in this man's company though the subject and tone of his conversation was quite

---

[61] People that belonged to you that lived there?

depressing. Still, he was obviously up for making a fresh start in his old family home. Not a bad start either, I judged. A nice night for it too; autumn demands still well in the future.

'Will you tell Uncle Ruairidh,' he smiled – his scythe-sharp mind having sliced through the available data, 'that there's a bag of carrots and one of turnips waiting for him in that shed over there?' He pointed in the direction of a large steel building, visible over the rise. 'And that Caoimhin "of the pipes" grew them for him.'

'Poor Caoimhin,' Ruairidh's confirmation. 'His heart is currently being fed by two rather scrawny collateral arteries.'

'Which for the Arts student are?'

'Blood vessels that grow to help the main furred ones; soon they'll just bypass them – like a plumber might. It's happening in the States with good results. These operations could give the likes of Caoimhin another ten years.'

'He doesn't look that old?'

'He's not. Glad to hear that man's out and about.'

Ruairidh's expletives on news of Ìomhair Dubh's interruption and Jane's swift departure were choice and amusing. We were now two men together – or at least getting that way – so why pretend?

'Such a bloody tosspot,' his final verdict. 'And she was fine, was she?'

'Yes, lovely. Eh, well, friendly.'

He gave me a strange look. 'You heard what Ealasaid said, *a Chailein*. Be careful, okay?'

'Can I ask what happened between you and them?' my mouth blurted, then coughed.

'No.'

'Okay.'

'That jar of lemon curd's almost finished. Will I get some more?'

'Thanks.'

'They'll be good, Caoimhin's carrots. Better collect them tomorrow.'

'Carrot and Lemon Curd Cake,' I said, to maintain the imposed safe space. 'Could be tasty?'

'Can you bake?' he asked.

'Never too late to start, Ruairidh.'

'Indeed. We'll organise a tutorial with herself. And Fionn and Gràinne wed where again?'

'Near Ceann a' Bharra, on Tiree.'

'Never heard that one before. It's usually by Glen Lonan in mainland Argyll, but well done, lad.'

I'd decided not to play back my 'pickings' to my uncle yet, using the excuse of not wanting to risk moving the tape and losing something important. I was, though, desperate to listen back myself.

The following morning would suffice post-Ealasaid. A box of books – personally delivered that evening, by a curious Joe Galbraith from Northbay – had given me the impetus to start work the way I hoped to continue.

Mum would never put pressure on me to visit her on Barra, but the more I thought about it the more the idea appealed. She was just across the sound and I was missing her in a way I'd never felt in Glasgow's West End. I would, though, need to justify my absence to Ruairidh with a gem or two safely in the can.

Chapter 8

'Tìr nan Òg, you said?' Oisean asked Niamh. 'Yes,' she replied. 'The Land of Eternal Youth. It lies far out west across the sea.'

'GRÀINNE HAD GROWN tired of Fionn...' I prompted Alasdair, having resumed our session on the Saturday night. Jane sat opposite and looked much more relaxed – oddly I felt, given her husband's rude interruption. Her children were spending the night at her parents, I learnt later – helping Papa lift the peats. Ìomhair was playing football in Eriskay with a dance to follow the game. I deduced she didn't expect her husband home until after sunrise. Was Ìomhair not getting a bit old for this type of entertainment?

League matches usually took place on a Sunday, but the teams had re-arranged this one to accommodate Scotland's last chance of progressing in the World Cup; we would have to beat opponents, Holland, by three clear goals. 'A tall order'– the view from the most hopeful. Impossible, the opinion of those who'd suffered the damp disappointment of the team's two recent performances.

'He had become an old man, Fionn,' I continued, 'and his young wife desired something...'

'Better,' answered Jane, with an obviously painful creasing of her eyes to form her now familiar, mischievous, warm, smile. No one was smoking and the strong sun had dipped gracefully behind a cloud.

'The left eye,' my uncle confirmed later in Taigh Eòrasdail. 'First thing I noticed when she came out to the car – new bruising. Quite artfully done too, *mo ghalghad dubh. Dia ach an trustar!*[62] Did she ever look at you straight on, Colin?'

'I don't think so. Nice she came out to the car, though.'

'You reckon?'

'And,' continued Alasdair mac Sheumais Bhig in Geàrraidh Bhailteas, 'didn't *Gràinne Nighean Charmaig a' Chuilein* fall in love with Diarmad! And who was Diarmad, *ma-thà?*' he demanded. Only the squat walnut-clock responded. 'But Fionn's nephew!'

'The son of Fionn MacCumhail's sister,' Jane quickly clarified, aware of my potential grammatical deficiencies.

'Indeed!' Alasdair agreed. 'Fionn adored Diarmad, and the younger one was just as fond of his uncle.'

Jane let out a little whimper and I could feel some of what she was responding to in her uncle's rhythm and music. Knowledge of the story's course and intensity would surely also have stirred her.

'And Gràinne tried everything she could to get Diarmad to go off with her!

'But he refused. Diarmad was a man of honour – who wouldn't insult the leader of the Fèinn or any others of that loyal band of warriors. Whatever she tried, it was useless, for Diarmad loved Fionn with all his heart, from a very early age. It was his uncle who first showed him how to handle and fight with the *claidheamh*.'

'Sword,' mouthed Jane, her lips rounded to maximise her voiceless enunciation. I was enjoying her helping me out in this way.

'Because,' Alasdair continued, 'from the day he was born it was fated for Diarmad mac Dhuinn to be a swordsman.'

I immediately saw Diarmad standing in a modern disposable nappy, wielding a massive Arthurian-type Excalibur. I watched his frame grow and change – develop mass and honed musculature and dark voice-lowering body

---

62 ...my black-haired charmer. For God's sake what a villain!

growth – but when I looked up, this six-foot warrior, stooping under the rafters of mac Sheumais Bhig's thatched cottage, still retained the same smooth-skinned, cherubic, face.

'Eventually when every other trick had failed, Gràinne visited a witch – the most dangerous and most powerful one on the island, in all the islands of Argyll.'

The *seanachie*[63] leant forward. Jane and I were already on the edge of our seats. I remembered to pull the microphone back a little to maintain the minimum eight-inch distance I'd gleaned from Ruairidh's crib-sheet of The Irish Folk Society.

'And with the crafty wiles of the witch – *A' Chailleach Bheurr*, I think they called her – Gràinne got round Diarmad, and he eloped with her.'

We spent the next while spell-bound as Alasdair rollercoasted us: from the village of Bailephuil to the lovers' hide-out in the great cave of Ceann a' Bharra; back to Tràigh Bhì and the Lochlannaich's bloody feud; MacCumhail's capitulation – a desperate bellow to Diarmad on the Instrument of Peril, Diarmad's unswerving loyalty and the Fèinn's energised defeat of those Scandinavians. I feared the worst in Jane's anxious look and Alasdair's slowing and lowering of his voice.

Fionn had captured his nephew and was insisting he complete a near-impossible task for pardon: they jump into a boat and Gràinne joins them.

Many hours later, Diarmad, sword-less and exhausted, spears the fiercest of wild boars then hauls it from a Lismore wood. Uncle Fionn then exploits his intimate knowledge by making his brave nephew measure the dead beast's length – snout to rump. A spike lodges in his weak 'mole' on the right ankle, fatally wounding Diarmad.

'Three times,' the *bodach* in Uist half-screamed, 'Fionn went to the stream, knowing full-well that a sup of water from his hands would save Diarmad. But he let every drop

---

[63] storyteller

trickle through his fingers and the young man died.

'And did she not just leap into the pit – in the fullness of health – on top of her lover! Then two dogs appeared and jumped in before the grave was closed.'

'And,' Alasdair's finale, 'that's what inspired the bard, Oisean, who witnessed the death of his cousin, and whose eyes shed the sorest tears, when he wrote:

"We buried at the bottom of the hill,
at the time of the laying out of the wild boar
Gràinne the daughter of Cormack of The Hound
two whelps and Diarmad."'

A long silence followed. I looked at Jane who had been staring at me. She pulled a little tobacco from her tongue, between forefinger and thumb, then adjusted her lank hair with the three dry fingers.

'There you are!' Alasdair gave us eventually. His voice was still low in volume but now spent by the intensity of the work of telling. 'They killed the fellow – and he was an honourable man,' he added, as if imparting inside knowledge to the select few. 'All the time Diarmad and Gràinne were sleeping together in that big cave in Ceann a' Bharra the sword lay there between them.'

Jane blushed, unexpectedly, and pulled a cigarette from her pocket, offered me one, which was oddly tempting, but I shook my head. She chuckled and obviously weighed up giving Alasdair one but then thought better of it; it might hasten the end of those formidable abilities in a man of 88. She then removed her own fag from salivating lips, placed it on the Wally-dugged mantelpiece, and withdrew to Alasdair's seòmbar[64] to which she had obvious rights. Jane returned with a half-bottle of Whyte & MacKay's and three thimble-sized patterned glasses.

Without offering or checking on my teetotal status, she

---

64 bedroom

filled all three to the brim and handed them round. Alasdair downed his in one and a trickle. Jane and I sipped ours in tandem and listened carefully and comfortably to the clock and the gentle, steady, intrusion of the sounds of the outside world.

'Getting closer,' she commented, and Alasdair nodded.

'Must have something to tell us,' his reply.

'*An treun,*' she clarified. 'A corncrake. Been threatening a *cèilidh* for a few weeks now. They say that if the corncrake doesn't visit before *Latha Cholm Cille*[65] you'll have a poor summer and a terrible harvest.

I later recorded some more avian lore from Alasdair: should a cockerel crow in the night or a hen at any time, this was a sign of imminent death to someone close. He followed this with a short story telling why hens loathed a soaking whereas water fell off a duck's back. During Herod's purge, the hens had pecked the corn hiding the infant Christ and almost betrayed him, whereas the ducks were far more circumspect. I wondered later, if this were the sort of thing Mgr Pàdraig would have preferred I didn't hear.

'I'll take you home,' Jane stated, not inviting any challenge. 'It's raining.'

It was in fact bucketing down – for how long I had no idea. I had been mostly oblivious to the real world for the previous two hours as we chatted with the machine off, at Jane's insistence. Only that one tot was shared; Jane took fastidious care of her great-uncle's health and his faculties. Perhaps, given the chance, he would have enjoyed a little more, but Alasdair never mentioned the bottle again. For my part I felt a little nauseous, and dizzy, having not eaten since an early lunch. While I was well able to throw back pints with the best of them, my straight-whisky constitution was obviously rusty and enfeebled by student life. Thankfully,

---

[65] St Columba's Day — ninth of June

Jane made tea and divided a substantial homemade scone among us.

This first proper recording session then seemed to suggest a possible pattern of activity – a longer item first, with or without drams, then some shorter pieces before my departure. Jane was happy to provide the transport home. 'Can easily collect you as well?' she said, more a question this time. I could tell she was keen. I was apprehensive – too much contact too soon and Ìomhair's potential displeasure expressed just as he saw fit.

'No, no,' I insisted. Ruairidh can usually drop me off. I looked at my watch. 'Must have got a few calls or...'

'He's in the operating theatre.' This was a statement. 'A girl from our village – Margaret. Everyone's talking about appendicitis. I think it's a bloody ectopic.'

'Sorry?'

'When the egg sticks in the tube; it can grow there a while before bursting and bleeding you to death.'

I shuddered at the thought. Jane's telling (like Alasdair's) of this information was imbued with dramatic relish. 'Better off being a hen, *a Chailein*,' she added with a chuckle, 'or keeping your legs closed until you're married.' The irony did not escape me. 'I'm always near tears when I see Gràinne's reaction to Diarmad's predicament – what a terrible, terrible, shame.'

Alasdair, who followed English perfectly well, had chosen to remain silent and his polite yawning suggested I was on the point of overstaying my welcome.

'I really enjoyed myself, Alasdair,' I said, extending a hand.

'Good for you,' his intuitive reply. 'You could come back,' he added, as if this had been one-off visit to complete that tragic story of infatuation, scorn and true love.

'Many thanks,' I replied, 'I might just do that.'

Jane's blue van smelt strongly of animals perfumed by tobacco-ash. I could also see some bags of cement – one torn and losing its contents and a few pointed tools that might have done the damage.

'You can come back any time,' she said. 'He liked you and the whole thing. The way you listened. There's not many listens as good.'

'Well, well, *a Chailein*!' Ruairidh's enthusiastic applause. 'And he gave you a wee whisky!'

'Jane gave me a whisky,' I corrected, 'and himself. Just the one.'

'There you go,' he said. 'What a story. What an amazing tale, Colin. You'll get more. You'll get gems, just as they come.'

'And you?'

'What about me?'

'How did you get on tonight?'

'Very well. Very well, I reckon.'

Reading carefully between the lines of confidentiality, the young woman was judged not to have appendicitis and, with a flushed cuddle and a flood of tears for Dr Ruairidh, he confirmed she wasn't pregnant either. Perhaps this diagnosis was more wishful thinking on Jane's part.

My uncle had intended calling on Iain Nìll Dhòmhnaill, but then remembered the back-up recorder had a battery issue. While some brawny lads had sunk the *bàrd's* electricity pole a good few months ago, a connection remained outstanding.

'Anyway,' he said positively – sincerely – 'your need of a fully-functioning machine was obviously greater than mine. Well done, *a Chailein!* If I don't get the old one going properly after Mass (surely just a loose wire) I'll take the Uher with me this afternoon. He said to call any time.'

I reminded my uncle of our invitation to the chapel house for the football.

'Yes, yes. It's all integrated into the schedule, Colin – as far as the schedule can be controlled. When does the match start again?'

'8.45pm.'

'Oh well, the good people of the South End will enjoy a swift service tonight, with no rambling sermon, if Mgr Pàdraig's going to eat in a measure of comfort.'

Against vehement protests, Ruairidh had insisted that Ealasaid now take the weekends off. We really could fend for ourselves, and she had more than enough to do with her own family. Her compromise was that she'd still give us breakfast on a Saturday, leaving sufficient cold meat until she returned Monday morning.

Ealasaid's generosity meant that Sunday morning, therefore, was the only real chance for a long-lie, but my uncle's drive to achieve on the folklore front, before the footballing social obligation, had him whistling, singing and stirring porridge at the unhealthy hour of 9.30am.

'You don't want any more bacon or eggs do you, Colin?'

'No, please!' It felt like I'd put on a stone since my arrival nearly three weeks previously.

'I'll talk to her,' he promised, as he had the previous week. 'It's too much every day, but I don't want to offend her. She's so kind.'

Apart from the odd walk on the shore, I'd hardly taken any proper exercise. I was missing the Uni gym and swimming pool: their quick energy boosts and lithe females.

'Were you thinking of studying today?' Ruairidh asked carefully.

'Tomorrow,' I assured him and myself. I'd succeeded in arranging the books brought from Barra on the shelf in my bedroom and had fashioned a desk from a dusty trestle table we'd discovered in a stair cupboard. Tugging a stiffened sou'wester revealed an ironing board with four heavy irons to be heated on the range; I couldn't see that any of them were in use, hence perhaps Ruairidh's assortment of crew-neck sweaters.

'Right, Colin,' he said. 'Let's go for a drive. Mass is at 11.00am in Ardkenneth. We'll easily make it. Ìochdar's quite a long village,' he then said, as we left the middle-district heading north – a dry enough day but no sun, and the peaks of the Uist triumvirate under cloud.

We'd hardly covered the first mile when a whiskered chap wearing a Harris-tweed suit (a retired gamekeeper known locally as *An Jock*[66]) flagged us down with a shirt dancing on a pole in the gale.

'They waant you at 'e hospital,' he commanded, in an incongruously broad Caithness accent.

'Thanks, John,' Ruairidh's sighed reply. 'We'll do Ardkenneth next week, Colin,' he addressed me.

'I'll easy tak the chiel,' offered *An Jock,* in a way that my refusing would have seemed both impolite and irreligious. 'I'm headin early tae the kirk onyways.'

I smiled a weak acceptance; from one who could still be snuggled deep under the covers with a good book.

My companion's service in the Church of Scotland would start half an hour after Mass but finish well after the long line of Catholic cars had wound their way back to the main road.

John Weir had joined Lord Edward's staff in North Uist in 1947 but later employment at Grogarry Lodge, then marriage to a local woman, had kept him South since, though he and Sara were a 'childless couple' he declared.

'All her faimily's here – and that's a gie muckle!' he informed me at Loch Druidebeag. 'That's oor nature zone – crofters beware! Only a sister left in Halkirk noo – she can hae it tae her sel.'

I was relieved to escape the usual interrogation of where I was from; how long I'd been here; when was I going; how I was connected to Ruairidh and what my future plans were. *An Jock* showed little interest in anything personal in

---

[66] The Jock

my regard – except to ask where I'd purchased my 'smert Sunday jaicket'.

'Glasgow,' I said vaguely, preferring not to reveal its second-hand origins – something I'd often boast about in studentsville.

The man from The Far North did though negotiate a lift back south for me after church, with a mother, father and three young boys.

'We quite often go up visiting,' the woman said, rolling down the window – letting a gale blast in the back where the four of us were packed. 'But especially today with my sister's strangulated hernia.'

I felt sudden panic for Ruairidh. But what could I do? Not much but sit in the back while the squished kids argued across me about plastic soldiers, marbles and comics. Their Gaelic was quick-fired and loaded with a keen sense of injustice. Sharing meant sharing – not hogging!

By the time I reached Taigh Eòrasdail, I was exhausted and collapsed on top of my cool bed. Was there something wrong with me? Surely the effects of the Uist air – though I'd breathed little of it that morning – should have long since worn-off? Anyway, the air here was unlikely to be that much more potent than the Barra variety unless there was an additive 'peat' component, or an Ealasaid Iain Alasdair stodge factor at play, but this was her day off and my belly still felt full.

Chapter 9

*'And what's it like, this Tìr nan Òg?' Oisean then asked.
'It is a most beautiful place,' said Niamh. 'In Tìr nan Òg everybody is always young. Nobody grows old and we are all very happy, and the sun never sets.'*

'COME ON COLIN – let's head for Daliburgh,' my thick head heard, then felt, as Ruairidh's soft warm hands began to rock me. The contrast between the anxious insistence in his voice and the gentleness of his touch confused my logical, bizarre, dream: it was now my turn to drive *An Jock*, but to 'The Chapel!' So why was Ruairidh making me go somewhere when I was already en route?

'How is she?' I asked, as Ruairidh's smart wee motor sped and swerved us to Mgr Pàdraig's – fortunately few other cars were travelling north.

'Who?'

'Margaret.'

'*Glè mhath*. Very well indeed. Went home mid-morning with a good liquorice laxative to help her on her way.'

'Didn't her hernia strangulate?'

'No, no. That girl's still quite unwell. I'll tell you though, Eric is a wizard in an emergency – as cool as a cucumber too. If I'm ever taken with an acute abdomen, Colin, just put me on the boat to Lochboisedale. I'll happily surf the Minch for seven hours to be opened by Eric Adams, than by these so-called city specialists. He saved that lass's life so beautifully – artistically – like Bean Eòghainn's faultless rendition of *"Mo Rùn Geal Òg"*.'[67]

---

[67] 'My Pure True Love'

'Absolutely, *a Ruairidh*,' I replied. 'So, we need three clear goals tonight. What do you reckon: Dalglish, Jordan, then Masson?'

'He's out,' stated my folkloric, non-footballing, uncle. 'According to Brùchd anyway – a skilled theatre assistant and a fine gate-erecter, even where one's not strictly required!' he laughed.

'Asa Hartford, *ma-thà?*'

'Could Gemmill get one, Colin?' Ruairidh pushed, as if this match now really mattered to him.

'Well...' I started, but a mad, one-eared, collie dashed diagonally at the car and was surely dead under the front wheel, except it somehow ran off delighted towards the rear and barked its own prediction. 'Woof, woof, woof, woof, *woof* – it will be a *draw*.'

Mgr Pàdraig's door was opened by Ealasaid: she obviously specialised in caring for Barra men and their guests.

'What a Christian!' Ruairidh returned her compliment and with a wide smile.

'She sure is, lads. *Fàilte gu Mendoza*,'[68] the priest exclaimed, leading us into his book-lined sitting room in St Peter's. His armchairs, while comfortable enough looking, immediately recalled a tense retreat in Mungo Hall during my fifth year, when I'd tried and failed, in deep reflective silence, to pray. Perhaps the clutch of St Pat's girls – with whom we had midnight-feasted the previous evening – were more troubling than the institutional furniture.

Four of Fr Pàdraig's chairs were already occupied. 'And this,' he introduced, 'is my brother, Calum. You'll have seen him about in Barra, Colin?' I hadn't, or if I had, I wasn't aware of it. 'And this is Niall' – he pointed to a very dark, bowl-haired, youth in the corner.

---

[68] Welcome to Mendoza

'Hello.' The lad's shot-out hand and turned-away head asserted their shyness. Niall was studying for the priesthood in Blairs' College, but home on holiday after his exams.

'And these two comedians,' Mgr Pàdraig continued, getting the desired laugh, 'What can I say: Morecambe and Wise? The original Steptoe and Son?'

While Ruairidh seemed quite relaxed with this protracted introduction, I wished we could get on with the game. Both teams had emerged, Holland in white, Scotland in their customary blue, but with fashionable diamonds down their short sleeves.

'We're actually the other Two Ronnies,' the older of the two men remarked. 'Except I'm Murdo and this is my son Alfonsus.'

'It's Allan!' the other one corrected with a jovial dunt. 'And I'm not his son or a relative – which is quite remarkable.'

Yes, the teams were on the park, but the sound was turned right down. They'd soon be singing. It was rumoured 'Scotland The Brave' might replace 'God Save The Queen' to give the boys an extra push.

'*Nach suidh sibh?*'[69] Mgr Pàdraig finally suggested, and we did – Ruairidh to the left of Murdo and me beside the fellow with the vocation.

'No Masson today,' my opener.

'Rubbishplayer,' Niall dispatched at a volume hardly above that of the mute TV and at 112 miles an hour. 'And Macari'snotineither forwantingtoomuchmoney,' he added.

I nodded agreement, having earlier scanned a newspaper in which the Man United player had criticised the SFA on several counts; his Old Trafford chip shop could provide a better bonus any Saturday than the current wages for a month's slog in Argentina.

'There is nothing at all wrong with the name, Alfonsus,'

---

[69] Won't you sit down?

Ruairidh addressed the slim, fine-featured chap who had rejected this title. Now, while it didn't bother me what this merry band chose to call themselves, any mention of my stiff Jesuit high school, would be gratuitous. 'Our Colin here…' my uncle started but then stopped on my fixing him with a piercing stare. Ealasaid's abrupt entry knocked him off track.

'Would you look at that!' he said in appreciation of her sumptuous tray – the first of three. 'Looks like you'll be poaching the best cook in Uist from me, Father?'

Ealasaid beamed, then coughed loudly, before almost skipping back to the kitchen.

'Yes, indeed,' agreed the priest, in a flatter tone than I expected, and then added obliquely, 'as good a head-hunter as the bishop me.'

Mgr Pàdraig's brother's patience had expired. With a lunge from his chair, Calum attacked the round knob in the middle of the TV set, thus heavily contrasting the picture and hyper-fuzzing the orange socks of the Dutchmen. Still sweating, he found the volume and the last verse of 'Wilhelmus' mercilessly drowned out Ealasaid's joy at meeting the needs of two masters. 'The oldest anthem in the world,' Archie Macpherson (in former-teacher mode) told viewers as the teams split to warm up.

'Maighread Bheag's day off then?' Ruairidh enquired, placing two sandwiches and a bun on his plate.

'Her father's not at all well,' was the priest's reply. 'Months since he's been to church.'

I could see the wheels whirring in my uncle's mind – Mgr Pàdraig's housekeeper's father *that wasn't at all well*. Had he ever seen him in surgery or at home? How much worse was he tonight? Would the man allow his daughter to phone the chapel house and interrupt this special occasion? Ruairidh bit greedily on his bread, chomped his bun and helped himself to a second cup of tea.

'Yes!' screamed Calum, when a Scotland header, from the edge of the six-yard box, shot homewards then cruelly struck the face of the bar; and 'Now!' when Rangers' Tom Forsyth's toe netted from fifteen yards to be judged offside. 'Bugger that,' he groaned, looking round only briefly, to sanction similar language from the rest. We were all pals, all grown men. His eyes didn't meet Mgr Pàdraig's.

'Behindtheballhewas whenitwasplayed,' young Niall insisted, a comment, which I failed to decipher until half-time when the discussion widened a little.

The Two Ronnies – Murdo and Allan – if usually an utterly dependable comedy duo – seemed subdued, bemused, as how best to contribute to this particular gathering. They did though echo 'Kenny, Kenny! Kenny, Kenny!' when Dalglish firstly had a goal disallowed and then, two minutes later, as he sent a sizzling shot just wide of the post.

'Quite an attractive city, Mendoza,' Mgr Pàdraig was explaining. 'Totally rebuilt after a major earthquake and right at the heart of the best wine region in...'

'No, no!!' we all interrupted.

'Neverapenaltythat,' Niall said. 'Neverever.'

Johnny Rep had fallen (or dived) over the gangly Scottish defender's retrieving tackle and the ref was generous; the 'Total Football' team went one goal up with ease.

'Not missing Cruyff that much,' Ruairidh offered. 'I mean they are playing very well.'

'Was Scotland's game too,' Mgr Pàdraig's brother challenged. 'All over now.'

'Is it all over now, *a Chaluim*?' the priest asked, when, in the final minute, Dalglish volleyed home a Jordan cross, from the left, high into the Dutch net. 'Who says Dalglish isn't as good for Scotland as he is for Celtic. He's there when you need him!'

As the commentary returned to the studio at half-time,

Ealasaid replenished her platters, added fresh tea and allowed Mgr Pàdraig to be Mum until he asked to be excused. Where had the chatty, opinionated, woman in Taigh Eòrasdail disappeared to?

We could hear the priest's undulating tones booming down the empty corridor.

'Yes, *a Mhaighread,*' he said on numerous occasions. 'I see, dear. I understand. And he feels no pain?'

'Will I call over now, Father?' Ruairidh asked, as he re-entered the room. 'What do I care about football and someone out there on his deathbed.'

'No need. She won't let you, *a Ruairidh*. Her family are all there. It's his time to go. Why spoil that?'

I thought that was quite a rude comment, and saw Ruairidh shaking his head.

'The older people in Uist who are dying,' the priest continued, as if my uncle was from Tunbridge Wells, 'God welcomes them like that beautiful Dalglish goal. Who are we to go meddling and potentially causing far more harm than good?'

'*Ach tha...*'[70] began Ruairidh.

Archie Gemmill's solid penalty score put paid to further discussion on the meaning of life, science versus religion.

'What did I tell you, Colin,' Ruairidh boasted. 'I said Gemmill would get one and he did. But what's he up to now?'

The goal of the game – Scotland's international goal of the century: the sublime hope of World Cup redemption through gutsy, grafting, beauty – sadly provided mere background music for the base entertainment unfolding in Mgr Pàdraig's, now uncomfortably appointed, living room.

The ball had gone out of play on the far side of the packed stadium, when Iomhair Dubh crashed through the Parish House front door and across a very definite line.

---

70 But there's...

'So here's where the blessed are gathered!' he roared, joining us. 'The reformed and the corrected, drinking tea at *Cupa na Cruinne*[71] – ha! And us, *Clann Ifhreann* – "poor banished children of Eve" – the children of the unpure woman I shall not name!'

'Enough, Ìomhair!' Mgr Pàdraig said very calmly, no hint whatsoever of anger. 'Won't you have a seat?'

'*Suidh, a laochain!*'[72] Calum echoed his brother.

'*Suidh, suidh, suidh!*' Ìomhair repeated, adopting the Barra 'u' sound. 'Ìomhair will sit among the blessed Barramen.' The offensive prick was quite a good mimic, despite a drooling, thick, tongue – missed again by his coat sleeve and an alcohol-drenched brain. 'All would love me to sit with them, but you!' he then slavered in my direction. 'Why might that be now, Mr Colin Quinn Esquire, eh?'

Johnny Rep had just unleashed the most beautiful of strikes from thirty yards and while Allan Rough got a hand to it, he couldn't keep the ball out. Scotland's dream was over – the two non-Barra Ronnies tutted and looked as if they'd like to leave immediately. Mgr Pàdraig poured stewed tea into a mug from the sideboard and chose Ìomhair a Club Biscuit which, after only a momentary pause, he unwrapped for him.

'RepsthecentreforwardnowCruyff'sgone,' Niall informed us.

'You'd be dangerous if anyone understood you!' was Ìomhair's crass return. The lad blushed instantly – particularly the tops of his ears, which went a deep, hot, crimson.

'*A mhic na...*' started Ruairidh, stopping himself abruptly.

'Aha! Good, kind, Doctor Ruairidh would now like to comment,' spat Ìomhair. 'He starts in our local, common – that right, Colin? – tongue. *A mhic na...* son of the "she" who is going to be a really bad "she". So bad maybe that

---

[71] The World Cup
[72] Sit down, lad!

she will be neglected, allowed just to die in front of our very eyes. She will never be invited to watch World Cup football in the comfort of the blessed *Barraich* and their sad sidekicks.'

'Time to take you home, Ìomhair!' Mgr Pàdraig urged, rising and unhooking his car keys from a tiny plastic font on the wall – 'A Memento from Knock'.

'He'll come with me,' said Ealasaid Iain Alasdair, who had returned with coat and scarf on, 'Won't you Ìomhair?'

The boor made a growl, which preceded a yawn, that might have brought sleep but for her. 'Now! Or you'll get a skelp – like your mammy's when your behind was foul!' The Ealasaid we knew was back and I truly believed her. Tonight's threat was over but what exactly might this low-life be capable of?

It was obvious that Ruairidh was itching to leave too but politeness made him sit out the rest of the match in deflated company.

'What a cheek,' said Murdo.

'*Abair bathais*,'[73] from Allan.

No one laughed.

Had they made the inter-language connection – the juxtaposition – I wondered, later in bed? I would have laughed now had my memory of the event not been so rank. Ìomhair really was the archetypal drunk – not even in the making – but fully formed – and still under thirty-five.

He stunk,' the Barra brother remarked.

'Goodness knows where he'd been before landing here,' Mgr Pàdrig added. 'Crawling in all the middens. Anyway, I'm glad he did come – at least we know he's safe. Poor Jane and those kids...' he began, as if about to launch into a long narrative but let it trail off. 'So, 3–2 the final score. Scotland played well. That was a great goal,' he added, forcing a little more enthusiasm, as the BBC replayed Archie Gemmill's 'epic' contribution.

---

73 What a cheek [lit: forehead]!

'As was that,' Ruairidh said, as Rep's cool, cruel, killer zoomed in from the right. 'I think I'll...we ought to give you some peace, Father,' he said a little formally. 'It was a lovely evening, thanks.'

'The phone's just out there,' the priest pointed – one on-call professional to another – anticipating Ruairidh's need to inform the hospital of his moves. I assumed, also, he knew where we were heading, but discretion prevented further prodding or probing.

We sat in Ruairidh's MG at the end of the driveway to Maighread's parents' small square house in South Lochboisedale. I was about to get out and open the gate.

'Hold on, *a Chailein*,' my uncle said. 'Ìomhair's allusions back there; "*the Blessed Barraich*". Mgr Pàdraig faced tough challenges in Dunoon; drink helped dull the pain. He's great now. Brand New!' Ruairidh's playful 'Glesga' inflexion allowed me to smile and nod sympathetically. The rain was now battering down on the canvas of the retractable, and fortunately watertight, roof.

'As for me,' he continued. 'Ìomhair's mother wasn't an easy customer; and had her reasons! You don't know the half of what goes on behind closed doors – here or in the poshest of homes in Duns or *Dùn Èideann*.[74] I thought you should learn some of that here, whatever you choose to do with your life. While that fool is verbally, and it seems physically, aggressive, his mother internalised much of hers; jumped and barked and obstructed... eh... good communication.'

I shivered and zipped my jacket. The smell of our sour breaths was now stronger.

'It must have been the second summer since her leaving Carinish,' he continued, 'the volatile, war-mad husband long dead. Jane invited her up here, I know that.' Ruairidh looked

---

74 Edinburgh

at me oddly and let his gaze linger. He struggled to raise his voice above the din. 'She came to the surgery claiming another touch of pleurisy but wouldn't unbutton her blouse – demanding antibiotics, ones she'd got six months previously. Bill Marr had made a full physical examination.'

It was my uncle's turn to give a shudder, and a tired sigh.

I steeled myself for the conclusion: not of fiction à la *Dr Finlay's Case Book*, but from the loneliness of rural practice in the bleak real world.

'Died that night, Colin. A massive PE.' My blank face, in the weak car-light, needed more. 'A blood-clot jammed in her lungs! Ìomhair and Jane were going to be christening the twins the next weekend – it was awful. Eric was very supportive and realistic but... so, there you have it.'

'Will I open the gate?'

'That's the dilemma, Colin. I've not been asked to see this man in my life.'

'But if he's very ill, surely you must – right?'

'I might Colin, but must I intrude on nature in a 78-year-old? Where's the cut-off when I must impose my agenda? When is it wrong to let people die?'

Mgr Pàdraig's car drew up behind us. 'They'll be glad to see you,' he assured Ruairidh. 'Both,' he corrected himself.

And of course they were. My uncle and I happily responded to the priest's prayers before and after the administration of the Last Rites, and we swallowed another cup of tea with the bereaved wife while the body was still warm. The nearest neighbour –on the phone – then called Ruairidh away to a fevered child in Geàrraidh Sheile.

'Soon,' I said, 'we'll all have phones in our pockets – like *Star Trek* – and we'll be contactable everywhere, day and night.'

'They'll be lucky here,' he said, nodding in the direction of a hidden Easabhal hill, 'in this wild weather and just over a week from the longest day. I reckon we'll get to hide in

Uist for many years to come – if that's what we want to do!'

Hide is exactly what I wanted to do – however unfair that might seem to Ruairidh in his intense state – and within the bosom of my own immediate family. Mum was still in Barra, and I longed for our easy familiarity. The Monday car-ferry left Lochboisedale at 6.30am – far too early; *Dan A' Phosta* however would be waiting at Lùdag's little slip at 9.15am, all-set to motor back across to Eoligarry for his second breakfast.

I'm sure he would have too, for Dan and his *Mermaid* were a hardy team, had the previous night's conditions not grown into a Force 8 gale. No vessels sailed to or from the islands that day except a cavalier, thrawn, *Isle of Arran* which discharged its green passengers on Islay after a seven-hour 'nightmare', or as the skipper told Gaelic radio 'a bit of a breeze'.

Chapter 10

'Can I ask you another question, Niamh,' Oisean asked the beautiful woman. 'Of course,' she said. 'Will you marry me?' 'I thought you'd never ask!' was her joyful reply, and the young couple sealed their love with a solemn kiss.

A GENTLE SUN blessed the winding, coastal road to Lùdag on Tuesday morning, though much evidence of the previous day's deluge was clearly visible in drenched driveways and puddle fields. The air contained a post-electric clarity and, as far as I could see, roofs were intact and there were few other signs of structural damage. This island had got off lightly – merely a capricious summer storm flexing its muscles.

Ruairidh had taken me as far as Daliburgh and sorted a lift with a local joiner who was due to collect two fellow *Uibhistich* off the first ferry north: Coinneach was now married and living permanently on Barra, while his Stilligarry neighbour, Roddy, had been over visiting for the weekend – an extended one.

'They may have had to drown their sorrows for Ally,' the boss reflected, 'but if those two grieving Schottlanders are not on this pier in twenty minutes' time, I'll go across and drown them for them. They got their 'Holiday Monday' – which we didn't, in that weather. Loads on just now. I can't afford to lose men for days or even half-days. This pair's pretty good though, I'll give them that.'

I nodded some understanding of Hebridean tradesmen; those who'd rise two days after a major football game – an exciting one at that – to catch a choppy wee ferry ranked among the good.

The boys jumped onto the jetty slip, looking quite fresh in donkey jackets and Doc Marten's – their tidy toolboxes equally consistent. They shook my hand as I waited to climb aboard; my driver knew my name evidently.

'Almost stayed for tomorrow night's concert, Donald John,' Coinneach joked with his boss. 'Will be one of the biggest Wednesday nights Barra's seen in a while.'

'Could easily get back for it,' his pal replied, 'if we knock off on time in Balivanich.'

'Very unlikely!' was the unequivocal reply and the three of them jumped into DJ MacPhee & Co's nimble Vauxhall van.

With Dan's supportive hand, I stepped carefully down onto the little boat then sat outside in the tight stern, allowing the sun to offer its warmth and counter the wind generated by his energetic pat-pat-pat engine. Another five passengers were already seated – including two Canadian backpackers and a very white-haired, but youthful-faced, woman, Katie. The boys had been chatting to her before boarding, thus my joining them, mid-conversation, conferred a relaxed freedom. I could sit back, allow my shoulder-length hair to fly around my face, and zone in and out of their chat at will.

A large family of seals stretched out to my left, sun-bathing on an exposed rock beyond the islet of Lingay. They were without an apparent care in the world – no hunters or pelt-thieves in these parts and all last-year's cubs now well able to swim in the event of any other threat.

The lads, too, were related: first cousins from Cape Breton of Barra descent – *Niall a' Ghreusaiche*[75] and the *Fìdhlear Bòdhach*.[76] Katie beamed, complimented their pronunciation and asked if they'd been following the World Cup – which they hadn't – then told them of tomorrow night's concert of which they were well aware, being 'huge' Runrig fans.

---

[75] Niall son of the Shoemaker
[76] The Handsome Fiddler

Laughing kindly, she described the location of her house and invited them to visit if passing.

I could see Mum standing just above Eoligarry pier in a bright, patterned, dress and white cardigan. Before greeting me, she yelped and leapt – with arms outstretched – onto Katie, whom she evidently hadn't seen for a while. Backward glances, nods and large smiles indicated that the woman now understood who'd been sitting near her on the boat.

'So like your uncle Andrew!' she exclaimed. 'I should have recognised you straight away, Colin, though I never got a good look at your face with all that hair blowing around.'

''S fheàrr,' I said, usurping the ladies' moment, 'a bhith dhìth a' chinn na dhìth an fhasain!'[77]

Katie's jaw visibly dropped as to slightly embarrass my mother.

'Been working with Ruairidh,' She offered to compensate. 'He'll have thick Uist Gaelic before the end of summer.'

Katie laughed at that. 'You're doing just fine. Keep it up, a Chailein.'

'We were always together as children,' my mother explained, linking arms with me. 'Years since I saw Katie. They're in England; near Hull. Her husband got the house in Lèanais. Throw your bag in here,' she said, as we reached an empty Chrysler parked just beyond the toilets and then, looking up at the sky and the incline ahead, my mother announced we were walking.

She had arranged with neighbour Iain Shìmein Iain,[78] when he dropped her off, that he'd deliver my bag in about an hour's time on his return from the winkles. I had no memory of ever ambling like this with Mum in Barra though we surely must have; no driving licence would have meant some walking – as it had in her youth – but there was usually a lift from someone.

---

77 Better to be headless than without fashion-sense!
78 John of Simon of John

We caught up a little, as we covered the mile or so up to the croft gifted by 'The Department' to my great-grandfather in 1919; Alasdair 'Bàn' had been a cottar in Bruairnis – hence, perhaps, Ruairidh's approval of Glasgow's Head of Celtic.

I learnt that a former primary school friend – 'Colin's wee sweetheart', they all used to tease me – had just got married, too young in Màiri Iagain Mhòir's view. Joyce did, though, look '*eireachdail*'[79] on her big day and a cluster of former All Saints' mums had gathered outside the church to see her.

Dad was in good form, she said, and becoming increasingly World Cup-focused, despite Scotland's failure. He now had his money on West Germany to enjoy repeat success. And my sisters were in Greece.

'What!' I shrieked. 'How?'

'On a plane. The Paisley Buddies. It's a club that...'

The horn of Dùchan's grocery-van consumed the rest of her explanation but I was delighted to hear that Celia and Flora were exploring a wider world.

'Neither of them planning to marry, are they?'

'Never heard a thing,' Mum confirmed. 'If they don't each come home with a black man.'

Oh, mo nàire![80] I thought. But to Mum Greeks, Italians, Indians, Africans were all to be found somewhere on the same racial – but not racist – spectrum. If they were handsome and seemed to care for her daughters, she would welcome and accept them. Hadn't she not married beyond her own culture – albeit to a Caucasian, Scottish, Roman Catholic?

My father – who'd felt some of the changes immigration had brought to working practice and expectations on the buses – was far less open, even in the run up to Christmas.

'Ye gee wan o rame a wee chance an' then afore ye know it the whole family's there pushin you oot the road. They're

---

79 absolutely beautiful
80 Shame on you!

made-up wi a sixty-five pun' wage that wilnae buy holf whit it bought five year ago!'

'A telt ye, Dad, ave no intention o "winchin anybody o any background" at the staff party,' Flora had replied. 'And to bring the conversation back to where it started, did your great-grandfather's family no come over here fae Donegal en masse?'

'At wis different, pet,' he protested, 'there wis a potato famine – people destitute – a navvy wis a lucky man, he could eat!'

'You'd hink there wereny famines in every second country in Africa,' I heard her whining later to Celia as they swapped tank tops and sorted each other's hair for the dancing. 'My heart puir bleeds fur aw they stervin weans. Is at stockin' line straight noo?'

'And how's himself?' My mother asked, when her own sister, Raghnaid – whose tea, pancakes, butter and jam were there waiting for us – had left the kitchen.

'He's,' I stopped. '*Tha cho math*.[81] Not saying a lot, but he must be missing Aunt Emily. Did she regret not returning to work?'

'I'm not sure, *a Chailein*. I never heard her or Ruairidh say too much about it.'

'Didn't really do Uist, though, did she?' I probed.

'No. But…'

'There in Duns on his return.'

'Exactly!' she said, and I knew my mother appreciated my slightly more developed sensitivity. 'I was only kidding you on there, for Katie's benefit, *a Chailein*. Your Gaelic's really come on. Not got a nice click yourself yet?'

'Nope,' I said, blushing. Unbidden, Jane's not beautiful but intriguing smile came into my head. I felt a sudden tug of desire at the memory; an uncomfortable stirring, sitting having tea and pancakes with my mother in Barra.

---

81 He's fine

'Is he collecting much?' my mother, hopefully oblivious, asked.

'Bits and pieces. I'm now on the trail of a major tradition-bearer for him. A natty *bodach* in a thatched cottage. Did you ever hear of Fionn MacCumhail and his crew, growing up here?'

'Of course.'

'What stories do you remember?'

'None, I'm afraid! And what about the Uni work?'

'Making steady progress, Mrs Quinn,' I reassured her. 'At the risk of seeming over-confident, I really don't expect young Colin to encounter any insurmountable hurdles in the autumn.'

''S mi tha toilichte,'[82] she laughed, enjoying my faux-unctuous fun.

'I packed a few other books for you,' she added, rising to add water to the teapot.

'So I noticed,' my reassurance. 'I really like Ruairidh's *Celtic Tales*.' Studying his neatly cut bookmarks had revealed membership of St Andrew's Med Soc and The Liberal Club plus a 1938 Physiology past paper. I made no mention of the 1977 edition of *Thinking of Being a Doctor*, which she had packed near the top. Nor did my mother. I wondered when she might. 'Gaelic's pretty tough in places but I'm enjoying them all the same,' I said instead.

'You're finding *the* Gaelic tough,' she corrected me and then giggled. 'Still a little this *cailleach* can teach you, *a Chailein*.'

'You said it!' I agreed and added, 'Years before you'll be a *cailleach*.'

My mother wouldn't be fifty until February 1980, though there in the freshness of her sister's kitchen – three blues of sky, sea and shore-shallow dazzling – I could see clear

---

[82] Happy to hear that

signs of ageing that hadn't struck me in Greenock. Discreet, punctuated, memories of times – mostly summers – spent in Barra had always been with a younger mother, however old her children grew.

'And this is Cailean,' my aunt Raghnaid informed Iain Shìmein Iain who seemed delighted to have the opportunity of delivering my bag and visiting the two sisters. Raghnaid had been widowed when their only son, Aonghas, was eleven. Always a home-bird and a constant support to her (if a little moany), he'd recently joined a boat of *Barraich* fishing out of Mallaig. My aunt was missing him terribly and was not at all certain that 'flighty' Seonaidh, another cousin, was properly managing their sizeable croft – the cows especially. 'Those raiders didn't risk their skins for future generations to be so casual.'

'Times they are a-changing!' my mother sang – bizarrely – prompting a sly smile from Iain Shìmein and a hurt scowl from her sister. '*Duilich, a Raghnaid.*'[83] She quickly adjusted herself and amended her tone. 'But they are, you know. Young ones are in search of...'

'A career?' Iain Shìmein supplied.

'Yes and...'

'Freedom,' Raghnaid added. 'I'm just used to things being just so with Aonghas and when they're not I worry.'

'That one will be back,' Iain predicted. '*Clann A' Bhàirnich*[84] will drive him crackers. They're chaotic.'

'If *she* lets him,' my aunt replied, confirming her main fear in this whole Mallaig debacle.

My mother's glance across once again enquired of my own romantic status. Was I keeping something from her? Had I failed to take my exams due to some liaison from which I'd run?

---

83 Sorry, Raghnaid
84 The descendants of 'The Barnacle'

'I once thought you might try for the priesthood, Colin,' Raghnaid said, as if with access to my mind.

'He's not like that,' my mother replied sternly. 'Just saving himself for the right girl. Between Ruairidh and visiting the *bodach*, he's surely not getting near girlfriends.'

For the second time that day, the wrong girl – little married mother, Jane MacDonald – made her presence felt, this time from behind as she bent to shine Ìomhair's boots; her own tackety ones were noticeably scuffed with frayed laces.

'Better be making a move,' Iain Shìmein Iain said, 'before those winkles overheat. Try and call in, *a Chailein* – tell us about Uist.'

'*Thugainn*,' my mother urged, 'let's walk this fine man to the gate. Leave those dishes, Raghnaid. We'll inspect the cattle for you.'

Had Iain Shìmein once been the wrong man for my mother? Or perhaps the right man at the wrong time? I'd never considered any other potential romantic paths for her, but I now knew that he had, at some time, been closer than just a very good neighbour.

'Cille Bharra!' Màiri Iagain Mhòir back home insisted. 'Dad's favourite tourist spot. It might pour for the rest of the time you're here. When are you leaving anyway?'

'I've only just arrived!'

This got a louder, freer, laugh and we continued on the road towards and past the last walled vestiges of Eoligarry Farm and its prosperous past.

It was lovely to be with Mum – spend some time alone with her on this much easier-feeling island of family and familiarity.

We soon reached the gate to the island's medieval cemetery; I hadn't been inside for years nor ever attended a Barra funeral.

After a stroll in silence through its beautiful, serene,

grounds my mother stopped at two ancient gravestones set close to one another. 'That's an arm carved there isn't it, *a Chailein?*' she checked. 'I didn't bring my glasses.'

'How come these guys got buried here anyway?' I asked.

'Ties to the Chief!' she fired back. 'MacNeils, surely,' added their proud clanswoman. 'Anyone can get in nowadays!' she laughed.

We then returned to the chapel on the north side of the cemetery where more of those loyal were buried. 'They're talking,' she said, 'of roofing this chapel, then doing it up; that Edinburgh lot might yet return the *Grieving Viking*'s rune-stone.'

'Which Viking was that?' I asked, turning towards her.

'Steiner,' my mother's certain reply. '"After Thorgerth, Steiner's daughter, this cross was raised". That's what's written on the back.'

Before leaving the chapel, my mother knelt on the stone floor and started praying. 'Oh, God, who chose thy glorious servant Finnbarr...'

'Canon Healy taught us it, Colin,' she said, having crossed herself and risen. 'The king was all for burning Finbarr's mother, a poor, pregnant, unmarried lass, but the wee fellow soon stopped him – from inside the womb! The rest is history, as they say.' I immediately heard her brother, Ruairidh's, voice; so frighteningly similar. Would he be missing me already, or was he also feeling a little freer?

'Did the same priest tell you about Steiner and his sad stone, Mum?' I asked when we were back on the main road. 'No, no,' she said, 'that was a professor. I met him on the beach the day before yesterday! The man wouldn't let me go until he'd written it all down for me.'

We visited Mum's other brother, Anndra's, family on our energetic return via Dun Scurrival, the small islands east off Rubha Mhìcheil – Fiuay, Flodday, Hellisdale, Gighay – like giants' stepping-stones across to Eriskay.

My favourite cousin, Seonaidh, had popped home, having encountered tractor problems while hauling a laden trailer. 'If I don't fix it now,' he said, 'Dad'll be up to high doh– after a long day in the factory.'

My uncle, *Anndra Iagain Mhòir*[85], worked just past the airport, in Suidheachan, crushing cockleshells for a Cumbrian aggregate company. Perhaps not what Sir Compton MacKenzie had planned when he installed his library and billiards table there in the '30s, but the famous house of merriment did now provide vital employment at a tough time. I had spotted fresh flowers at the writer's modest headstone as we left Cille Bharra.

'Did you see her pets then?' Seonaidh asked my mother, referring to Raghnaid's cattle.

'Yes, yes!' We'd both seen them. 'They're...'

'As fit healthy and gleaming as they've ever been!' he completed. 'Aonghas will get a shock when he comes home – how solid they are.'

Seonaidh was a kind, likeable lad and much of the criticism levelled at him by Raghnaid (and by extension, Aonghas), was based on jealousy at his easy-going, optimistic, nature.

I promised I'd call over the following evening to watch the Holland game. We could then head up to the concert in Castlebay, he suggested. Did I know Runrig?

Though I'd heard of them – before eavesdropping on the two Canadians – I had to admit I'd yet to listen to any of their music.

'Gaelic pop songs,' he said. 'Marion's got their LP. It's quite good really.'

'I should come too!' my mother joked.

'So you should!' his generous reply. 'Much better than that "Grease Lightning" rubbish. You've not got that one have you, *a Chailein?*'

---

[85] Anndra son of Big John

'I'll watch the film first,' I replied, which amused my cousin. Last time we'd talked music Seonaidh was getting into Johnny Cash but still fond of Status Quo. *Grease* fell safely between our tastes – safe to slag off!

Mum and I continued our walk down to the shore and when we returned home it was after six. I had never felt her so liberated, nor spent so much time with her unburdened by domesticity. Raghnaid of course had washed, dried and put away the dishes and a pot of soup was bubbling on the stove with a cottage-pie browning nicely in the oven. I asked to use the phone.

'*Dia, Dia,*'[86] my aunt's reply. 'As if he has to ask! It's on the desk under the stair, dear.'

Ealasaid's voice, at first tentative, was then effusive. 'It's you, *a Chailein*! He'll be delighted to hear you phoned and will surely call you back. Was it nice today in Barra?'

Yes, it was. It was gorgeous and easy.

And that was that: no further hint as to my uncle's absence at tea-time, nor Ealasaid's continued presence in Taigh Eòrasdail. I almost asked her what she was cooking, but louder chatting, indicating my own meal was ready, made me depart her pleasantries a little abruptly.

By 9.00pm my eyelids were a lead-weight, and my head had begun bobbing, but I pushed my own *modh*[87] to 10.00pm and firmly refused toast – anything at all to prolong the agony.

---

[86] God Almighty
[87] politeness

Chapter 11

'Why, this will be the best wedding ever to take place in the Gàidhealtachd,' exclaimed Oisean. 'I'm sorry, a luaidh,' said Niamh, 'but if we are to marry, that must happen in Tìr nan Òg. And once there, you must promise not to return here again. Tìr nan Òg will be your new home.'

MY MOTHER'S LOUD whispering to a normal-volume male woke me around seven in the morning. One of Seonaidh's sheep had gone missing.

'The daft thing will probably be having coffee in The Heathbank Hotel, but best find her, eh, Colin, or my name will be mud around here for weeks to come?' This earned a guffaw from my mother; 'Ha, ha, ha,' I heard three times as she slippered her way to the toilet. Raghnaid would surely be up in a minute.

Uncle Anndra's factory was under pressure to meet a deadline for a new contract in Singapore. My other two cousins – AJ and Iagan – had booked on the early ferry intending to trade their cars in Glasgow. They'd promised, through the *Exchange and Mart,* to appear at the appointed time.

I was delighted to accompany Seonaidh. Our jaunt would be good exercise and I'd hopefully also be of some practical help. 'It's one of my own, Colin,' he said, 'a total nut-job! Aonghas's perfect sheep are all still out on Fùideigh, of course. I only took a few off after shearing them – skinny looking things.' Seonaidh's dog, a slick black and white collie suddenly appeared, crouched in anticipation and then came with a whistle to heel.

Our trek up and down Beinn Eòlaigearraidh started

steeply, and I spotted a good few cows on the shore, who'd obviously abandoned the top-notch grass; unless they just fancied a paddle before the tourists arrived. But what an amazing view we had across hill and moorland, beach and ocean; all complemented by the red, blue and yellow carpet under-foot and a huddle of guillemots and terns winging up and west.

Then, for the next quarter of a mile or so, the going levelled out – barring divots and ditches – across the narrow strip of land between the beaches of Tràigh Mhòr and Tràigh Ìais.

'Talking of Fùideigh,' Seonaidh said, as I watched a private-plane land to our east, 'Did you ever hear about the night Niall Sgrob spent on that wee island?' I shook my head. 'A Tireeman,' my cousin continued, 'who'd speed straight to Mingulay with his bull, on *The Sluagh* – *'The Fairy Host'*!

'Anyway, this particular night, Niall Sgrob continues on to Fùideigh and stops at the shepherd's house to ask for food. "*Nach tu thàinig aig deagh àm,*"[88] the fellow says, "I'm just about to have my porridge before going to bed." Niall Sgrob sits down and eats a bowl with him. "You'll stay the night, my friend?" the shepherd asks, "it's late now."

'"Sorry, I can't," replies Niall Sgrob.

'"Well, *ma-thà*," says the man, "there's no boat to Eoligarry at this hour."

'"What need does Niall Sgrob have of a boat?" was the answer he got, and in the blink of an eye *The Sluagh* had transported himself and his bull back to Tiree.'

A nice story spontaneously told – from a younger cousin, walking and breathing outdoors on a younger-feeling island!

When we reached the sheep, it was in a sorry state, having descended or slipped down a steep cleft almost at Cleat on the west-side. Its struggle to try to climb up and out would have exhausted the creature, her own caring shepherd reckoned.

---

[88] You came at a good time

The animal was lying there whimpering and shaking and I wondered whether my cousin would just put it out of its misery. But no, he fed it a bottle of 'special brew', as he called it, looked it over for any possible injury, then carried it on his shoulders up to the higher, more level, ground.

After a few ineffectual, faltering, steps the poor thing limped off on its own. Bob (the dog) monitored its return home from a discreet distance – never too close, never too far away.

'Can you believe the water-level around here is so low again?' Seonaidh said. 'This summer could still get as hot as the one before last, Colin. She would just have gone on down to find something to drink. Did Ben More on Uist go on fire recently?'

I told him it had and that the smell of burnt heather was still strong when the wind was in the east.

'And do you like the place?' he then asked.

Stunning beaches flanked both sides, and a much more accessible, compact, drier, landmass stood before me. 'I think so,' I started. 'It has its own...'

'Too bloody long and spread-out for me,' he interrupted. 'And those hills are spooky.'

Our return home was much faster, though we'd spent time at the strange stone-imprint, known to Seonaidh as '*Lorg an Deamhain*',[89] but by 11.30am I, at least, was soaking my own bones in a delightfully warm Radox bath. Mum took control of breakfast, letting my aunt interrogate her nephew about the conditions on the hill and what else did we see around '*Slighe na Ciste*'?[90]

'Little wonder,' she said, when he'd gone, 'if you're going to let your sheep stravaig all over the place accidents will happen, and you'll have to face the consequences.'

---

89 The Devil's Mark
90 The Coffin Route

Ruairidh had rung briefly at the end of his morning surgery to apologise for not getting back to me earlier. His evening had got complicated, he euphemistically told my mother. He'd call from Taigh Eòrasdail after 6.00pm – all going well.

As there are no fresh-water lochs in Eoligarry I was keen to fish Loch Ni Ruaidhe – a fair walk given my earlier jaunt with Seonaidh; but then Iain Shìmein Iain stopped and picked me up within yards of the house.

'Head into the Gleann Dorcha,' he advised at Loch an Dùin, 'and when you see a wee wooden bridge... but you were there before, surely, *a Chailein*. There's little chance the *Cailleach Ghlas* or any other spook will disturb you on such a nice day!' Iain laughed at this. 'It's great,' he said, opening the car door for me, 'to see your mother in such good form.'

It took less than twenty minutes to walk in on the soft moor but given the renewed strength of the sun and its harsh glare on the water, I wasn't too surprised still not to have caught anything after an hour and a half of 'dancing' my grandfather's flies.

Then came a definite, but fleeting, bite which drove me on for another while before abandoning this contrary, frustrating, sport for a Spam sandwich and a Blue Riband.

Afterwards, I sat in my favourite spot – facing the crannog where they'd kept the *Nighean Ruadh*[91] from her numerous Viking suitors – and devoured two further tales from Ruairidh's book.

What glorious weather to savour and not a breath of wind; too hot perhaps for the midgies, but not the copious *canach*[92] which fringed the loch in a delicate white cotton, or for one intrigued orange butterfly that alighted and lingered a while very close by.

Respite from Ruairidh and his rather intense set-up was

---

91 The red-haired girl
92 Bog Cotton

certainly welcome, but my mind was back on old Alasdair as Beinn Ghunnaraidh drew closer in the trickster sun; a famous local storyteller, now long dead, had lived in its vicinity.

Despite the challenges, there was a clear need, now, for me to focus on recording a body of material from the *bodach*, while he was willing and able, and I had the time and space to do it. This would also give me more freedom from Ruairidh's day-to-day doctoring, which was only right, I felt, for him and definitely for the Uist folk!

Ìomhair was a serious concern, but not, I hoped, an insurmountable one. Jane would have a plan, which might mean her having less involvement in the process. That would be a pity as we were getting on well. The two previous sessions had confirmed my own skills: I could establish a rapport with older people, show interest in their lives and treat them with due respect. Alasdair was now ready to impart some of his hidden treasures, so why I lazing on a hillock in Barra failing to fish?

I'd succeed. My productivity would increase. Jane would be fine. Her antipathy towards Ruairidh was surely Ìomhair's. She held nothing personal against him, as far as I could see, and had little to be mindful of when dealing with me, bar her husband's boorish outbursts.

I phoned my uncle on my return to assure him I'd be back soon. Then, impulsively, I said 'Why not tomorrow, Ruairidh?'– with an Alasdair session the next day. We chatted about another story in his book, *'Conall Gulbann'*, recorded from a Donald MacDonald, also from Milton. Ruairidh confirmed him to be a great-uncle of Alasdair's from whom he and his brother, Iain, had gleaned much of their material. Donald had worked until seven days before his death at the age of 93, planting potatoes on the machair.

Ruairidh didn't say whether he had re-visited Iain and Joan given the now close connection with Alasdair. My diligence with the *bodach* would not have escaped them, or anyone else for that matter. In a half-hour or so, I'd be heading to Anndra's house to watch the Holland v Austria game: another 'great' escape.

My uncle's busy brother on Uist had also caught some juicy radio snippets I'd missed at Raghnaid's. 'Churlish, stupid fans,' he said, had booed the Scotland players while they'd tried to relax at their hotel, before thick fog forced a move to Buenos Aires – where the team's digs were in a dodgy backstreet, deemed by one of the players as 'unfit fir hoors'. The dejected squad would reach Glasgow Airport tomorrow afternoon where a much smaller, angrier, crowd were expected to meet them. Ruairidh made no mention of any Uist folk planning to travel out this time.

Unlike in Daliburgh, only one other spectator, a Jim Bryce, had joined father and son for the game, although it was expected that their neighbour, Eòghainn, would arrive at some point. Jim Bryce was the newest recruit to the Barra airport fire-crew.

The Dutch were now most people's favourites (except my dad's!) and talk of Johann Cruyff's absence and its potential effect dominated the pre-match chat; the elegant player had opted, a little strangely – neurotically thought some – to spend more time with his family.

'When a politician says that,' Jim joked (in my Aunt Seonag's absence), 'it means he'll spend much more time with his mistress, but with added privacy.'

While we all laughed, none of us felt Cruyff's decision was in any way suspect. Something quite significant must have rattled the Barcelona captain.

In true reverse (and ultimately futile) Scottish football logic, it was also a shared opinion that the further Holland progressed the better this would reflect on us. Should the Dutch win the World Cup, then Scotland might prove to be the only team to have beaten them. Perhaps the baying fans in Argentina would reconsider their actions. Seonaidh doubted this.

The major change, silky-toned Hugh Johns (on the box!), informed us, was that the keeper who had let three past against Scotland would not start the game. Ajax's Piet Schrijvers would replace him between the posts.

Jackie Charlton, the 1966 living-breathing-now-commentating-legend, was making one of his first contributions when Holland took the lead.

My cousin let out a whoop and Uncle Anndra asserted, 'That's it now!' And it was: by half-time, the men in orange were ahead of their rather static opponents by 3–0.

Mum had considered accompanying me to keep her sister-in-law company and help with the sumptuous spread. In the end, she stayed with her own sister who'd been caring for us so well. Wednesday was not a traditional Raghnaid *cèilidh*-ing night and a Holland v Austria football game was not going to make her break the habit of a lifetime.

A 5–1 final score underlined the Netherlands' strength and was perhaps also a sign of the scale of Scotland's previous achievement. To have beaten this team by three clear goals belonged to the realms of fantasy – the reality of which was our early deflating exit.

Another question of course was: if Scotland were able to beat the team who put five past Austria, why could they not have scored a couple against Iran?

'Delusions of grandeur?' I remembered hearing once on *Sportscene*. 'We'd be happy in Scotland wae delusions o' adequacy!'

Meanwhile, In Buenos Aires, Holland's conquerors of '74 – the mighty West Germany – failed to score in a scrappy 0–0 draw with Italy. Many felt Germany could still do it again. Anndra wasn't so sure. 'Watch the home nation,' he said, numerous times. 'They've got such a vocal crowd behind them: the voice of the people. Let's just see what they do.'

Scouser Jim's arrival had turned the conversation exclusively to English – even between my aunt and uncle, which I found most odd, though I did understand there was a football co-efficient at play too.

'Might hear commentaries in Gaelic one day?' I offered the party, as the first of the Group B matches began. 'What?' Seonaidh snapped, 'Between Brazil and Peru?'

I shrugged. Were we going to hear Runrig? 'What time you thinking of heading up to Castlebay?' I asked.

'Pretty soon,' he said. 'When Eòghainn comes.'

'What's he doing?'

'Watching this in his own house, I suppose.'

My mental arithmetic told me the game would end around 10.45pm. Might the concert be finished? 'Hopefully not, *a Chailein*,' I was assured, with a smile.

'Can we maybe go a bit earlier?' I tried. 'I don't want to have too late a night if I'm going back to...'

'Better wait for Eòghainn.'

Brazil took the lead, after about fifteen minutes, with a gorgeous thirty-yard set-piece. A second, lucky one on the half-hour, brought another whoop from Seonaidh. 'They're good too you know!'

'Good!' said his father. 'Three World Cup wins in a row; no team will ever equal that feat, nor will we ever see another Pele. Brazil will just do what they want to do.'

I knew that this great team's three victories had not been consecutive but didn't challenge my uncle's statement and nor did anyone else.

Eòghainn, who either loved football (in his own home), or whose socialising timescales were even more horizontal than most, still hadn't appeared by 10.15pm.

Seonag brought us bowls of soup and roast-lamb

sandwiches. 'It's looking like a late one – or should I say an early one!'

'What the f...!' Seonaidh almost completed, as a Brazil player, whose shirt had been held fast by the Peruvian defender, fell to the ground following a scything tackle from another. Former Scotland star, Iain St John, howled incredulously and his opposite number wondered whether the ref might award two penalties.

Zico, who'd only been on the field a few minutes, competently put his team 3–0 ahead from the spot.

The Argentina v Poland game was just starting at 11.15pm and I about to make my frustrated excuses, when a delighted, totally relaxed, infectiously charming and tipsy Eòghainn Buchanan arrived.

'Well, well, *a Chailein*,' he exclaimed. '*Dè idir bha gad chumail?*[93] Been up there waiting all night long and you with nothing better to do than watch that hellish football!'

'Ha!' I blurted, stretching to finish my tea. There had been no alcohol offered in my aunt's house – not for any specific reason as far as I could see – but I was glad when Seonaidh took his car keys out as a signal of soonish if not imminent departure.

''*S aithne dhu...* you know Jim?' he asked Eòghainn.

'No!' Eòghainn replied, emphatically, and let out another loud laugh.

'You're an awful lad, Tickles,' Jim Bryce accused.

'I see,' was Seonaidh's return. 'Not just on first name are you, but on nickname terms. What do they call you then, Jim?'

'That would be telling!' My cousin's life-long pal replied. 'He'll find out one day when the time is right.'

'Right *erru*,' Jim asserted, 'Mack a shaw! This poor guy's been expecting to go to a dance for the last two days.'

---

93 What the heck's been keeping you?

'I thought it was a concert?' I asked.
'Both, no?' Seonaidh checked with Eòghainn.
''N e?'[94] Eoghainn asked '*Oh, ma-thà,* that will be great. What's the time? *Dia, Dia,* we should be heading.'

At 12.15am we entered a packed community-hall and from the news on the streets – Castlebay Square to be precise – we hadn't missed much.

The band had come on stage just after nine, played a couple of numbers and then, with the consent of the few assembled, agreed to re-start the gig at 11.30pm – around the time Argentina went ahead, and talk of us leaving Eoligarry finally became a reality. With its churches, hotels, shops, hall and pier all in easy walking distance from clusters of houses on either side, Castlebay had no equal on Uist. It was good fun to be back 'up town'.

Runrig were a five-piece outfit: comprising a bearded lead-singer, two lanky guitarists, a sturdy drummer and a humorous wee accordionist who sounded quite Glaswegian. The look was clearly untraditional. I felt I could hear some influences of Wizard and Wishbone Ash in their rhythms and riffs, but their songs were very definitely – and bizarrely – Gaelic. Popyish Gaelic, as Seonaidh remarked, but with references to the well-loved Highland themes of homesickness, cultural pressures, romance.

The singer's voice was particularly sweet and melodic, and, without any great prompting, he had the audience joining in the choruses with him – they seemed to know them all; as did the Canadian cousins who were crooning their hearts out right at the front!

This was a very different sound and representation of Gaelic culture to that being chased by Ruairidh – and now me – from tradition-bearers in South Uist. Runrig's approach,

---

94 Really?

as far as I could see, was to embrace mainstream modernity in their music, but to use their native, ancient, language as the medium of that expression.

It was also clear from the band's pride in their North Uist, Skye and Scalpay roots – the story of their people's journey – that these performers also cherished and celebrated their unique identity in a fast-changing world.

I was suddenly overcome with the strangest of feelings: that I was taking part in history and that this World Cup Wednesday in Barra was somewhere near the beginning.

Would there be, say in twenty years' time, a healthy number of rock, blues and heavy-metal bands all doing their own thing, but with a strong sense of Gaelic being wholly appropriate when it came to their creative output?

Or would this outfit be a one-off soon to evaporate? Would Runrig have to modify their approach to survive and reach out to a wider audience at home and maybe even abroad?

Seonaidh and Tickles were safely ensconced in a group of friends – half-bottles aplenty in and out of jackets and hip pockets. While I could quite comfortably join them, I preferred to stay detached and observe – to savour this experience alone.

The accordionist came into his own when the band began to play a series of traditional tunes. It always surprised me how well the Barra youth danced – particularly the girls – and this innovative band, having energised them with their songs, fed their feet exactly what they needed. I rarely danced, but watching was fun.

Given the fullness of the experience and the heat generated by the sweaty, invigorated, bodies, I decided, just after enjoying the spectacle of a Strip the Willow, to step out for some air.

The sky was cloudless and the temperature balmy. The chat at the door of the hall was for the most part male-dominated and jovial; then a momentary change of tone drew my attention.

'He's not the only one!' I heard spat.

'They're all taking drugs – every damn one of them.'

Oh, dear, I thought, surely no cousins are involved and was then relieved to hear, 'Willie Johnston was just the idiot that got caught!'

I passed in front of The Top Shop, crossed the road, and was about to head down The Street to the pier when I sensed hurried steps and laboured breathing.

'*A' falbh cho tràth, a Chailein?*'[95] a husky, sexy, voice asked from a few yards behind me. Was there a reason for this unaccustomed use of Gaelic? Did everyone here know what I was up to in Uist, or was it an age thing – my now being almost 21?

'Just getting a bit of air, *a Chatrìona?*' I replied to this attractive young woman of Mingulay descent; what would her take on Niall Sgrob have been?

'I thought you looked lonely,' she said, gazing out to the bay and its iconic castle.

'Really?'

'Did Seonaidh and Tickles run off? That pair can be...'

'No. They'll wait for me.' We were now facing each other – our history there in her smile and ever so slightly parted full-fleshed lips. Catrìona used them to kiss me gently, almost chastely, on mine. No thrusting tongue – no saliva – all very safe.

'Thanks,' I said.

'You're welcome. You okay?'

'Yeah. How are you?'

'You know. Aren't they good?'

'Who?'

'Runrig. Who else?'

'*Seadh, seadh,*' I agreed, 'Wonderful.'

---

[95] Heading off so early, Colin?

I held Catrìona's hand, and we cut across towards the Leideag road-end. You'd have thought we were in a Mediterranean country, so still and warm was the star-blazed night. Monday's storm might as well have been one of Alasdair mac Sheumais Bhig's myths.

'I saw your mother the other day,' she offered, leaning her head on my shoulder.

'Were you chatting?'

'Màiri always talks to me.'

'Of course,' I agreed and turned her round.

'Is she nice, Colin?' she then asked me.

A response such as, 'My mother is very nice,' would have been cheaply hurtful and negligent of what we still meant to each other.

I shook my head; and in that dim-lit, cool, thatched cottage in Milton, Jane MacDonald looked through me to a deeper, less definable, place. *She* wasn't exactly *'nice'* – but she was a definite factor hindering my intimacy with Catrìona. I owed it to Jane to be careful – restrained – here in Barra. I owed it also, bizarrely, to Alasdair mac Sheumais Bhig.

'Your own folks well?' I asked, and Catrìona smiled a little ruefully as she loosened her grip.

'Yeah, fine.' Her dad – *The Calm Stonemason* – had died a few years back. Her mother had re-married not that long ago to the surprise of many.

'I'll try and call in.' That wasn't a lie. I would try to visit. But not this time round.

I then kissed her lips in a similarly 'safe' way and led her back in the direction of the dance. I could hear yet another chorus of *'Tillidh Mi Dhachaigh'*[96] blaring out through the open, frosted windows and screening.

'Fancy a gin and lime, friend?' she impishly enquired, removing a small bottle from her inside pocket. 'Angela was in Benidorm.'

---

96 'I Will Come Home'

'Good for her!' I enthused.

Catrìona then magicked two small limes, halved them with a penknife and squeezed the juice through the narrow neck before giving the gin a good shake.

Our saliva, if not our tongues, shared this fresh, refreshing, delight and our entrance to the hall and final waltz were as they should be: *modhail*.[97]

Catrìona MacNeil was a dear, important, person to me and it shocked me how easily I'd let her be absent from my thoughts when obviously my heart had not forgotten her.

I was, though, glad to be returning to Uist and leaving behind the familiarity of Barra with its fast-modernising living presence of my own past.

Paradoxically, Uist was about the present: Ruairidh's getting through this extended locum with a few spoils in the can of lore from Colin Quinn. My role was to support that effort as best I could, while knuckling down to study for my exams. That island's strange privations – especially no telly without a *cèilidh* – would be usefully focusing.

---

[97] well-behaved

Chapter 12

Oisean dearly loved his father, Fionn, and the mighty warriors of the Fèinn and the thought of leaving them behind, to never see them again, disturbed him greatly. But Niamh had won his heart, and he agreed to travel with her to Tìr nan Òg.

MY MOTHER'S DISPLAY of affection at Eoligarry pier was a close hug and a longer than normal kiss on my cheek. It had been most enjoyable spending time with her and *'Clann Iagain Mhòir'*, people who'd known me forever and who tolerated my foibles for the most part.

Mum's heightened confidence also secured a lift back to Taigh Eòrasdail with the local councillor, a 'Lord' John, who had a meeting in Benbecula about rocket fuel – 'the real stuff!' he assured me.

For two years he'd sat directly behind my mother in Rudhachan's infant class and sniffed incessantly summer or winter. 'What a character, though,' she added. 'You could be bold with John without worrying.'

Just as she'd been this morning – attacking his car and insisting he roll down the window. *'Seadh, ille.* And who's picking you up off the ferry? O, very good, you can take my son, Colin, down with you then if my brother's busy?'

I wondered did the good 'Lord' have a choice in the matter. Fortunately, the man had sorted a lift from his neighbouring counterpart (a most guarded Dòmhnall Francis), as there was no sign of Ruairidh in Lùdag or of his having arranged anything for me.

'I totally forgot, *a Chailein*,' he confessed as we supped our soup around 1.00pm. 'I reckoned if I got cracking early on the house calls, we'd have time for a proper lunch.' Ealasaid had hung on to tell me this too and prepare my room – perfectly! 'But as to how you might get down here, well that was another matter. Who was it again, you said, brought you?'

I retold him and wondered had my uncle been up through the night or perhaps he'd had a tough morning.

'Ah yes. Could do with some rocket fuel up himself that Dòmhnall Francis grump – for goodness' sake he's not fifty yet. As for the "Bold Lord" he's been using the stuff most of his adult life. Do you know he sat…?'

'Behind Mum,' I completed, 'in Rubhachan's class – and usually "coryzal".'

'Sorry?'

'Coryzal,' I repeated. 'Is that not the term for showing signs of having a cold?'

'Where did you hear that?'

'Dunno,' I teased. 'Maybe I read it.'

'Well, well. I think you heard it and contextualised it. You have a good ear, Colin for words, expressions, feelings. You enjoyed Barra then?'

I recounted some of the highlights, including our foray into Castlebay on Tickles' eventual appearance. 'You know, Ruairidh,' I started, 'there's this new band called *Run…*'

'Listen, Colin,' he interrupted, 'I'll drop you at Alasdair's house on my way back to the surgery, okay?'

I nodded assent. Tomorrow's intentions were now obviously today's duties.

'This is the best time of the day for the old fellow,' he said. 'He gets tired in the evenings. And the kids will be in school, until the end of the month. When we hit July, it might get more complicated.'

Ruairidh gave no indication as to whether he'd had an update on Bill Marr and his 'doolally mammy' or if this was just wishful thinking on his part. He had though, he confided, spoken to Jane.

'By the way,' he said, 'while you were watching an excess of football, I had a wonderful visit with Iain Nìll Dhòmhnaill. He recited some of his own *bàrdachdan*[98] – which are super – but then he talked about the creative... eh... "muse" and told a cracker of a story he'd heard from an uncle. You know the one about the youngest daughter of the nobleman and she marries the prince in the end? Like Cinderella, but with no mention of the older two sisters being mean to her – just the hellish fix of having to marry her father.'

'The wrongs of incest?' I asked.

'Indeed. All too bloody sanitised now: for mass consumption and Walt Disney money-spinning.'

'Will only get worse,' I predicted, with an incongruent smile. 'Or better,' I added, perhaps a little provocatively.

I thought Ruairidh was going to say something profound, personal, even. His body tone had changed, and I looked at him directly, but he averted his gaze out of the dead-fly-silled window, which was, as ever, shut tight.

'Does it matter?' he asked.

'Sorry?'

'If one dominant, indiscriminate, culture destroys the others in its quest for supremacy?'

I shrugged.

'Who cares? Do you care, Colin? Do these people who come to see me here and tell me how good it is to have a Gaelic-speaking doctor?'

'Yes,' I parried. 'We do! We care. A lot!' Then cruelly, I thought afterwards, I added. 'I also wish Aunt Emily were alive and that you'd be returning to her from Uist, like you used to. Unlike in the stories though...' My uncle had left the table.

'Sorry,' I said, trying to break a long silence, as Ruairidh crackled up behind Jane's blue van in her familiar parking spot.

---

[98] poems

'No need, Colin,' he said. 'Your frankness is refreshing, if not entirely accurate, or should I say, complete?'

Was my uncle not then pining for Emily? Hadn't they been as tight a couple as we all thought? Many relationships experience difficulties that remain unknown to others. How would my own Dad be or feel, in similar circumstances – apart from being utterly lost as to where his clean shirts were: 'Your side of the wardrobe, Tom? No. The dispenser? No. The washing-line? No. Oh, dear still in the shop un-bought? Impossible – indeed. Aha, hung under those new cardigans! What a shock!'

'Life gets complicated, the longer you bother living it,' Ruairidh stated. 'Your past assumes a distorted significance which makes your present anxious, pressured, rather than enjoyably lived in as it once was.'

'And the future?'

'The future towards which you've been striving all these years, Colin, with "once I've done this – if we only sacrifice that for another three, five, ten years – we can do that, we'll then have achieved such and such". It all proves rather illusory I'm afraid.'

'Right.'

'But you were right too. I do miss Emily very much. I just wish we'd lived more of the present of our past; let ourselves play a little more often. Oh, oh, watch out, looks like folkloric trouble but maybe with some present-day fun.'

Two twin girls and a younger boy appeared over the brow of the hillock and stared at us before running off at full pelt.

'Obviously not in school today then,' I observed.

'Might have chickenpox,' Ruairidh replied with a half-cough. 'There's lots of it about – I take it you're safe.'

I wasn't sure.

'Actually,' my uncle then said, 'it's not so very funny. If they do have them then old Alasdair might...'

Ruairidh bolted out of the MG and I followed him up over the hill. There was an upended cart at the gable-end which I'd not previously seen. The children were playing a hide and seek type game inside it which involved one of them being the horse.

'They haven't got spots have they?' Ruairidh challenged Jane before greeting either her or her great-uncle.

'None,' she replied. 'And the two big ones took them before. So did he,' she said, pointing to the nonplussed super-neat, super-tended to, *bodach*.

'Why are they off school then?' Ruairidh asked.

'That's my business,' Jane replied 'I'm their mother. They won't come near you,' she said to me in a warmer tone, an assurance that this recording session would proceed without interruption.

'But the wee lad's never had them?' Ruairidh pushed, using Gaelic strategically.

'The only thing wrong with him,' Jane replied, 'is that he's spoiled by his mammy.'

This felt such an odd remark, as if Jane were borrowing someone else's phrase – about another child. Was her own mother kind to him and the twins? I hoped to God she was and that was why I'd never yet seen her in Milton.

'Anyway,' she said, 'I didn't let them in the house and nor will I. Even if it pours, they can go hide themselves in the barn.'

'*Glè mhath, ma-thà,*' said Ruairidh. 'Very good…'

'Are any of you ever going to sit down?' Alasdair mac Sheumais Bhig demanded.

'No thanks, Alasdair,' Ruairidh replied, perching for less than a minute. 'I must go. Make sure and tell the boy a good one today! He'll manage long difficult stories now. He's got a good head on him and full of Gaelic.'

Jane sat down with an eager expression on her face – not

only had she made tea, but she'd baked a fresh scone and pancakes which following Ealasaid's sumptuous lunch looked daunting to say the least.

'Post-prandial,' I muttered to myself – gearing myself up to make this a successful afternoon with Alasdair.

'What?' Jane demanded with a toothy smile. 'You're funny,' she then added rather seriously.

'My mum sent me up some books,' I told her. 'Including one of Ruairidh's with lots of interesting bookmarks. Would you mind if I left your fine baking until a bit later?'

'Your choice,' she said gently, appreciatively I reckoned, and then with a roar – again belonging to someone else – she added, 'But you have to eat them before leaving... every bit or you'll just fade away, *a Chailein!*'

This produced a laugh from Alasdair and a quickly lit cigarette followed by an abrupt but equally quickly dealt with coughing fit from his carer.

'*Seadh, ma-thà, Alasdair,*' I started, '*Ciamar a tha sibh an-diugh?*'[99]

'About time someone asked!' he said without a hint of humour.

'I'm only...'

'*Mach!*'[100] screamed Jane, as the door opened and her youngest rushed in.

'They ran away on me,' Donnchadh, blabbered, with arms outstretched for a cuddle, which was ignored. 'And I'm hungry...'

'Take a pancake on your road out,' she barked, and the wee lad snatched my thickest one and skipped out into the summer sun on a hunt for his two worn-out sisters.

'You'll get another, Colin,' she assured me giggling, as if at hilarity, 'if you're good and diligent.'

Alasdair mac Sheumais Bhig glanced across at her then

---

[99] Well Alasdair... how are you today?
[100] Out!

turned back to me. 'Is that thing ready?' he asked.

'Yeah,' I assured him – nudging slightly closer and positioning the microphone at the appropriate distance under the *bodach's* chin – a little closer than last time I judged.

'Did you ever hear told of Tìr nan Òg? "The Land of Youngness",' his translation.

My eye had been drawn to its being part of the title of a story I'd yet to read in Ruairidh's book. I shook my head.

'Where everyone stays young forever,' he clarified. 'Unlike me, they won't get old and worn and useless. They don't decay like the summer sun facing winter's menace.'

I smiled in appreciation. '*Seadh, ma-thà*, might you tell me about this Tìr nan Òg?'

'It's far far out west,' Alasdair continued, pointing to the near part of his house. 'Further than St Kilda.' He spat into his spittoon, and Jane passed him a clean handkerchief from an ironed pile.

But before you reach New York! I might have added, in different circumstances with a different person and probably in a different language.

'That's the place where Niamh came from,' he said. 'And this girl here could tell you everything about Niamh,' Alasdair continued, looking affectionately over to Jane. 'She has heard plenty about her. And she was just as likeable and every bit as pretty.' 'In her day', my tightening gut heard. I wished it hadn't and cursed Ìomhair.

Jane blushed and cast an eye down at her long-ashed cigarette and hurriedly stubbed it out, thus cleansing her lungs of any non-mythical badness.

'Except that one was from Tìr nan Òg not Tìr a' Mhurain.'[101] We both laughed. 'But there was a fellow in Uist at the time they called Oisean. *Oisean mac Fhinn ac Cumhail* – Ossian the son of Finn McCool.' Yes, the full title in Ruairidh's book

---

[101] The Land of Marram-Grass ie South Uist

was 'Oisean of Fionn and Tìr nan Òg'. 'But he didn't enjoy fighting and warring and killing,' continued Alasdair. 'He could hunt, all right, Oisean, but he never killed a man. The rest of the Fèinn were so keen on all the slaughtering they could do. You wouldn't want to be long in the company of these people – especially if you were a *Lochlannach*!'[102]

'Or a *Leòdhasach*'[103] Jane interjected, and Alasdair chuckled. Had she imbibed, I wondered, one of Ìomhair's many prejudices, or was it always in her; a consequence of years lived remote from such close island neighbours but now, through administrative change, urged to be willing partners in The Western Isles' Council's new shared archipelago? Neighbours who would work together for the greater good, travel north and south to visit one another due to improved roads, piers and ferries.

If Jane had completed her education in Stornoway rather than Lochaber, would she be leading a different life? Perhaps, but then she mightn't now be spending this time with Alasdair mac Sheumais Bhig. Certainly, her children did not seem too burdensome – although 'best behaviour' warm summer-day rules did not necessarily shed light on the day-to-day norms of survival in their house. Was it also that Jane's mother didn't care too much for Alasdair, which was keeping an already busy woman at a distance? My experience of all this was limited, but recent time spent with Mum on Barra had made me think more carefully about parents as people.

'Jane's not far off the mark,' asserted Alasdair to get us back on track. 'The Lewis people were Vikings or at least descended from them: but anyway...' he was off, and time for Jane and I to respect this – in thought, word and action.

'Oisean son of Fionn MacCumhail was a *bàrd* and poet and people would come to listen to him from all over, as far

---
[102] Viking
[103] A Lewis-person

away as Greece and the Low Countries' – mighty Holland in other words, Belgium too, presumably?

'And lo and behold who joins the usual lot one day but a beautiful woman on a white horse. They'd never seen the likes before, you know.'

A flicker of an eye in Jane's direction confirmed this to be Niamh.

'And after the crowd all dispersed, she stayed back and went up to speak to Oisean. She praised his poetry – how much it had affected her – and asked, could she return the next day? "Of course you can," he says. He would be delighted to see her again. And with that she jumped on her white horse. That night Oisean was doing his very best to get songs and poems ready for her visit, because he had fallen terribly for her – this Niamh woman – although he had absolutely no idea who she might be or from where under the sun she might hail.'

I could see a tear in Jane's eye, and I feared the worst for Oisean, Ruairidh and herself. They were all doomed. Only Alasdair mac Sheumais Bhig and myself would survive this ordeal; he by his having outwitted death so adeptly where so many had failed – killed in wars or slain by TB and its ilk, when the wind changed direction.

Why I should prosper, I wasn't sure, but I felt I knew for the first time, in Jane's tear and Alasdair's vividly painted emotion of Oisean's attraction to Niamh, that I would survive. How, though? What would ensure this? Unaware of his own skill, Alasdair eased my panic and brought me back to the medieval present.

'At first when there was no sign of Niamh, his heart wasn't in it at all. Though he did his best for many had gathered that day – some very learned ones among them.

'And then she arrived, a little flushed – as if she had hurried or was worried she'd miss him. As soon as that lovely woman lowered herself from the horse and took her place with all the rest, Oisean immediately found songs and poetry of the highest quality and everyone who was anyone gave a mighty applause when he brought the show to a close.'

Jane was examining her coarse, nicotine-stained, fingers – biting a bit of hard skin here and there. The light shining on her, filtered by the tiny window, accentuated her dimples and gave her a cute double-chin. I saw that her pullover was stained in several places and ragged at the cuff on the right. Her jeans were too tight – particularly across the front. I wondered if she needed the toilet after two large mugs of tea. She'd never go at this juncture. Nor would I, but I'd have to soon.

The thatched cottage suddenly darkened, and Jane rose then stretched to light a tilly-lamp. Her face slimmed in the process and a ripe muskiness wafted across.

'And didn't Oisean,' continued Alasdair, 'fall in love with Niamh and she with him.' His two Wally Dugs looked mournfully at each other and jealously at the three migratory geese as they flew over a Coronation tray.

'And it wasn't long before he asked her to marry him.' Alasdair's own voice quavered at this point. Did he, I wondered, regret not marrying, and had he wished for better than boorish Ìomhair for little story-gobbling Jane?

'"I accept," Niamh says. "But if you, Oisean, son of Fionn Mac Cumhail want to marry me, that must happen in the land where I come from."'

'"Which land would that be?" Oisean asked.'

'Tìr nan Òg!' blurted tiny, pretty, young Jane and overly masculine, neglected, mid-twenties' Jane.

Alasdair raised his hand.

'"And" she says, "if we get married there, it wouldn't be right for you to return to Uist. But Tìr nan Òg is a wonderful place, you'll see for yourself, Oisean, the sun never sets, and the people there never get ill or age."'

Alasdair sighed.

'Well, although it hurt him greatly to leave his father, Fionn, and the rest of the Fèinn, Oisean could only agree and on a gorgeous spring day the pair of them set off on the white horse to Tìr nan Òg.

'And after a long journey over the waves – they reached the pleasant shores of the place where the bride-to-be was raised.

'What a stir there was there waiting for them – and at the head a *bodach* wearing a crown with a woman dressed just the very same.

'"Who are these gentry?" Oisean asked.

'"Oh!" she says, "That's my mother and father and their servants. Did I not tell you I was a princess?"

'"Never! Well, well," said Oisean, "And I'm getting to marry you."

'And the next day they held the wedding. What a fabulous do with the highest calibre of guests and food neither you nor me has ever tasted.'

I tried to think what the best food I'd ever had was – I'd certainly not eaten it at any of the conventional hotel weddings I'd been to.

'And for months after that, the two of them were as happy as the day was long and Oisean was fond of Tìr nan Òg and its people. But after a while he began to miss Uist and all those he had left behind. He grew tired of this endless sunshine.' Alasdair looked out of his tiny window, 'He'd just love to feel a wild stormy day once again!'

Jane gave a 'you-can-have-them' look, we get enough rubbish weather here!

'"I'm going home," he says, one day to Niamh. "But I'll return."

'"You promised, Oisean, that you wouldn't."

'"And now I'm now promising you I'll return. I must see

everyone – and Uist – one last time, that's all."

'After a lot of persuading, Niamh gave in to him eventually, on condition he travelled there and back on the same white horse on which they'd come.

'"Whatever you do, Oisean," she said, "do not get off the back of that horse. If a single part of you touches Uist soil, it will not be to your benefit! And that was the agreement on which they parted."'

Alasdair paused, blew his nose properly and peered at his range before opening it and adding two sizeable peats – they would certainly outlive this telling of the story.

'It wasn't so terribly long – although the distance was great – until they were getting close to Orosay. The horse came ashore up there – very near where the seaweed factory is today, though there was no sign of it in those days.

'At first, he didn't see much different about the place – the houses – all were as they'd been except they had chimneys just like my own two! But then he spotted some nice new white houses and motorcars. *Dùn na Cille* and *Dùn an Doichill* – every *dùn*[104] there was – were covered in thistles and nettles. Oisean couldn't understand what on earth was going on. But then there were the people, as fashionable as any Glaswegian walking down the gangplank of the *Dunara Castle*.'

A quick glance down revealed drab, neutral, un-trendy clothing; was this a deliberate attempt on my part to assimilate? It may, though, have had more to do with a mounting pile of laundry. Despite Ealasaid's remonstrations, I didn't want this woman hand-washing my Y-fronts.

'And when he got to his own house,' said Alasdair, 'it was just a heap of boulders and not a single soul who belonged to him to be seen.

'He and the horse just kept on past. Still Oisean sat in the saddle.

---

104 fort

'Then he stopped a man, and he asked that man if he had ever heard tell of the Fèinn – Fionn MacCumhail and his band of warriors?

'The man said he hadn't. Neither had the next one. Nor the next; but that fellow sent him to an old *bodach* – older even than me.'

We all laughed and this lightened the atmosphere. 'Stop!' I yelled, snatching and turning the tape.

'Oisean carefully positioned himself and the horse, then leant over and knocked the *bodach*'s door. The man of the house came out and Fionn's son put the very same question to him.

'"Well," he says, "If my great-great-grandfather hadn't reached such a good age – like myself – I dare say I wouldn't have ever heard of them – the Fèinn. Now it was Fionn that was the leader, yes?"

'"Yes!"

'"And there was, Diarmad, he was quite a swordsman."

'"You're right!" cried Oisean, "When were that lot last here in Uist?"'

A shadow of sadness crossed Jane's face, and she opened and then closed her cigarette packet and, oddly, I thought, rolled up her pullover sleeves. What action was she getting ready for?

'"Oh," says the *bodach*, "just let me work it out. Well, it will be three hundred years – at least!"

'When Oisean heard that figure, he understood immediately what had happened. He was coming near the end of his first year in Tìr nan Òg. For every day he'd spent there, he had lost a year in Uist. Three hundred days there – three hundred years here.

'"And wasn't there," the *bodach* said, "one they called Oisean who was a great poet?"

'"There was, indeed!" said Oisean. I'm just history now,

he thought. He thanked the old man and pointed Niamh's horse in a westerly direction.

'Who did they meet on their way, but two lads trying to shift an *ulpag* – a huge stone – off the road and into the ditch. They requested Oisean's help.'

I could see that Jane had gone emotionally beyond the end and its almost certain negative outcome. I had too. It didn't really matter what exactly happened. Somehow Oisean would renege on his second promise to Niamh and never see her again; Jane would return home to be beaten up by Ìomhair. I now knew this to be true, from the awkward way she had sat and a sudden wincing as she changed position halfway through the story. Her previous black eye was an error. Ìomhair's next assault would surely be better hidden.

And not too long after the end of this story, Alasdair would die and take it and hundreds of others untold with him. And my recorded version would then be what? Another part of the final cultural will and testament – as alive as a Wally Dug?

'Not necessarily,' said Ruairidh, as I played him the entire performance later that evening. 'I should apologise, Colin, for being a little maudlin earlier. I've had a good, satisfying, day as have you by the sounds of things. Jane's kids behave themselves?'

I'd almost forgotten about them until we emerged into the late afternoon freshness. They were completely absorbed in making a daisy chain.

'He did well today!' Jane said, placing a hand on her lower back and shielding her eyes, with the other one, from the strange sun.

'Very well. Amazing, really.'

'Did you think he'd panic?' she asked.

'Who?'

'The white horse – when he saw Oisean as an old, wrinkled

man of about three hundred? Did you think he'd just leave him lying there, that he'd gallop back to Tìr nan Òg?'

I admitted I hadn't really considered any other options. I'd accepted the events much as Alasdair had presented them to me.

'Know what, Colin?' Jane said, linking her arms through mine – my chest began to heave into my neck. Could her children see us? We were over the brow of the hillock, but what if the wee guy, Donnchadh, ran to her? What if big ugly Ìomhair appeared? 'I always wanted Niamh to come and fetch him,' she said. 'If Oisean got back to Tìr nan Òg all those years would soon fall off him and he'd return to being a handsome, young, man.'

I'd said to Ruairidh that if the weather stayed fine, I'd walk to the main road and head north. I gently eased my arm from Jane's, to open the gate, and suddenly wished I'd kissed Catrìona MacNeil long and hard on Castlebay pier to simplify all this.

'Once,' Jane said, 'I asked my uncle to change the ending for me. But I could see he didn't believe in it and the next night I just got him to tell me it as it should be.'

'It's a great story,' Ruairidh enthused, 'and so clearly and eloquently told. Alasdair has such a strong, inflective, voice for a man of his age.'

'Perhaps,' I said, 'frequent renditions of the story have retained his youthfulness?' I heard Alasdair's own 'youngness'.

'That's an interesting thought, Colin. Though I don't think the old fellow's done much practising for a good few years, since Jane was a wee girl. How was she anyway?'

'A bit stiff looking actually.'

'No bloomin wonder,' he replied. 'The miles she puts in chasing after those cows – in old worn boots too; a prime candidate for lower back pain, I'd say.'

Come on, Ruairidh! I thought. This was far too plausible.

My uncle knew much more but was choosing – professionally or selfishly – not to delve any deeper: so that my recording could continue without angst.

'Still more chickenpox in the South End,' he added. 'None of those MacDonald kids erupted yet?'

'Never came that close,' I replied. 'She's got them well-trained.'

'Something like that – *na truaghain*.[105] As Oisean discovered, Colin, if you trade your youth for something else – better, bigger, whatever – you won't get it back and others too will suffer the consequences.'

My uncle was right. Perhaps my certainty earlier that I'd survive was partly due to the fact I'd enjoyed my youth and still was; our generation had been given or indulged youths in ways previous ones simply hadn't. Barra had affirmed this.

'Do you know,' Ruairidh began, 'there's actually a Japanese story about that, *Harashimo*...'

I could feel my eyes closing. The post-dance early start in Barra, then the intensity of recording in Alasdair's stuffy cottage and my growing concern for Jane had done me in.

'One for another day, Colin,' he said.

And with that my uncle departed to re-visit a breathless *cailleach* who wouldn't go to hospital; she refused to 'abandon' her fifty-year-old son with Down's Syndrome, despite numerous offers of help.

I was tucked up in bed by 9.30pm and having located 'Oisean of Fionn and Tìr nan Òg' in Ruairidh's old book, managed the first two lines before letting it clatter to the floor as I fell into an exhausted, forever-and-ever, trance.

---

[105] the poor-souls

Chapter 13

It was a sad day, the day Oisean son of Fionn MacCumhail left the Gàidhealtachd. All the Fèinn gathered on the shore and many a tear was shed. But off they went, riding on the white horse, Niamh on the front and Oisean behind her.

THE RADIO WAS blaring in the kitchen, when I awoke with the immediate feeling I'd slept in for something important – an interview, first day at work, an exam? Smells were strong and salty and yes, fishy.

'They can prattle on as long as they want, Ruairidh was saying at the table, buttering bread and nodding to me to sit down beside him opposite a shapely salmon. 'Scotland are never going to win a World Cup. That was as much our fantasy as it was poor wee Ally's. The public has to take its share of the blame too – for suspending oodles of rational disbelief. Oisean will still be okay even if...'

He didn't continue and I grimaced and began to cut my fish as I would meat or bread. My uncle looked at me impatiently, then attacked it using the flat edge of his knife, expertly removing spine and bones in one and leaving the pink flesh beautifully intact.

'I did consider becoming a surgeon, Colin!' he said. 'But in the end, I reckoned I lacked sufficient grit. Perhaps that I was too touchy-feely.'

'Ha!' I laughed, I hadn't heard that expression before and certainly didn't see it quite fitting Uncle Ruairidh.

'If they waant tae boo us, they kin,' Willie Donnachie was saying on the radio – with little apparent expectation of any other response. 'But that's no gonnae chinge any'hin.

We done whit we done and we done wur best.'

'Perhaps in difficult circumstances too,' the smooth interviewer suggested.

'Aye!' the Man City defender agreed, 'Whit a heat John, know?'

'Enough!' Ruairidh announced, rising and creating a correspondingly full silence; our cutlery scraping through the fish onto the china plates echoed throughout the dining room.

This was the only sound to be heard except the wind, which had got up despite the deceptively bright sun-stream spilling through and bathing the breakfast table. Hopping from near the barbed wild roses to a rusted scythe, in the walled garden, I spied what looked like a robin – but surely not in early summer – a thrush then?

I raised my eyebrows and nodded towards the scullery. Ruairidh's smile confirmed that Ealasaid was still present. It couldn't be that late then. My uncle shrugged his shoulders indicating he didn't know why she was being so quiet.

'Shh,' I connived, pressing forefinger to lips, then tiptoed out of the dining room. I was about to burst open the scullery door when an odd feeling made me grab a chair, instead, from the back porch and prop it beside the wall.

I then stood on it and heaved myself up to three small glass-panels. Two of these were frosted – the other, perhaps previously replaced, greasily transparent.

Ealasaid was sitting with her eyes closed and her joined hands clasped round some long black beads. Her lips were moving continuously and now I could just hear the Gaelic murmurs.

'Some sort of anniversary?' was Ruairidh's interpretation. 'It's not a month since poor Norma died, is it?' he added. 'I wouldn't be surprised if some keep Month's Mind.' To me it felt like many months had passed since I'd played gaily with those dogs. Again, I found Uist's time dimensions out of keeping with those of the world I'd come from – but working in the opposite way to those of Tìr nan Òg. When I returned to Glasgow would I find myself considerably younger than this Uist version of Colin Quinn?

Perhaps it was the company I was keeping – Ruairidh, Alasdair mac Sheumais Bhig, Jane – not exactly Motown, Funk or Reggae dudes. And me? Well, a bit more than I was allowing myself to express here.

'*Seo a-nist thu, a ghràdhag,*'[106] Ruairidh said to Ealasaid when she returned to collect the piled dishes. 'Lachie's salmon was better than they serve in The Ritz. You tell him that; and that everyone deserves a day off – especially those who work hard at a fish-farm.'

She smiled wanly. 'Lachie always turns up for his days-off. It's getting windy. A gale coming, I reckon. Look how dark it is now. Make sure you take a proper jacket, Doctor!'

'A good working-day for the student,' Ruairidh returned, to include me. 'That's the plan isn't it, Colin? You're going to pass these resits, aren't you?'

I felt the intended jab but chose to say nothing. It was immaterial – totally irrelevant to Ealasaid – to repeat, that while I'd take these exams in late August they wouldn't technically be resits as I hadn't sat the original ones.

'You'll get plenty done this morning,' he'd decided. 'You can then come out with me in the afternoon. That'll do.'

Was I being given a reprieve, if not sacked as a bogus medical student? Or had the charade begun to run its course of usefulness for Ruairidh – perhaps with good reason – no matter how his sister in Greenock might feel about that?

'Who's playing tonight, Colin?' Ealasaid asked. 'Poor Ally,' she then said, 'I just said a Decade of the Rosary for him there – and for his wife, they've been hard on her too. She seems a very nice person. I hope this doesn't ruin them altogether.'

---

[106] There you are, dear

'They'll be fine,' Ruairidh assured her, as a doctor of his years might, no matter his personal beliefs. 'Time's a great healer!'

My first day's proper studying for these finals was surprisingly quite effective – buoyed I'm sure by Ealasaid's utter decency; self-indulgent sloth was not an attractive option nor Byron's muse quite as fey as I'd first thought.

By 11.30am I'd made sufficient progress, I reckoned, to allow me the luxury – the privilege perhaps – of commencing to transcribe Alasdair's vivid story.

Ruairidh had passed me some helpful notes on this too: an attempt to take down verbatim what is being told and how best to strike a balance between this and an *'err-urr-uhm'* ruined work of art.

Writing in Gaelic didn't faze me as it terrified many: Mum for one, Raghnaid another. From where, though, had I gleaned the basic rules – 'broad to broad, slender to slender'? No idea!

Dwelly's tome was a useful resource as was a new little dictionary Ruairidh had left lying on the dressing table: *'Abair Facal! –* Say A Word!' or was it actually 'What A Word!' like *'Abair latha math'*, What a lovely day! Which today, as Ealasaid had predicted, definitely wasn't.

I played Jane's exclamation numerous times. It seemed imbued with such hopeful, enthusiastic, innocence; perhaps like Oisean's when he agreed to Niamh's terms of marriage. What, apart from pregnancy, had been Ìomhair and Jane's terms? If the couple were loving in those early days, why did it then sour?

'The good news or the bad?' Ruairidh asked, as we headed south on calls.

'You don't want me to accompany you any longer? You want me back in Greenock? I've spoken out of turn once too often?'

'Hold your horses, lad!' his smiling reply. 'I was referring to our next two visits. You are most welcome to come with me whenever you want to, Colin, but also if you've got other important things to crack on with then that's fine too.'

'Oh,' I said. 'Ta.'

'By the way, Dr Marr's hoping to return soon. I spoke to him on Wednesday. His mother's settled into her new home or whatever it is. He's just to sort out the house and a few legal bits and pieces.'

'Ok, Ruairidh,' I said, 'I suppose we should get the bad news over and done with.' Unless that was the bad news – our departure date – I thought.

'Actually, it makes more geographical sense,' he replied, passing the Smercleit road-end, 'to do the good news first.'

A familiar dark car was parked outside the house of the woman I'd suspected of depression, and whose child I last saw precariously balanced on her brother-in-law's bike.

The weather was becoming wilder, but immediately, I sensed a more positive energy around her home. But whose black car was there? Not the husband's – he had a van. I was never good at retaining this type of information. There were some in Barra who could remember number plates on first sight, others who'd recognise a walking style when the person was still a tiny dot on the moor.

Mgr Pàdraig met us at the door – being shown out by a very different Theresa Steele: in her dress, her open face willing to crack spontaneously with laughter and her ability to cope with the social niceties to allow the priest to leave at his leisure and us to enter.

'Hurry, Doctor,' she urged Ruairidh, 'you'd think we were back in winter.'

Mgr Pàdraig was halfway to his large Volvo when he hailed me.

'Might as well sit in a minute, let them get on. How's the story collecting going?' he asked, as I settled on the passenger seat, rubbing rain droplets from my face with my sleeve. A recent, more naïve version of Colin Quinn might have waxed lyrical on Alasdair's prowess and yesterday's great session.

'Quite well, Father,' I replied.

'*Tha sin math*. That's good, Colin,' he said. '*Tha feadhainn eile ann cuideachd,*'[107] he then added. 'There are other storytellers, other stories. Sometimes,' he continued, 'we can get overly focused on one particular informant. Others slip past us who are just as important, perhaps more so. I've learned this to my cost in my own work.'

'But Ruairidh…' I began and then realised this wasn't about our joint approach. This was about me. 'Thanks,' I replied instead. 'I'll bear that in mind,' then stupidly added, 'Do you think Holland will beat West Germany on Sunday night?'

'Hard to say. Colin. The Germans look very competent, and they'll have the psychological upper hand from '74. Are you coming over?'

'Eh… I'm not… eh,' I stuttered.

'Ìomhair's banned,' he assured me. 'Don't you worry and remember my advice.'

That was good news, for those attending. They'd all get to watch the game in peace – and without serious cursing – but I certainly wouldn't be among them.

Ruairidh was on the doorstep, mirroring Theresa's exaggerated movements and doing his own hand gesticulating. A sudden, heavier, downpour propelled him to his sportscar, and I shook the priest's hand, waved to the woman and joined him.

'Become really miserable,' he said. 'The weather,' he laughed. 'That woman's a hundred times better. Her house is immaculate. Good old Mgr Pàdraig.'

I swallowed hard.

'You or I might have had her on a six-month course of

---

107 There are others too

pills, Colin, when all she needed was to talk to the right person at the right time. He's some guy, as our transatlantic chums would say.' I wondered if the Canadian lads were still on Barra, and if they had visited Katie.

'Ruairidh,' I began, but I could sense he wasn't in the mood for listening. Now wasn't the 'right time' to put a pin in his ebullience. One thing I was sure of, though, was that I didn't want to go to St Peter's Chapel House on Sunday night to watch football. Tormod Mòraig's place would be far more relaxing.

Ruairidh's next call – 'the bad news' – made my decision resolute.

From the tyre marks leading from her parking spot onto the road, Jane's blue van must have only recently departed. She'd phoned the surgery, Ruairidh said. The old fellow was out of sorts and had a sore back.

'Must be quite bad,' I suggested, 'for Jane to call and Alasdair to let her.'

'We'll see,' my uncle said. 'They're getting to like us – one of us anyway.'

Jane's initial hostility now did seem quite foreign, compared to the warm wide-eyed admirer of her uncle's stories. Then again, she'd had little contact with Ruairidh in the intervening time.

'She won't be long!' Alasdair assured us. 'Gone for painkillers, she has. Thinks they'll do some good for this *diabhal droma.*'

That phrase stuck in my mind for months after – '*Diabhal droma.*' *Diabhal* being so painful it resembled the devil's work and *droma* the genitive case of '*druim*' – back. Elegant Gaelic indeed for something so sore.

'There, Alasdair?' Ruairidh checked. His thumbs were on a tenderness trail.

'The right side, I said!' her uncle was shouting when Jane

rushed in, a bottle of Aspirin in her clenched hand. 'No. Not the left!'

Ruairidh had the old man stripped down to his semmit and was prodding around his loin – his hand on his brow suggested a slight temperature, confirmed by the thermometer under his right oxter to be 100°F.

'Are you running to the toilet, Alasdair?' he asked.

'I wish I could,' he replied. 'And I had one to run to!'

Quite a witty response too, I thought, for an 88-year-old in discomfort.

'Is there a smell off the chamber-pot when you empty it?' my uncle then asked Jane.

'He deals with all that,' she blushed, perhaps as an unmarried sister might. Jane was full of contradictions.

'Did you keep any?' Ruairidh asked him.

'Any what?'

'Urine. In the pot?'

'I donated it all to the nettles,' Alasdair confirmed. 'See how well they've grown since I neglected the rhubarb.'

Suddenly Ruairidh turned to Jane, 'How's the wee fellow today?'

'Well enough for school.'

'Was he hot this morning?'

'They're always running temperatures, if you kept them off for...'

'Alasdair,' Ruairidh insisted. 'We're going to take off that vest!' While his under-garment looked clean, Alasdair's protestations seemed to indicate that there was a set ritual to its removal and that this wintry Friday in June was unorthodox and inauspicious.

'You should,' Ruairidh said to Jane, 'take wee Donnchadh,' – I didn't know he knew her kids' names – 'home from school. He's got chickenpox and his teacher is at a dangerous point in her pregnancy.'

'Shingles, Alasdair,' he confirmed. 'I can see the first spots – there'll be more yet. Keep them dry, Jane!' he ordered, 'And give him that Aspirin three or four times a day. Your stomach okay, Alasdair?'

'Indeed,' confirmed the old bachelor, 'as strong as a horse's!'

'We'll see, Colin,' said Ruairidh in the car. 'They can turn out quite nasty in old people – their defence is poorer – that's why they get them: the chickenpox virus re-awakens. Thankfully they're not round his eye – which is far worse.'

'So, the kids gave him them?' I asked.

'No, it doesn't work that way round, but they may have helped weaken his immunity.'

'Surely,' I reasoned, 'if Jane had seen any spots on Donnchadh she'd have kept him off school and far away?'

'You'd hope so. But unfortunately, with chickenpox you can be infectious for days before the spots appear! You feeling okay?'

I felt fine and, on earlier reflection, had remembered a conversation between Mum and her sister when her young baby caught them. Hadn't they placed me about the same age beside Celia and Flora, so I'd take them? Or was that German Measles? I'd need to phone. She was due back in Greenock later in the day. Perhaps best left until morning; let her compliment Dad on his domestic maintenance. I wondered, would my parents indulge in anything remotely romantic on her return from Barra and the house devoid of infant or adolescent demands? I'd ask her straight on the large, old-fashioned, phone from Taigh Eòrasdail at 9.30am in the morning.

'Hope I didn't interrupt any wild passion?' I'd say, 'Just wanted to know if I've definitely had chickenpox?'

I laughed at the thought – both of their passion, though it surely was there at some stage – but more at my attempting such a forward tone with my parents.

From my recent sojourn with her in Eoligarry, it did feel though much more likely I'd receive a warm, if still perfectly evasive, response from my mother.

'Ave absolutely no idea, son,' my father replied the next day at 11.00am – regarding my chickenpox, not whether he and his wife had just had hot sex. 'You probably did. See they Germans, they're gonnae win that Cup again. You watch them the morn. Holland's good but without Cruyff they're no that good.'

'How else would Scotland have beaten them,' I mused.

'*Gu dearbha fhèine ghabh!*'[108] Mum confirmed. Since I was the baby and had caught them from the family across the road (originally from Mull) whom she visited quite often, she put me into bed with my older sisters who'd escaped them in their infancy.

'That's good news!' Ruairidh said from behind Thursday's *Scotsman* – 'Callaghan's Socialist Expiry Date looms' the headline and below it 'Autumn or Spring, Sunny Jim?' and then, rather bizarrely, my uncle added, 'There's a disco in the Gym Hall tonight.'

I thought for a moment he was going to suggest we went together, which would certainly have been weird. Was my uncle becoming a tad eccentric?

'I could go and visit Iain and Joan MacDonald, Colin. Their noses might be a bit out of joint with all the attention we're giving Alasdair. They're a lovely couple and she's a fabulous singer. I'll call in on himself en route.'

'I can't just go to a disco on my own,' I said, 'even if I wanted to.' This expression of modernity felt alien – but of course just like in Barra and Barrhead, the young people here loved TV and pop music and went to discos. However, my experience to date had been of another, more traditional, Uist. Apart from Jane (hardly a contemporary role model) I

---

108 Of course you did

didn't know anyone remotely young.

'Do you students not backpack across Europe and...?'

'Yes. Well, I might go to a disco – or at least a café – alone in say, Czechoslovakia, but not Uist.'

'Very few cafes over there these days,' Ruairidh replied. 'The Russians have recently clamped...' He couldn't hold it in much longer. My uncle's laughter and re-filling of my coffee cup confirmed his wind-up.

'There is a disco, Colin,' he chuckled, glancing up purposefully, 'and you've been especially invited by Patricia and Steafan.' The door opened and I tightened my lazy-looking dressing gown.

'Steven will do fine,' a lad, about my age said. 'How are you enjoying your holiday?' he asked me.

'Yea, not too bad.'

Patricia beamed. 'Much nicer day today. I don't know where all that water came from.' She was a pretty young woman with lustrous auburn hair.

'Probably the Atlantic, dear,' parried Ruairidh. 'Steven and Patricia live in the house at the other end of the village, Colin. You'll have heard of *Clann Fhearchair*?' I hadn't. 'Your dad's side, yes?' he asked.

'Mum's.' Patricia's finely formed face beamed again; she seemed very cheery. 'We're thinking of a walk along the shore if you fancy it? Get some fresh air before all that stuffy dancing.'

'Will we call back about two?' Steven asked. 'Give you time to get up!' He said this in a jovial, non-judgemental, way.

'Sure,' I replied. 'Thanks.'

'Do you want that lift tonight?' Ruairidh offered.

'No.' Patricia was certain. 'I'll take Dad's car. You'll need yours for calls!'

'Would four get into that wee thing?' her brother joked.

'Just about,' Ruairidh returned, 'of our proportions. How's Edinburgh?'

'Cold, but decent and no resits.' I felt my uncle's reflex look across.

'*Math fhein*, a *Steafain!*'[109] he enthused. 'And will you be following in your brother's footsteps, Pat?'

'Not exactly,' she replied, a little bashfully. 'Off to Glasgow – well Bearsden – teacher training.'

'Sounds posh,' I kidded, keen to join her conversation.

'Or like hard work from what they all tell me,' Patricia's first more serious comment of the visit. 'Come on, *a Steafain*,' she urged her brother. 'See you shortly. You can come too,' she then said to Ruairidh, and probably meant it, unlike my mother's enthusiasm regarding the Runrig dance.

'Shouldn't really stray too far from a phone,' my uncle's reply.

'No,' she said, and perhaps only then did I fully consider the physical limitations the job imposed. GPs could be up and down the island – with advance warning on their whereabouts – but they couldn't just spontaneously comb a beach or climb a hill.

Ruairidh would value that extra freedom when the locum ended, though there would be no Aunt Emily waiting in their splendid house to offer a brandy and enjoy the time with him. Eric Adams and Bill Marr, who worked here all year round, had to cope with these restrictions on a permanent basis.

'Engineering,' Steafan confirmed, when I asked him later, as we strolled south on the shore – no significant wind to influence our direction. 'Your uncle was always on at me to be a doctor, but five years seemed a long time and I do like getting my hands dirty – but not bloody!'

'No shortage of work here either for Civil Engineers on these dodgy roads,' said Patricia. 'And you're thinking of changing tack?' she asked me, offering gum which both her brother and I accepted.

'Sort of...' I began.

---

[109] Excellent, Steven

'If mac Sheumais Bhig and spooky Jane don't turn you into a ghost hunter. Did you know that little hillock you cross is a *sìthean?*'[110]

'Hush, *a Steafain!*' attractive Pat cautioned, 'They're fine!'

'She's not. She's touched, that one.'

'Enough!' she commanded and stopped walking. 'Excuse my brother's insensitivity, Colin. He's spent his life trying to get away from Uist and isn't yet able to appreciate some of what we have – what loads would pay a fortune for!'

'Wouldn't have to pay her much,' Steafan said. 'Maybe that's why Ìomhair...'

'*Stad!*'[111] I asserted in defence of what I'd shared with Jane – what she and Alasdair had given me generously, freely – and in defence of my uncle's respect for the oral culture. 'They're just people – like you and me – who've treated me very well. Come on let's jog a bit.'

Surprisingly, both brother and sister were willing and steadily we covered about a mile and a half, on firm seatangle-strewn sand, until we stopped a little out of breath on the edge of a crop of rocks with crab-pools aplenty.

'That was great,' Patricia said, predictably positively (this was her role – to smooth things, especially when her brother was contrary), as she dabbed at the few drops of sweat on her freckled brow.

'Great,' Steafan said, 'Sorry, I shouldn't have...'

'Don't worry about a thing,' I sang out, in a recognisable, if poorly imitated, Bob Marley voice.

Pat continued the tune beautifully, her singing voice totally Hebridean.

Steafan looked quite uncomfortable with this sudden extroversion but didn't speak until we'd finished. 'The old Wailers,' he joked, 'Or is it the Whalers?'

---

110 a fairy-knoll
111 Stop it!

'Ha, ha, boom, boom,' his sister countered. 'Let's hear your singing!'

We did later, at full throttle, but quite tunefully, when another of the Jamaican legend's numbers came on halfway through the night in a packed island Gym Hall. I could see why Pat had been keen to store up plenty of fresh Atlantic air, to feed her relaxed, rhythmic dancing.

Two cousins had joined us and the fivesome made a comfortable, inter-changeable, unit. The girl, Agnes, looked a cross between Steafan and Patricia whereas Paul Antony, with his wispy fair hair, bore no resemblance to either.

Another song we all got into (or down to?) was 'Night Fever'; I'd taken a charming girl from Ayr to see the Bee Gees' feel-good film and thought we'd had fun, but she never returned my calls.

Thoughts of Susie and our efforts to boogie in Balivanich were soon swamped by four guys (squaddies we heard, though it was hard to believe) whose torn jeans, gyrating scrawny bodies and safety-pin'd jackets told their own story: Punk had found Benbecula.

'You'd just love to give them a good kicking,' I overheard, in the toilet, and the sound of gluttonous swigging. Ìomhair Dubh's voice was unmistakable.

'Tough guys, so they think,' his companion replied, clinking his bottle.

'I've thumped much harder ones before,' Ìomhair enthused. 'You know what, *a Chailein*,' he then snapped and began pounding the cubicle next to mine, 'if I found anyone – any! fucking! one! – near the wife, I'd torture him. I'd do much more than that to the wee shite!'

'Out we go!' his pal insisted. 'Don't you go starting anything just now. There's plenty time.'

A plausible coincidence, I reasoned, in the car home. Uist, like all the islands, was full of Caileans – and Donalds and

Iains and Alasdairs! Why should Ìomhair and a mate choose to follow me into the toilet to frighten me? Why wouldn't they though? Thankfully there was no sign of them when I returned to the hall.

No major brawl had started before we left the disco, and I was glad of that but still unsure if that made Ìomhair's pretext any less believable. I wasn't sure either, from the look of the Punk Rockers – especially if they were army boys – that Ìomhair would have fared as well as he'd boasted. Had that, in the end, been the deterrent?

Pat's driving was sober and safe, and her large-framed night-glasses brought a new, sophisticated, dimension to her youthful face. My uncle's car was at the back of Taigh Eòrasdail when she and Steafan dropped me off and I was glad of that. I could see that he was tired and much in need of a couple of nights of uninterrupted sleep to charge his own batteries.

'*Oidhche mhath, ma-thà,*'[112] I waved to my new young friends. 'Thanks for the invite.'

'Any time,' Steafan called. 'See you soon.'

Auburn Patricia reversed gently without revving or tooting and disappeared into the star-filled summer morning with the first glimpse of 'White Boy' Bob's 'rising sun'.

'*Don't worry 'bout a 'ting,*' I hummed, as I made tea and slapped not lemon curd, but peanut butter, onto untoasted plain bread.

It was that night, and Ruairidh wasn't disturbed.

---

[112] Good night, then

Chapter 14

The white horse began galloping west on top of the waves at a tremendous pace. They soon passed Skye and then St Kilda and before long had reached the shores of Tìr nan Òg where a regal reception party was waiting for them. 'Oh, did I not tell you?' said Niamh. 'This is my father, the king of Tìr nan Òg,' 'Which makes you a princess,' Oisean laughed, 'whom I'm going to marry!'

ONLY THE SOUNDS of birdsong and Tormod Mòraig's heifer accompanied my waking. Other crofters did keep their cows between our house and his, but my ears had grown accustomed to Marjory's entreaties: quasi-desperation for breakfast.

Not being one for the kirk, Tormod Mòraig allowed himself an hour or two extra on a Sunday morning. All his animals – cows, sheep, chickens and the two dogs, Sleak and Salamander, were well nourished, well looked after.

Marjory, he maintained, had some kind of 'hunger' disorder. 'It's not that she eats more or less than the rest, but what an almighty racket she makes waiting for it – like a demented toddler.'

'Pre'-prandial tantrums was it? I resolved to try out my adapted terminology with Ruairidh.

It didn't look as if we were going to church either. Had Ruairidh received a more urgent call? If so, he hadn't left yet. I could hear him moving around further down the house – trying to be quiet and failing.

I wandered through and helped myself to some Cornflakes; ten lid-flaps and a £2.25 postal order would secure a lurid green and red, Corn Rooster-emblazoned space-hopper. I'd survive, I reckoned – especially here in Uist – without such a luxury, though some independent means of transport would be useful. Alasdair mac Sheumais Bhig's was do-able by bike, but how then would I carry the large recording machine?

'Never thought of learning to drive?' my uncle had asked in the first days of the holiday. 'I'll show you the basics on the machair.' He hadn't yet. Perhaps I should raise the issue today, I thought – bike-less and space-hopper-less. My lacking this skill was a nuisance and a burden on others. I was about to suggest we give it a go when, between mouthfuls of toast (with lemon curd!), he said, 'Evening Mass in Daliburgh okay and then...?'

'I don't want to watch the football at Mgr Pàdraig's, *a Ruairidh*.'

'Tell you the truth, I'm not that bothered either. A lot of fuss, as if tonight's game's a decider, but he's invited us and...'

'No!' I said. 'I can't. I've got to pay Tormod Mòraig a visit.'

Ruairidh raised an eyebrow of disbelief. The idea that someone, me especially, who hardly knew him, would be obliged to visit such a socially undemanding person was plain daft.

'I don't believe we're to be such a large party,' my uncle pushed. 'Just the two of us; and Ìomhair of course!' he grinned.

Once again, I heard those foul, whisky-rich threats, thumping through the toilet door and my heart began thumping in tandem. A stray pubic hair nipped on my zip; I hadn't at the time, but I felt the jab sitting there, at 11.30am in Taigh Eòrasdail.

'He's banned, I know.'

'So, what do I say to Mgr Pàdraig, then?'

'What would you like to say?'

'Yes!' the firm reply. 'He's an important, eh, ally and friend, to have here.'

'Is he, Ruairidh?' my naivety asked. 'Well, why the heck

is he trying to put me off Alasdair mac Sheumais Bhig?'

'What!' Ruairidh exclaimed and then said quickly, 'So you all enjoyed the disco last night?'

'Yes; fun. Nice people and,' I continued – not letting him sidestep every difficult topic – 'how was your night with Alasdair's brother?'

'Delightful, Colin. No problem at all. Iain and Joan are fine. She sang "'*S trom an t-eallach an gaol*"[113] so beautifully. *Chan eil duine ann an Albainn,*' Ruairidh began quite tunefully, but getting louder, '*Ris an earbainn co i!*'[114] In fact Iain mac Sheumais Bhig was telling us about a fellow – Murchadh Caol[115] – whom I intend visiting briefly before church tonight – suss him out for a possible future visit. It's Lays he has mostly – a good few apparently and no one's ever recorded him.'

I could sense my uncle's enthusiasm and didn't want to dampen it nor hamper his work in any way.

'Ok then, I'll come with you. It will be fine. We'll...'

'No, no, Colin' he said. 'You must visit Tormod Mòraig, as promised.' I couldn't meet his eye. 'He'll appreciate your company. His apparent self-sufficiency puts too many off; unfairly, I reckon.'

'Are you sure, *a Ruairidh*?' I felt like a selfish teenager.

'Absolutely. I'll manage Murchadh and Mgr Pàdraig. Anyway, you've got a busy day ahead of you tomorrow. Alasdair's shingles hasn't come to much, thank God. He's expecting you after two. So, you'll get a good morning's studying in. Jane'll collect you – save you time – Ealasaid will leave lunch.'

Less than an hour later, Ruairidh was called to a village further north, Dreumasdal. Although within the boundaries of the

---

[113] 'Great is the burden of love'
[114] There is no-one in Scotland... whom I'd trust with her identity
[115] Thin Murdo

neighbouring practice (as was the man with the leg), this patient, originally from Eriskay, swore by Bill Marr and wouldn't change. The rest of the family were registered in Benbecula.

Seònaid was most apologetic and insisted I come inside with my uncle. There was now a change in his introductory tone if not fully in its content.

'Colin here is keen to learn. We might make a doctor of him yet, if he's not smitten with folklore.'

I gave a smile that committed to very little and remained in the nearby kitchen as they went down through the house. Was this then Ruairidh's dream of another life lived, in which he could have had ample time (and resources) to dedicate to the pursuit of his true passion?

But how? Who or what would have financed it – even with a First and a PhD in the right area?

Few from Ruairidh's background enjoyed that luxury. This was the realm of the Ian MacKay-Frasers of this world, landed aristocrats of independent means, and in his case significant drive and diligence too.

'They call him *Fear Cholla*,'[116] Ruairidh had repeated mid-lecture on the greats of Celtic Studies. 'What a scholar too!' he enthused. 'Seminal works, time and time again – in the field and in his huge library – with a squad of kids to boot. Ever visited Coll?'

I'd only been to Barra and now South Uist.

'The *Lochmore* used to stop there, and at Tiree. Always wanted to get off. That's when I first met *An Èileag* – now there, Colin, was a singer and a lovely man.'

Later I mused, staring out of Seònaid's kitchen window at two pewits competing for shrillness in an overcast arena, had my uncle taken the Arts path and secured one of very few posts in say, The Scottish Archive, would that have given him enough status to support the other things in his life? Or

---

[116] The Coll Laird

was it a case of his having grown accustomed to that status – and the income – that made quitting impossible?

'*Seadh, a Sheònaid,*' I heard him saying, 'You're just a young woman and there's no heart disease in the immediate family. Far too much chasing after that toddler, I bet!'

'Someone has to!' she replied. 'Did you hear they're planning a Refuse Area near *Coilleag a' Phrionnsa*? What next will they dump on my pretty wee island?'

'The Eriskay people should just refuse!' I tried on Ruairidh on the way home, which got a 'Ha-ha! Yes, well, if only local democracy worked like that, Colin. It's a lovely spot, whether the Bonnie Prince ever set foot on it or not.'

Seònaid Anderson, he told me, had become a granny at the tender age of 41 and was providing much of the weekday childcare since her daughter worked mornings in the Army's NAAFI store in Benbecula.

'How do you rule out a heart attack?' I asked, as we approached Taigh Eòrasdail – a clammy drizzle now which was fast eroding the perfect rainbow that had appeared through the shimmering light.

'Not always easy,' his reply. 'But Seònaid is a worrier and a stooper, a guzzler too I bet. Won't give herself the time to digest her food properly before rushing to the next thing. Her age too is hugely on her side.'

'Heartburn, *ma-thà?*' I said with a knowing smile.'

'I reckon so. Màiri still bad with it?'

Since starting new medicine (in time for last-year's Royal Jubilee!) Mum had suffered little of her customary acid-chest but dared not come off whatever magic was in them.

'There's your man, Colin,' Ruairidh pointed, as a rather less tidy than usual Tormod Mòraig made his way across his field.

'They ran away!' he moaned, referring to his cattle. 'Some fool left the gate open all night. Marjory was the only one who remained, scared she'd miss her dinner. What a calamity!'

'Should I still come over tonight?' I asked – implying prior acceptance of a specific invitation; we had though agreed on more football.

'You're coming tonight, are you?' Tormod replied, blasting my bluff from the top of Rueval to the stars. 'I'll expect you then, *a Chailein*,' he added usefully. He then looked at my uncle, 'I don't do Sunday drinking, Doctor. The rest went but that stayed.'

'Nor does he,' Ruairidh replied unnecessarily, 'Keeping well, *ma-thà*?'

'No real complaints. If I didn't have to chase them whores!'

The three of us laughed a tad dirtily.

'*An t-Àpainneach*,[117] his grandfather,' Ruairidh explained, as we moved off, 'Mòrag's father. He was brought in to labour on this farm – Eòrasdail Tack – before it was divided into crofts. Told me himself, one day, when he had a bad flu. A hardy 'annual' though – he'd never have called me.'

My agreed, fixed, encounter with Tormod spurred me on to do some effective studying that afternoon. Having never taken the time to get to grips with it, I was now enthralled (if that's the right word) by Poland's tragic story of foreign occupation – decades entirely off the map – and now an enslaved Soviet colony; with a far better football team than Scotland! The light drizzle became heavy – but with no need to light a fire – infusing Taigh Eòrasdail with a rather foreign almost tropical atmosphere. While the high-pressure effect made listening to the radio, any music, most irritating, it proved quite a useful cocoon in which to work.

I was vaguely aware of Ruairidh popping his head round the door prior to departure. He seemed in good cheer – looking forward to meeting Murchadh Caol and with a platitude ready for the priest.

---

117 The Appinman

I did reflect, having finally finished a rough transcription of *Oisean an Tìr nan Òg*, that Alasdair's ending was far more poignantly told than I'd let myself hear it live.

'And when the white horse turned round, it almost jumped out of its skin. The young handsome lad, whom he'd taken back across the waves to Uist, was now a wizened, ugly old man of more than three hundred years of age. It fled as quickly as it possibly could – far out west. I never heard what became of Oisean – did he even survive that day? Whatever his fate, I do know one thing: he didn't set eyes on Niamh or Tìr nan Òg ever again.'

There certainly wasn't anything too sacred or religious about Alasdair's lore – so far. Was Mgr Pàdraig concerned that once the chink in the MacDonald armour had been breached that it might close permanently afterwards, like a clam-shell, before age and infirmity (those two chestnuts again) demanded their own priorities?

Or was he simply jealous of my level of access to the old fellow and the time I had at my disposal?

If it weren't something completely different? Like, say, a long-standing blood feud between his and our family on Barra: totally unbeknown to me or Ruairidh?

Alternatively, does he think young Cailean is showing amazing prowess 'in the field' and should spread his skills more evenly? This, however, seemed least likely.

It had to be the blood feud thing, I chuckled, searching for something to take to Tormod Mòraig and getting hot in the process in my coat and boots. I'd call Mum, she'd possibly answer honestly, if I asked her the right way.

'Yes, *a Chailein* – every year for a hundred and four years, we have slain one of theirs and them one of ours.'

Poor Mgr Pàdraig! My far-fetched fantasy had demonised him rather; a man who'd invited me to watch a great game. Perhaps he also wished to make amends for our previous TV *cèilidh*-ing episode aka: Archie Gemmill's classic goal fails to match up to angry Ìomhair on the razzle. What a tosser indeed! How personally dangerous a tosser, I still wasn't sure.

The quarter-final proved a football spectacle and Arie Haan's blistering strike from thirty yards was exciting beyond belief. The German keeper stayed rooted to the spot, while Tormod Mòraig and I did a little Sunday sitting room dance before returning to our ginger beer and black bun (found in a high cupboard) for treats: like Holland v West Germany.

Now at 1-1 – the first World Cup goal lost by Helmut Schön's team in four years – Hugh Johns fancied Holland's chances. A win, or possibly yet a draw, against Italy would take them nicely through to the final for the second consecutive time.

Gentleman Jack Charlton however cautioned against 'premature chicken-counting': this was still West Germany. In his career he had won – and lost (!) – in similar circumstances; a cool second-half header from Müller supported this view.

'We'll just have to see how it all turns out, Hugh!' the big man said. 'And let's face it, Italy might not be playing their best ever football here, but they are man for man a much stronger side than the Scots!'

Both Tormod Mòraig and I felt that one and I would have loved to have yelled at the top of my voice: *'Thalla thusa, a chac!'*[118]

But despite his earlier bawdy humour, such crudity would not have been appropriate from me at this moment in Tormod's house. I didn't know him that well – at all really, when I came to think about it. Who did, I wondered?

Tormod did though tell me that when his grandfather arrived in Uist from Appin, he thought he'd reached the ends of the earth – if not a loch-infested moon.

'But,' he continued, 'I'm certainly happy he came here. There are still plenty Gaels left in Uist – becoming an

---

[118] Get lost, you shit!

endangered species in Argyll!'

As we parted at this door, we both stopped to observe a man repairing the thatch on the house beside Loch an t-Seileasdair, the last inhabited one in Eòrasdail. At almost 10.45pm he was still there measuring and bunching appropriate lengths of new marram-grass to insert into the two-toned curvaceous roof. It wasn't so clear a night and the sun had long since gone down.

'Could do it with his eyes closed,' Tormod observed. 'There's no one quite like Raghnall in Uist these days. He'll be much in demand in autumn.'

'Come from nearby?' I enquired.

'No, no,' Tormod confirmed. 'He'll drive back across to Hacleit yet, but he never lets Bean Eachainn down. She was very good to them all as children.'

From the gate, I waved back to Tormod and across to Raghnall who was finally removing his heavy wooden ladder in almost darkness from the old lady's roof. A man of singular talent: another one. These islands were teaming with individuals who were particularly skilled: as joiners, stonemasons, ploughers, peat-stack builders, scythers, stookers.

The list was endless of artistic and aesthetic abilities being honed over many years within the craft of the day-to-day demands of croft-life.

I wondered how song and story – apart from the obvious work-related stuff – had attained such sophistication and status over the centuries. Were these not rather impractical ways to spend one's time in a society that was so heavily reliant on manual skill and endeavour for survival?

Holland's late equaliser would surely see them through to the final. Raghnall, the thatcher, Tormod reckoned, should complete his goal in one more session. He'd had to go to extra-time tonight, but in the world of juggling crofting-crafts and paid employment there was little use for penalties; he'd just have to return another day when the weather was right – fifteen miles up south from Benbecula.

I wondered if 'disgraced', 'drug-taking' Willie Johnston would perform the equivalent for someone who had been good to him as a child? What might he do – play keepie-uppie with the grandkids to let her out to the shops?

Further fantasies followed me home until a starling's shriek revealed Ruairidh's car at the back door.

I found my uncle hunched over a large textbook with only the feeble 40w table-lamp lit.

'More light?' I asked, pressing the switch.

'Thanks.'

'I wonder does Bean Eachainn have songs or stories?'

'No idea, Colin. Who?'

'You know,' I said, 'the *cailleach* whose house that fellow, Raghnall, was working on – by the loch? She certainly looks old enough.'

'Age has nothing to do with it, Colin,' he snapped, slamming the tome shut. 'It's about interest, memory, artistic sensibility and prowess.'

'Time?' I enquired

'What?'

'Having the time to devote to such practice. Surely even if you've got the rest, if real-life demands steal your extra-time, you'll end up not that much better off than those who had no talent in the first place.'

There was a long pause, which I thought of filling with an enquiry about Murchadh Caol or Mgr Pàdraig, but an image of Willie Johnston, Raghnall and Alasdair mac Sheumais Bhig wearing Scotland strips and tartan bunnets kept me amused in the silence.

'Shh,' Raghnall was saying, 'we're going to hitch down to the Mexican border – Willie's got plenty contacts in Colombia

– very good friends, you know – we "borrowed" a wheelchair for the *bodach*. Mum's the word, or Ìomhair will come and his ugly face will put them all off giving us a lift!'

'Did you know, Colin,' Ruairidh was saying back in Taigh Eòrasdail's dim reality, 'that in 1942 I won the Urquhart Diagnostic Medal? It was a highly contended award for it went beyond St Andrews. Unlike most exams it wasn't about amassing and regurgitating screeds of facts. It entailed assessing real patients with real illnesses – minor and major – and reaching the correct differential diagnosis, then narrowing to the most likely one with an appropriate management plan.'

'Wow,' I said, 'Well done. There you go. Not bad at all.'

'Among them was a young woman who'd lost the power in her limbs. She'd... anyway, it was Guillain-Barré syndrome, a rare, eh, condition. And there was an older chap with a foot sprain – nothing more. The x-ray was completely normal, though lots confused his rather large posterior talar process with a fracture. Ten cases overall we had.'

I felt that this wasn't going to go anywhere positive, but resisted any softeners of my own. I did though add, 'Can I make us supper? Black bun and ginger beer only go so far.'

'She did have a heart attack,' my uncle said. 'A mild one, but still and all, a bloody infarction. The ECG at the hospital showed acute changes.'

'Sorry?'

'The woman with the heartburn, Seònaid. That wasn't what she had at all.'

'Oh, shit.'

'Exactly. Time for me to quit this nonsense.'

'*Fuirich, ma-thà,*'[119] I said, 'I'll put the kettle on. Two sugars, right?'

'Only one, thanks, Colin; since turning sixty.'

---

119 Wait a minute

Chapter 15

Oisean and Niamh's wedding on Tìr nan Òg lasted a week and a day and everybody who was anybody from throughout the land came to pay their respects to the happy couple. They all feasted and danced and sang from dusk until dawn.

BILL MARR WOULD be back by the second weekend of July. He phoned to confirm this the following morning after Ruairidh had left; Ealasaid and I were still chatting.

For the first time in my stay at Taigh Eòrasdail she had sat down beside me. Normally there was a need to dash off, unless that was the impression Ealasaid liked to give to save any possible awkwardness.

I offered, and she accepted a cup of coffee.

'Yes,' she said. 'I was once quite fond of coffee, during my Palace days in Oban – those shifts were so early – coffee was the only thing for it.'

It was clear she wanted to talk.

'The hotel would be full in July and August, and everything had to be "just so" for Smart Alick. We had this boiler to light by 5.00am, to be ready for the keen breakfasters – or those on an early boat. The Tiree lot left so early while the Uist and Barra ferries would leave so late.'

'Do you think he's okay, Ealasaid?' It felt safe enough to confide in her.

'*Cò, d' uncail Ruairidh?*[120] Yes, yes. He'll be tired, that's all. He's had a long stretch on-call, *a Chailein*. He's very

---

[120] Who, your uncle Ruairidh?

well-liked and an excellent doctor. There's lots prefers him to Marr – a nicer way with him altogether.'

This gave me some reassurance. I had begun to fear a little for my uncle's well-being. Perhaps his diagnosis of Seònaid Anderson's mild coronary as heartburn could easily have been done, especially Ruairidh claimed, without a portable heart monitor.

Her getting to hospital would have meant an hour's round-trip, with grandson in tow, on a Sunday afternoon. Clearly, she had attended later – perhaps the daughter insisted where the doctor hadn't? Ruairidh would be glad to complete this extended locum and to see Bill Marr safely back at work and to his fine view of Ben Coinnich and Lochboisedale Bay.

'*Is ciamar a tha i fhèin,*[121] lady-muck?' Ealasaid asked.

'Who?'

'Jane, of course.'

The image of her arm through mine in broad daylight came unbidden to my mind's eye. She held me gently, longer than she had then, and our parting laugh was light and untroubled.

'Mellowed,' I said, intentionally vaguely. 'She's quite, eh, enjoying her uncle getting recorded, I reckon.'

'That's not all she's enjoying. But they say he's very good,' Ealasaid confessed. 'Alasdair mac Sheumais Bhig wouldn't have told you the time when the two of them were there: him and Dòmhnall. She's obviously been working on him to perform. Before it's too late!' she stated, just as I'd often thought.

'Well, you should have heard him telling about Oisean and Tìr nan Òg, the other day,' I said. 'It was beautiful.'

It would have done little harm to play her a fragment – the whole tale even – but I chose not to. It seemed like a transgression of my duty to Alasdair (and Ruairidh). Also, I was not sure Ealasaid could remain seated to hear him out,

---

[121] And how's herself

and I didn't want to preside over a tense situation: her needing to get on and my detaining her with 'rubbish'.

'She'll have...' Ealasaid stopped, 'Jane will be, eh, moving in on you if she hasn't yet?'

'Sorry?'

'She has a history of it. Why, did you think you were the first?' Ealasaid's laugh was rough. What proof did she have? 'Plenty more where you came from, Colin,' she added, 'though that's the first time Jane's used the *bodach* to eh… get what she wants. Just you be careful!'

I didn't feel comfortable. Whom to trust? A stuck, frustrated, spinster or a rather sad (in so many ways save in her uncle's presence) Jane MacDonald?

'And the beatings will only get worse,' Ealasaid added, coming closer, 'the more Ìomhair winds himself up. *"An rud a chì na big, nì na big"*,[122] Ìomhair saw too much, too young.'

God, how horrible! How widely was all this known – and accepted? Had Steafan's caustic warning been accurate then? Was Jane a bit touched and not just a poor bullied sort – her arm once again thrust itself through mine – or was she possibly playing some twisted game with Ìomhair and me, encouraging her husband to come after me for real?

If ever-dutiful Ealasaid were not merely a fanciful gossip, jealous of Jane's obvious fertility and her bond with her great-uncle, and perhaps – I thought, when she'd gone – the hours she was spending with me?

The bright early morning had dulled and Eòrasdail was now settling into a more recognisably Hebridean – rather than tropical – drizzle.

Despite our conversation, I was able to settle quickly into Monday's first topic. I now had a proper timetable, which meant starting the day with an hour's Psychology (the easiest to get into) then alternating between History and

---

[122] What the children see, they will do.

English Lit. Something I'd never heard of before was Cultural Psychology. Different cultures, proponents claimed, foster not only distinct social values but also logical reasoning. Time spent in Uist with Alasdair mac Sheumais Bhig and Jane made this theory relevant. As did my experience of Ìomhair Dubh!

Should I pursue more of this stuff if I passed my exams – plan some original research comparing say those who stayed in their Gaelic communities and those who had left?

The Dr Ruairidh Gillies / Prof John Boyd connection did though feel a tad too close for comfort, especially if my efforts failed to match my uncle's ideals.

So, was it going to be Psychology or back to European History – which I'd found, given the opportunity to focus, I'd enjoyed? On the other hand, could I really try moving to medicine – for me? Whatever I ended up doing, this newfound interest and application should surely ensure autumn exam passes. Time to crack on, though!

I made myself another coffee and listened to the rain splatter the lower windowpane, then yanked in the net curtain, which had got caught outside and was soaked and torn. Marjory must be on the machair. The starlings were taking advantage and dominating the soundscape. Any radio programme – especially Radio 1 – would violate their sacred space to hold forth, inform us of their views on weather; changing village life; their hopes for this year's journey and perhaps to give a prediction of the upcoming games? Would Holland (as most predicted) reach the World Cup Final again? And their opponents in Buenos Aires: the illustrious Brazil, or would Wednesday night see Argentina show another of Scotland's victors, Peru, that their desire for success on their home turf was beyond challenge?

Interesting days lay ahead in the world of football in the Southern half of the American continent, less so, I felt, for me in the Southern Hebrides. I didn't intend visiting Alasdair until tomorrow afternoon – let him settle into his shingles. While Jane would, of course, have a phone, the thought of chatting through our stiff black device to Ìomhair Dubh was not a pleasant one. What might he choose to threaten in a one-to-one situation like that? So, Ruairidh had informed Jane – through a neighbour from whom he'd removed a fat tick in a very tricky place.

Come on, Ealasaid, I thought, as I switched to *The Language of Shakespeare*, Jane is simply ensuring that her uncle's knowledge be retained for future generations. If she did perhaps have a bit of an odd way about her, that didn't equate to chasing me or other men. Ìomhair would have made damn sure of that!

So, why had thoughts of her influenced things with Catrìona in Barra? Had Jane supplied a timely excuse to end what should have ended long ago – kisses of convenience, beyond that of late?

It was 1.30pm before I looked up from my books. I'd been there in that world of words and ideas for much of the previous two hours. The stillness and silence of the house were today comforting, productive, and conducive to concentration. The starlings were gone. Tormod Mòraig's cow was still on the machair. I could hear a dull thudding sound in the distance – perhaps a fencepost being secured – then it stopped.

The steady ticking echoed in the wood-panelled hall and again its sound gave moment and movement to my task. Just two weeks ago the noise was bugging me as I struggled to settle, and a wish to yank its plug or eviscerate its batteries grew intense, but of course this 1916 pendulum clock relied on neither for its constancy and potential immortality.

I turned the Uher on and rewound the tape to the beginning.

'*But there was a fellow in Uist at the time they called Oisean. Oisean mac Fhinn ac Cumhail – Ossian the son of Finn MacCool. But he didn't enjoy fighting and warring and killing. He could hunt, all right, Oisean, but he never killed a man. The rest of the Fèinn were so keen on all the slaughtering they could do with their...'*

The story was a beautiful piece of art to sit back and listen to – luxuriate in – alone on a dull June Monday in Uist. From this safe distance, and as the key facilitator of my work, Jane was whole, wholesome, without blemish. Why wouldn't she slip her arm through mine at the end of such a successful session? Why not be on a high: Alasdair mac Sheumais Bhig so ably cheating death once again and her fragile youth unbroken?

I had heard the soft knock and assumed my uncle had made it back for lunch, which was soup left by Ealasaid as her sister was due off the boat in Lochmaddy. A second, louder rap, and then Patricia's opening the door, confirmed he hadn't yet.

'Is that him?' she asked.

'Alasdair? Yes.'

'I didn't want to...'

'You're fine.' She was absolutely 'fine'. It was lovely to see a young person like Patricia.

'Should I come another time, *a Chailein*?'

'Not at all. He'll soon finish it,' my promise.

We sat in companionable silence for a minute or two, which didn't feel at all awkward. If Steafan had come it would have. The quietness continued a little beyond the story before hunger rumbled my stomach. I invited Patricia to follow me into the scullery.

'Lentil-soup, *ma-thà?*' I offered, reaching for the matchbox.

'You do that too?' she teased.

'I stir it well on the stove. Ealasaid does the rest.'

'What a life you two guys have got!' she remarked, not bitterly. '"*Air allaban,*" as they say – "in foreign territory".'

I'd never heard that phrase before but was aware that my abilities to express myself in a less-domestic way were fast improving. I was enjoying the experience.

She sang a verse of a song:

'*Air allaban tha mi 's mi an* àite *fliuch, fuar...*'[123]

'Very nice,' I said and immediately followed that with, 'You've a great voice, Pat. Got many songs?'

'Should do,' she replied, adjusting her slim frame in the seat, 'my grandfather and mother... I was in the choir; we went to the Aberdeen Mòd – with Princess Anne, ha. No thanks, Colin, *cha ghabh mise sgath*,'[124] she continued, in a noticeably playful tone.

'Come on!' I said, pushing a bowl and two slices of bread in front of her, and like my mother – or more like Aunt Raghnaid – not taking 'No' for an answer.

'Not at all salty,' Patricia approved, tucking in.

'No, Ealasaid is quite modern, that way,' I laughed, kindly I hoped, and met her own soft smile as she raised her head.

'They've all got blood pressure,' Pat added, her turn now to be a woman beyond her years. 'Her brother took a stroke, young, then a heart attack, but he was big too, Iain, and... do you really enjoy the stories, Colin, or is it something else you're searching for?'

'Like what?'

'Don't know. That's what made me ask. Are you searching for something particular?'

This was a difficult question for which to find an honest, accurate, answer.

'It was my uncle...' I began, 'Ruairidh was the one that asked me to come here – keep him company, help him with his work.' So, what now was my own motivation – my genuine interest in all this? Jane MacDonald smiled – like a

---

[123] I am in unfamiliar territory, a cold, wet, place...
[124] I won't eat anything.

six-year-old in a doll's house – and thrust her arm through mine with wide oval eyes on the hillock Steafan said housed fairies.

Was I still, though, largely seeking Ruairidh and by extension my mother's approval? 'Cailean's a good boy; few of his generation show interest in that sort of thing. This will help put him on a straighter path!'

Patricia was certainly a nice-looking woman – far more so than Jane – who until now had given few sensual cues. No flirting, that was it; even Ealasaid *bhochd*[125] flirted in her own 'harmless' way. Perhaps Pat was going steady and had switched off something; or was Jane MacDonald a key cooling factor?

'What do you think of them?' I asked her.

'What?'

'Stories, *naidheachdan*[126] – that sort of thing?'

'I'm fond of lots of the songs,' she said, 'but I'm fonder of the people, than of what they might have or care to give us. Do you know what I mean?' Her open, fresh, face took on an air of seriousness.

'Yes,' I assured her. 'That's admirable.'

'I can't imagine,' Pat continued, 'spending weeks of my life in the company of some old wretch just because he (or she!) was a "fab" storyteller.' She laughed loudly, lighting her sea-green eyes. 'Read too much of *The Jackie* in my time, Colin, can't you tell? "Fab" Alasdair mac Sheumais Bhig and "dishy" grand-niece Jane tell all to "cool" Col's listening ear and the Uher that never lies!'

'Ha-ha, you know your technology too.'

'It's written on the top cover. Over there,' she pointed. 'I should be off.' She had never declared a specific reason for visiting; the thought of Patricia just popping in without any

---

125 poor Ealasaid
126 shorter or less-weighty stories

pretext, appealed greatly.

'One for the road,' I said rising quickly – exposing my eagerness for her to stay a little longer.

'Ok then,' she said, 'but make it small, *a Chailein*, I'm driving.'

I had hoped she'd sing a parting song, but now had to find whisky. I liberally siphoned the last two thimble-fulls from the bottle in another high 'press' in the damp porch; sniffing it first to make sure it wasn't paraquat or turpentine.

'Now, dear,' I said, in a couthie wee voice. 'You will sing me something very nice – the one you began surely?' I fed her the opening line of the chorus, and she was soon off to a densely forested land full of forlorn emigrants – '*air allaban*'.

This she followed with a poignant love song from another local poet. 'Wow – fantastic!' I cheered, 'Amazing the effect Barra beauty can have on a receptive Uist heart!'

'Yes,' she agreed, 'and this girl was certainly special – still is, I hear. Sorry I don't really have any stories, Colin, well…' She then adeptly told of a girl courting a handsome man she met by Loch Chill Donnain while washing the sheets. As he naps on her lap his wavy locks reveal fresh-water foliage: a sure sign of a water-horse. The maiden cuts herself away leaving the straps of her apron still knotted in his hair, and, thankfully, never sees him again.

I could hear Patricia's competent, unadorned, giving of this story to her class, but still retaining the credibility and authority of Miss MacInnes.

'I didn't expect to be doing any of that,' she said, as I opened the door. 'Aren't you good at getting what you want, Colin!' I smiled and accepted the compliment, though it did also suggest a manipulative side that mightn't be such a virtue.

'I didn't expect you to be doing any of that either!' I echoed. The whisky and the performance had injected warmth into her light-coloured cheeks. 'Honest,' I added, though I didn't need to, and walked her out through the porch.

Pat's father's Ford Avenger patiently waited in the rain; presumably she'd been elsewhere and just kept on through the village. The MG's hoving into view caused a sudden pulsating panic. I wanted her to go now – perhaps wave to Ruairih on the road, but not for him to find her here at Taigh Eòrasdail. She obliged and promised to return soon. Would that be alone, I wondered, or with Steafan?

My uncle seemed upbeat after his busy morning: a longish post-theatre surgery, then house calls 'all over the bloody place. That road out to Strome is still rugged, Colin, I'm glad my first visit was in daylight – might yet have to stumble back out in the shadow of darkness, but not if I can help it.'

'There's soup,' I said.

'Excellent. Not smelt a snap since breakfast. Herself will be back for tea I take it?'

'Yeah, yeah, family taxi-service only. She's not abandoned us, yet! Tasty isn't it.'

'Two bowls, *a Chailein?*' he remarked, spotting Patricia's and mine, still un-steeped on the table.

'We had a visitor, who sang songs and gave us a story – all recorded!' I pointed next door.

'Weren't you lucky!' His eyes twinkled. 'As I said – really nice people, *Clann Fhearchair* – and what a sweet singer, her grandfather – no wonder Patricia's good. She couldn't have escaped getting at least some of those talents. But fabulous,' he added, 'that she was willing to share them.'

Pat hadn't pressed me further on the question of what I was looking for in this work. Her own fresh, controlled, contribution had though gone some way to answering one aspect of what I was enjoying, the delight at receiving generous rewards by showing some genuine interest.

Like Ruairidh in his many and varied consultations, my presence and willingness to use the recording machine, legitimised others to open up and give freely. What a privilege. What a blast!

'Eric Adams is on evening surgery tonight and he'll stay on-call for the next 48 hours,' Ruairidh said. 'He was most supportive about Seònaid; said he wouldn't have brought her to Daliburgh at that point either. Let's do something enjoyable after tea.'

Local ghillie, Eàirdsidh Fhionnlaigh, was waiting for us at Loch Olaidh in the west-side village of Stoneybridge, his small rowing boat under canvas and tied down securely; the 'residents' of Àrd Mhìcheil cemetery certainly enjoyed a fine view down on us and out to the eternal cycle of the sea.

'You're sure now, *a Dhotair Ruairidh?* Eàirdsidh pressed, freeing the boat. 'I'd be delighted to row you both out and back. Many's the day I did it and if God spares me my health, many's the day I'll do it yet.'

'Too kind, too kind,' my uncle's answer. 'See these arms, *a bhalaich?*[127] It's high time their muscles did something useful. There was once – not that long ago – when the oars were rarely out my hands. We won't even be two hours, *ma-thà.*'

Compared to the dull, drizzly, day the evening had become quite pleasant and there wasn't a drop of rain or a breath of wind to be felt as we clambered aboard *Beileag Bheag*; this was Eàirdsidh's hand-made *currach*, named after the *cailleach* who supervised its construction and brought him tea.

'Beileag Aonghais,' Eàirdsidh informed us. 'Her father would build dinghies – bigger boats too. She understood all about it. Poor Beileag died the day before the launch: life's cruel hand, *fhearaibh,*[128] eh?'

Our Shepherd's Pie full bellies sat safely on their seats as we made our way out towards the middle of the loch: Ruairidh was a surprisingly strong oarsman and with a good

---

127 my lad
128 men

sense of backwards direction.

He had primed Ealasaid, and she got us fed and 'ready to row' in record time. It was her turn too for the dishes, she declared, against some mild protest. *'Thallaibh!'*[129] she exhorted, 'Enjoy yourselves. Be kind to Eàirdsidh Fhionnlaigh.'

'Will get you something fresh for breakfast,' Ruairidh promised, and he did: four decent-sized brown trout teased from the still loch with Eric Adams' top-class flies. It was this special equipment which proved key, for after some intense but disappointing feeding and pulling with my own rod, I swapped with Ruairidh and soon brought our tally to half a dozen. The sunset ahead of us would have been outstanding on a clear evening, but even with residual cloud and plenty of moisture in the atmosphere, it was beautiful in its fuzzy orange-redness.

'I was thinking, Colin,' Ruairidh said, 'of cutting the locum short. I mean, Bill mightn't get back mid-July, his mammy could go bonkers again. What if it's the end of the month or we're into August? You've got your studies and...'

'Doubt it very much,' I interrupted. 'Dr Marr will have considered the matter carefully and given an accurate timescale. He has to. He's here all year round, Ruairidh.'

'Remember Colin,' my uncle continued, 'I've been here about six weeks now. It's obviously taking its toll. Brian Scott in Benbecula has a good bit of anaesthetics in him, and covered before, when they've failed to get locums.'

What should I say? I wasn't going to offer any false or unfounded reassurances to my very experienced uncle. Instead, I focused on the water. An otter appeared near the north bank, or perhaps it was another large rat. Then I said:

'I think I'll get a bit more from Alasdair mac Sheumais Bhig yet. It's crucial having you around to discuss the spoils with.'

Put another way, what would justify my on-going presence

---

[129] Away you go!

in Uist without him? I could always move in with Ealasaid, but perhaps not the ideal solution!

'Well,' he replied. 'Yes, Colin. You're probably right. It would be daft for you to lose this unique opportunity. Perhaps I'll return next summer – before then even – just to visit and record. I've never, ever, done that.' Never allowed yourself, I thought.

'Ok, *'ille*,' he said, 'why don't we head back? Put that poor man out of his misery.'

I grabbed the oars and made a rather ineffectual swipe at the water.

'Eàirdsidh's a worrier, like his father – that's the stroke now, Colin! – and he relies on this wee vessel for supplementary income. Let's say our man is a lower-key, tour-guide; he knows just where and *when* to fish.'

This was subtly expressed. One could never have accused Ruairidh of suggesting that Eàirdsidh Fhionnlaigh might occasionally poach or take cash-in-hand payments. The thought, though, did cross my mind when Ruairidh added to this 'supplementary income' with a swift thrust into a grateful palm.

'We've had a super evening and have these beauties to...'

'...prove it,' Eàirdsidh finished.

'No, Colin,' Ruairidh said to me later in the car. 'The fish don't prove we've had a fine time; we do! The fish are extra – added-value, the economists might say – though I'm looking forward to tasting what Ealasaid does with them in the morning.'

We had gutted and cleaned them immediately and thrown them into the box provided before waving to Eàirdsidh, whose well-checked *currach* he had swiftly fixed under cover with ferry-rope and boulders.

'I was hoping to call on a Benbecula woman soon,' Ruairidh said. 'A real font of songs but doesn't do any public singing these days. You're at Alasdair mac Sheumais Bhig's tomorrow afternoon, are you?'

I nodded.

'Give him and his shingles another day. I'll send word. Come and meet Oighrig Thòmais with me. She's charming.'

Indeed she was and elegant, in an unexpected (almost French) way for a woman in her mid-70s who hadn't left Uist for long periods in the last twenty years. Her songs were plainly and poignantly sung and like Patricia, there was no fuss – no falderals – about them but Oighrig did imbue them with an intensity I hadn't felt with Patricia.

Her rendition of *'Nach gòrach mi gad chaoineadh'*[130] was beautifully rich and lived in; there was no sign of a photo of a husband or children in her house and while Ruairidh could surely have filled me in on her circumstances he opted not to, and I respected this.

Oighrig was so unspinsterly, that whatever her own story, her singing told of love won and lost. I could see her in Amsterdam as an Eva; in Rome as Emiliana and in Seville as enigmatic Estela.

As it was, she was Oighrig in Nunton, her neat pebble-dashed bungalow matching a well-looked-after Volkswagen Beatle and her hair held a perfectly judged hint of blue.

Ruairidh told me she had been the secretary for a building firm and had run the place with unequalled efficiency and wicked humour; the men pleaded with her to stay but she walked out the door on her 60th birthday: very fit and very contented.

Holland versus Argentina was Oighrig's doorstep prediction for the World Cup Final 1978. 'Surely the Peruvians will give their neighbours the chance,' she said. 'They're out anyway and Peru could do with major investment – starting with the roads, then tourism. So they're saying anyway,' she added,

---

[130] 'How stupid I am to be crying over you'

most amusingly. Who I wondered? Commentators Coleman or MacPherson? South Uist's WRVS? Or more likely the young lads of her own village? Yes, definitely the Nunton boys!

Chapter 16

Not a word of a lie had Niamh spoken. All the people on Tìr nan Òg seemed very content and none of them were old in any way. And the sun never set. Yes, for the first few months, Oisean and Niamh were deliriously happy.

OIGHRIG'S FOOTBALL PREDICTION was exactly right, and while I hadn't heard any warnings of pre-match fixing, it certainly was being hotly debated following Argentina's 6–0 victory.

'Rubbish!' England manager, Ron Greenwood, told the *Today* programme on Thursday morning. 'There's no team in the world could have withstood that colossal attack.'

My sense of these games came solely from the unique visuals that radio demands, but the idea of returning Patricia's delightful *cèilidh* had certainly tempted me. There would, though, have been little chance of getting her alone.

I used the imposed restrictions to bash on with productive mornings for Uni and equally focused evenings of listening back and transcription; Ruairidh seemed fine with this – just letting me do my own thing – as long as I was happy *and* occupied!

Alasdair mac Sheumais Bhig had been in tremendous form on the Wednesday and told a fun tale of how Fionn MacCumhail tricked the Scottish giant, Angus, by pretending to be a huge baby. Alasdair yelped with delight as Angus ran off home, destroying the causeway they had both carefully constructed between County Antrim and the Isle of Staffa.

This he followed with an eerie story about a Benbecula shieling to which two MacPhee brothers are lured by bone-beaked hags and where they meet a bloody death.

Alasdair insisted I return the following two days, and his

offerings were no less impressive. It was then I heard him sing for the first time when, mid-way through some fairy lore, he gave the verse of the spurned lover. Jane, who had been silent throughout, joined him spontaneously on this, and her youthful accompaniment complemented that of the elder statesman but was also born of it.

Unlike Patricia and Oighrig, Jane's voice – not nearly as musical – contained a stark hunger and a *'langan'*[131] of under-performed, un-trained, naturalness, which caught me deep within my core.

Not for the first time in Taigh Alasdair mac Sheumais Bhig did the two of them move me close to tears. The weird fragility of it all: grand-niece and *bodach* in unselfconscious communion, a million miles from the kailyard, concert-hall, kitsch of *Wee* Andy Duncan; even Norrie Ross (whose full-page advert in *Am Pàipear* promoting his new LP warned – '*Your Norrie sings!*'). So much could have conspired against their having this relationship; their even knowing each other in this world was remarkable. In addition, I could see a new bruise on the side of Jane's face. Perhaps this Ìomhair guy did enjoy advertising his power? Which wasn't to say that were you to remove Jane's jumper and jeans you wouldn't find worse! And what were Jane's parents doing about this? Had they washed their protective hands of her when she laid her premature bed with Ìomhair? Or had they chosen just not to know – not to interfere in the couple's personal affairs?

And what were we, as professionals – Ruairidh at least – willing to do about it?

'Not much we can do,' he had stated. 'No concerns have ever been raised about the children, so it's up to Jane to contact the police if she believes she's in danger.'

On Friday she seemed edgier, less able to settle, less trusting that Alasdair would perform as well or that he'd remember all the relevant facts. Her prompting him and

---

[131] deer-sound

initial correcting him on the location of a particular story seemed unnecessary – verging on rude if she hadn't couched it in some odd, caring, language:

'O sweetheart. Now, was it not in Kilbride, you told me, that happened? Remember, the boy was working for Fear Bhaghsdail?'

'Yes, yes,' Alasdair accepted a little ruefully. Had I exhausted him during the previous two visits? He showed no signs of pain, nor was he off his tea and scones.

He did though come into his own again as he moved emotionally through this story. It concerned the daughter of the landlord and a local boy in her father's employ. The young couple enjoy a secret courtship until it becomes obvious that she is pregnant. Her father orders that the lad be killed and in the end it's the son from this tragic liaison – born two seasons and a month later – who avenges his father's death. Not unlike Fionn MacCumhail, it struck me.

When Jane challenged her uncle once again as he commenced his final story, Alasdair mac Sheumais Bhig was more than capable of putting her in her place.

'No Jane! Both Diarmad and Caoilte were there that day!'

Jane was wrong and she admitted it by lighting another cigarette from the one she was smoking.

'*Siuthadaibh, ma-thà!*'[132] she smiled. 'You are the fellow who knows.'

The Fèinn had been out hunting and had caught nothing and were winding their weary way home from Ben Gulbainn – 'In the Spittle of Glenshee, it is' – Alasdair declared, 'where this all happened. I was there; the term I spent on that farm near Pitlochry.'

Alasdair then told of the dog, Bran, trapping a young deer or *mangan* (yes, Jane definitely sang with the '*langan*' of a youngish deer!).

---

[132] On you go, then!

Fionn shows mercy towards the animal and later that night great passion for Sabha – a stranger with the same beguiling, oval, eyes. Sabha's worst fear is The Dark Man of the fairy-people, but her new lover pledges she will meet no harm in Almu.

Soon the Fèinn must travel to Morvern to rout the Lochlannaich and a triumphant, ardent, Fionn returns to find Sabha gone despite orders never to lose her! His fruitless searching becomes his torment and Fionn withdraws from valour until, three years later, he meets a young boy whom the baying hounds cannot maul, but spare. The lad makes no sound save those of a baby deer. 'Oisean,' Fionn says. 'My little deer, my little son,' and he lifts his boy high on his shoulders and never lets him fall.

No one made a sound in the house while Alasdair spoke. Even the batteries and tape of the recording device seemed to mute their whirr. Jane did not light up and hardly moved. No sheep ventured over the hillock to *'meh'* at us.

My concern was that the tape might run out before the end. I hadn't anticipated quite such a long story. It must have taken Alasdair a good twenty-five minutes or more, but fortunately I had wound a brand new one while Jane sorted tea.

'Sabha,' he laughed poignantly as a postscript, 'was Oisean's mother. He was half-deer and half-human.'

I wondered whether Oisean's being of deer lineage had helped his bardic skills in any way. Did Niamh know of his 'genetic' origins before she convinced him to travel with her to Tìr nan Òg?

Given his rather exciting, dangerous, and finally favourable start in life, Oisean's death back in the *Gàidhealtachd*, as a shrivelled, wizened old man, seemed acutely painful.

But then all sorts of things conspire to interrupt, or hamper, our life journeys – no matter how promising or important our initiation was.

Had my mother's desire or need to leave Barra and settle south taken me to or away from Tìr nan Òg and could I return now that her deed was done?

For Alasdair mac Sheumais Bhig at 88 and Jane MacDonald at 26, this was what they had, and this was what they were still doing x years later – x times 4 years later in Alasdair's case! Their lines had continued unbroken from the seventeenth century. Alasdair's days away working were just that – days out to enable a return to normality that would continue unhindered.

'I really like Oisean,' Jane said, as she accompanied me back across the hillock. 'I adore him as a wee boy, but I also like him as a handsome grown man, and how Niamh is charmed by his poetry and everything. Isn't it cruel, though, what lies ahead for him?'

'Why do you think what happened, happened, Jane?'

'Because he wasn't satisfied? Wanted something better than you could get here? *Gun robh pleit air* – that he was a bit full of himself,' she helpfully expanded, 'Better than the rest?'

'Yea,' I said, considering these possibilities.

Jane stopped walking. 'Or did he just marry the wrong person, *a Chailein*, who would change him to be someone no longer faithful to himself?'

I shook my head and caught her melancholic eyes. 'Any of these, *ma-thà*.'

Jane once again (she hadn't the two previous days) put her arm through mine, then turned me round and thrust her smoke-flavoured tongue into my mouth. I reacted, perhaps like a startled half-deer, before pulling away and seeking out the village road.

'He's wanting you here tomorrow,' she shouted after me, laughing. 'The kids will be at my sister's.' Then she added, as a coy throwaway, 'There's football on in Barra. A friendly!'

Chapter 17

In a couple of months' time, Oisean and Niamh would be celebrating their first anniversary on Tìr nan Òg, but Oisean was not as happy as he should be. 'I just want to go back home to the Gàidhealtachd one more time – to see my father and the Fèinn; then I'll return here forever.' 'But you gave me your promise,' Niamh reminded him. 'I know,' he pleaded. 'But I've changed my mind. Please – just once!'

'IT'S ME THAT'S first on-call today,' Ruairidh said next morning, 'so I can't do anything too wild.' My uncle had donned the weekend apron, which looked comical, and was dispensing Ealasaid's eggs, Patricia's mum's crowdie and the Co-op's bread. 'Not sure of your plans, Colin. Want to come out with me, if anything happens?'

'Eh...' I replied.

'Or' he said, 'if you've got studying or... that's fine.'

'Mac Sheumais Bhig,' I began, 'is keen I visit.'

'Again?' Ruairidh's incredulous chuckle. 'For the fourth time this week? That man's old now. He might need some rest.'

'And he's got shingles.'

'Very mild. Are you and Jane hitting it off now?' he asked inappropriately, salaciously, I judged.

I coughed loudly, propelling crowdie fragments from the back of my throat.

'Well, yes. No! Not at all, like... she's married.'

'To that thug Ìomhair,' my uncle reminded me. 'Sorry Colin, I shouldn't probe. Patricia was back here yesterday.'

'Really?'

'With Steafan. Ealasaid met them; tried to interrogate them,' he laughed.

'Did they say what they wanted?' I asked.

'Don't know that they wanted anything specific. She was quite disappointed. So herself's expecting you to record Alasdair this afternoon, is she?'

I had made no promises and felt little desire to taste stale tobacco, but I did want to see Jane: look into those striking oval eyes, witness her delight at her great-uncle's skill, feel the raw physicality of her presence. 'Could do a bit of both,' I offered, mixed loyalties once again besetting me. 'Maybe come with you in the morning? As you said, *a Ruairidh*, see what happens.'

What happened was this:

A car crash on the Loch Aoineart road: an eighteen-year-old being driven by his twenty-one-year-old cousin, home on holiday, in a souped-up Ford Capri, neither of them wearing seatbelts.

They had taken the bend on the north road at an idiotic speed, lost control and tumbled down the embankment just before the little bridge over the sea-loch. How they were alive beat me. The Police, Fire and Ambulance crew, who reached the accident ahead of us, concurred.

This was the first time I'd seen Ruairidh in 'real' action: efficient fact-gathering from the other professionals; a systematic approach to assessing the scene; his skill at checking and assisting Airways, Breathing, Circulation: 'It's ABC first, Colin. Always!' his only words as we turned, with only the slightest deceleration, off the main road.

This was no man 'old before his time', losing a little of his soft diagnostic skills, but an energised, fast-thinking, physician of considerable experience.

It was satisfying – exciting I had to admit – to be involved.

I helped hold splints and oxygen cylinders and leash arms and legs onto stretchers, once the firemen had cut open the casualties' mangled tin-can.

Mercifully the sun shone – this would have been far more difficult in rain of any sort. A lone sheep, perched on a crotal-covered rock, which must have leapt out of its fleece at the time, looked on mournfully, shuddering often.

Both boys were known, but their families had yet to be informed. We would hear later they'd been preparing for a birthday party of the local guy's sister. The Glasgow one had agreed to go to the shops, with a wink to 'wee' cousin to come along for the ride. They never did reach AC MacDonalds.

I could see the palpable relief on Ruairidh's face when both answered coherently through the shattered passenger window; the driver seemed the brighter of the two – his young companion moaning in pain.

'Mìcheal comes first,' he commanded. 'He might have a fractured pelvis.'

I observed Ruairidh carefully maintain his neck position until a securely fitted stiff collar relieved him. My knowledge, mostly gleaned from TV – *Z-Cars* and the like – told me that spinal injuries were a common and serious occurrence in Road Traffic Accidents. They could kill immediately or cause long-term harm.

While Mìcheal's pelvis escaped injury, he had broken a femur – as he flew forwards and twisted on the tumble – and ruptured his spleen. The damage required six pints of blood: all supplied, on demand, by family members who shared his blood type. His sister, whose party this event had abruptly postponed, donated two of these.

John, the driver, had escaped with mostly minor bruising though his chest x-ray showed rib fractures which, Ruairidh explained, could still puncture his lung.

Eric Adams and Ruairidh Gillies would be heavily involved

for the rest of the afternoon; my uncle considered his colleague's orthopaedic skills to be exceptional for a remote General Surgeon. While Mìcheal lay prone in theatre and far away, John was closely observed in the ward for any deterioration.

I spotted what must have been the sister with two other siblings and their parents sitting ashen-faced, while two solicitous and tactile nuns comforted them and fed them tea and shortbread. I did wish to speak to them, connect with them in some way, reassure them that given the circumstances the boys were in the safest possible hands and would surely survive.

But, at this point, I didn't possess the facts, nor indeed did I have the authority to make such a judgement. I said nothing and sought fresh air.

A judgement I did make, on my escape from the hospital, was that the unpredictability and possible seriousness of cases facing rural doctors should never be underestimated. Bill Marr and Eric Adams coped with this 'unease' every day, all year round, and had won my utmost respect – as had Uncle Ruairidh who chose to support them on his 'holidays'. This was a most challenging, and ultimately rewarding job, but not one for Colin Quinn!

A dark Volvo swung out from in front of the Post Office and stopped, 'dead', just ten yards on. Mgr Pàdraig pulled down the window.

'*Dol dhachaigh a bheil?*'[133]

I wasn't sure where I was going. Yes, I suppose I would be heading back to Taigh Eòrasdail – but for the moment all that was important was to be alone in fresh air to make sense of the last hour and three-quarters.

'I'll be fine,' I said vaguely, and remembering my manners just, added, 'Thanks though, Father.' Then, absurdly, I praised the weather.

---

[133] Going home?

'They're saying,' the priest pushed, 'that the young lad's come off worst. It's prison that's waiting for the other one.'

I hadn't thought of any consequences beyond the immediate life and death ones. Mgr Pàdraig, however, would be well-versed in these matters.

'Was on the point of losing his licence anyway.'

'Oh?'

'Are you walking to Eòrasdail, *a Chailein*?'

This direct questioning and detailed information were too much at this time and irritatingly intrusive. I wished Mgr Pàdraig could just go. I then wondered, bizarrely, if he had given Mìcheal the last rites before they took him to theatre – should he never wake up.

'You're both of course very welcome tomorrow night. Ruairidh said he would come to Mass first. Maybe you're busy again?'

I had no idea what he was talking about. Two young lads had just been wrenched from wreckage – one of whom was currently being operated on – and here I was now strolling alone on a pleasant summer afternoon. Tomorrow? Tomorrow night?

The priest prattled on. 'Calum fancies Argentina, but I think Holland will want to make up for last time. The Dutch, of course, loathe the Germans. Their treatment of them during the war, it was terrible. Some of that unresolved "hate" will be put to good use tomorrow night in El Estadio Monumental.'

I didn't follow Mgr Pàdraig's logic for the World Cup Final, but I did know the lingering, simmering, hostility to Germany felt by an older generation; there ready to boil over for a range of circumstances.

'Yes, thanks,' I said. 'That will be great.' What else could I say? I wanted rid of this man burdened by his own *fèin-fhiosrachadh*[134]. Now where did that expression appear from?

'*Glè mhath, a Chailein,*' he said. 'We'll expect you both.'

I thought this would be the cue for him to roll up his window and leave me to my thoughts, but instead, he asked me to sit in a minute. Whatever this was, it wasn't going to be a lucky-bag full of sugar-rich sweets.

I sat on his black leather seat and held my breath to stem the toxicity of polish – but did not close the door fully.

'Alasdair, mac Sheumais Bhig, down in Milton there,' he began, as if I didn't know exactly to whom he was referring. 'He's not getting any younger.' Do many octogenarians, I thought (and would love to have said), race back to youth without the help of dementia?

'He was exhausted last night,' he continued. 'This work's taking a lot out of him. Maybe you've both got enough now?'

What! While clearly, I had first gone to Alasdair mac Sheumais Bhig at my uncle's behest, this was now very much my project – Jane's and my project. *I* certainly hadn't got enough.

'She's concerned about him too.' Who, Jane? Nonsense! She'd been the one driving me on, keeping our joint spirits up, requesting I return today – 'He's wanting you here tomorrow… there's football on in Barra.' Or was the priest perhaps referring to Jane's mother – the one left caring for the children (and what all else?) as we both cajoled her uncle and forgot about Ìomhair?

'*Tapadh leibh, Athair,*'[135] I said, opening the door, then added in suitably nebulous code, 'I'll speak to Ruairidh.'

'See you very soon,' he said. 'This is the final Scotland never saw!'

'Yes,' I agreed, and he was off. This was also the final Ally

---

134 experience of the world
135 Thanks, Father

MacLeod would never see either, unless he watched it on the telly with a paltry wee bevvy – Sweetheart Stout perhaps?

So, what then was Mgr Pàdraig's game? Any advances on control, envy and good old-fashioned nosiness? All of these, potentially, but also the fact that he and Ìomhair Dubh were second cousins!

This revelation was supplied, unsolicited, by cheery-chappy, Dòmhnall Chaluim. He tooted generously as I wandered in a dream-like state by Abhainn Ealtraidh, my gaze out beyond the moor-lochs east of it; Donnie Wright (Decorator) was printed neatly on the side of his pristine white van and below that, Lochboisedale 342. Of course, he'd heard about my recording efforts and was most positive about old Alasdair's skills.

'All that was needed was someone to take an interest,' he remarked. 'The ones here these days...' But he didn't complete this sentence: there was no need, we'd both heard it too often in its numerous iterations of despondency. 'Behind Ben More, his people were – you know, his ancestors!'

'A remote spot!'

'You said it! But beautiful and peaceful. Nobody bothers you there. Did you ever go?'

I admitted I hadn't been anywhere near the mountains of Uist. Perhaps it was time to expand my horizons.

'You'd enjoy it, *a Chailein*, and you'd see how those people lived. Many went to Eriskay, but Alasdair's lot came out here – three families. Then Mgr Padraig's mother moved to Barra: a sister of Ìomhair's grandmother she was.'

But Ìomhair was from Carinish, in North Uist. Donnie Wright – or '*Dòmhnall Ceart*' as was stencilled wittily across his boot – could quite easily have told me the genealogical ins and outs. Instead, I thanked him within a mile of home and began walking in the warmth to see if it might soothe a now pounding headache. Fortunately, no cars stopped, including

Ìomhair's which I realised later was the one that had roared past, making me leap into the verge and almost impale myself on a barbed-wire fence.

'God only knows when your uncle will get home!' was Ealasaid's opening gambit, to which she added, '*Diabhail* speeders! He's been in trouble twice before – the Glasgow one. They can head to the depths of Hell!' She then winced and asked, 'They are going to live, Colin?'

'Both boys spoke to him,' I said. 'I'm not really sure what all injuries they had.'

I could have added more. Who was in theatre; who'd needed blood and the speed of delivery. But I didn't, not only for reasons of confidentiality, but because I knew I'd imbue my account with a hope that might prove unfounded; complications could still give a less favourable outcome.

'Don't say anything – to anybody, Colin!' Ruairidh had ordered through his surgeon's mask as he headed down the corridor with Eric Adams. 'It's always the safest way. You've been a great help.'

'Clunk-click every trip,' Ealasaid said, sitting down beside me at the dining room table. 'I hear that the only seatbelt in the car was in the back. And will the powers that be up there now widen that awful road? Is it a death they need? I've made Irish Stew – so he can heat it up easily, whenever he comes in. It's my sister's last night – Barra tomorrow. Clive's from Crewe; he always wanted to see something other than Uist.'

'*Seadh*,' I remarked, 'Understandable.'

'Ha!' she brightened. 'Listen to the *Barrach* talking! I'd almost forgotten.'

I, too, had almost forgotten! The intensity of the last few days had consumed me to such an extent that I couldn't really picture much of a before or after.

'Ever been over yourself?' I asked. She shook her head.

'*Agus an do chuir ur càirdean miann annaibh?*'[136] – another nice Gaelic expression – a definite Alasdair mac Sheumais Bhig and Jane one.

'Almost went once – twenty years ago, if not more.'

'But?'

'Chose Lochgilphead instead! And before you ask, yes, I've been to Eriskay loads of times. Why wouldn't I with my great-aunt married there, though Ceanag is now here in Uist.'

How old was Ealasaid, I wondered – perhaps still in her forties? – and decided on or programmed for this lifestyle from many years previously? She wasn't an unattractive woman. Had she fought them off too hard at the start?

'So,' she said, 'it's seven o'clock. Are you better eating now or are you going to wait for your uncle?'

'Both,' I joked, and patted my bulging belly.

'She's an excellent cook,' Ruairidh said, as he slumped into his armchair at 9.45pm.

'Absolutely,' I agreed. There had been an extended period of silence as he ate.

'Young Mìcheal wasn't quite as straightforward as we thought, Colin,' he began. 'Bled into his chest too. Two and a half hours on the table, blood pressure beginning to fall and…' my uncle checked himself. 'It's a hard balance to strike – the longer the surgery goes on the twitchier I get about anaesthetic safety. We get our fair share of boy-racers in Duns so it's nothing new but…'

'How's John?' I asked.

'Off home. Often the way. The older driver walks away, leaving the legacy of his madness in his wake. Maybe the psychological scars will have a positive effect yet. Doubt it though.'

'She's made apple pie,' I offered.

---

[136] And have your relatives instilled a desire?

'Tomorrow, Colin, unless you...?'

'Already scoffed my first bowl.'

'A growing lad...'

'Eats as a quern-stone grinds,' I finished for him.

'Ever seen one?' he asked. '*Brà* – a quern-stone?'

I shook my head. I'd heard Mum use the expression a hundred times but never bothered asking.

'Well,' he started, livening, 'You have two stones – an upper one and a lower one...' my uncle stifled a yawn and then failed with another longer one. 'Would you mind,' he said, 'if I kept this until the morning?'

I smiled; how terribly polite, from a caring, 'shattered', uncle. 'No, no!' a horribly spoilt Colin Quinn might have screamed. 'I've waited a lifetime. Tell me now, you old saddo, stuff the rest!'

Instead, a much nicer nephew got up from the table, placed my dinner-plate on top of his near spotless one and allowed my free hand to rest on his right shoulder.

'That was good, *ma-thà, a Ruairidh*!'

He still hadn't risen from the table on my return to collect the cups and saucers.

'I was very proud today,' I said, clearly, confidently, 'of what you did out there and that you were my uncle.'

'*Tapadh leat*,'[137] he replied. 'I appreciated your being there.'

In my safe uncomplicated bed, I read a sunny tale about *Boban Saor,* where the crafty joiner, pretending to be his son's apprentice, tricks the king and escapes unscathed and well paid!

Were there any parallels here with Ruairidh Gillies and his novice nephew? I felt there might be but had not identified them before sleep gained the upper hand.

---

137 Thank you

Chapter 18

After much persuasion, Niamh agreed that Oisean could return to see his father and the Fèinn one last time – on the white horse that had brought them to Tìr nan Òg. 'But, Oisean son of Fionn mac Cumhail,' she said, 'whatever you do, you must stay on the horse. If any part of you touches the ground of the Gàidhealtachd, you will pay dearly.'

'WHERE WERE WE, Colin?' my uncle asked, the next morning. He then raised his voice, 'As Ealasaid will tell you' – who was certainly not taking this Sunday off, sister there or otherwise – 'there were two stones.' She returned to the dining room – dishtowel in hand. 'The upper one with the hole was really the *brà*, as it rotated. Am I right, Ealasaid, and…?'

'How old do you think I am, Doctor? I've certainly heard of quern-stones but never seen one used. "'*S fheàirrde brà a breacadh gun a bristeadh,*"[138] they'd say – whatever that's supposed to tell us.'

'This bacon's beautiful,' he then shouted, although Ealasaid hadn't moved. 'As was last night's stew – delicious. Your own meat, was it?'

'No, but I knew her well!' That got a laugh, which sent Ealasaid back to the scullery from where she returned with waffles and a bottle of maple syrup. 'Clive and Rona brought me these things from England. Eat your food before it gets cold, the story of the *brà* can then be told, word perfect.'

My uncle did this at length over coffee, which followed the tea. I let him and listened well while observing his neat

---

138 Better to pick a quern-stone than break it

illustration taking shape on the back of the Irish poets' booklet.

'Anyway,' he said, putting down his pencil. 'That's how it was done. And what a bannock it made for Rodachan in Borve. Right, I'll call in on young Mìcheal's family before they head to church and then join Eric in the hospital. Do you need a lift, Colin?'

'I'll take…' began Ealasaid. 'He can sit in Mass beside me.' She let out a daft giggle, which would have been embarrassing previously but wasn't now given her huge kindness over the previous twenty-four hours.

'Are we not going to St Peter's, tonight, *a Ruairidh*?' I asked. 'Mgr Pàdraig's expecting us afterwards.'

'He is?'

'For the World Cup Final?'

'Who's playing again?' my uncle asked genuinely – the accident had erased it from his mind plus our agreement to attend.

'Argentina,' I said. 'And bonny Scotland.'

'Ha! Holland?'

'Yip.'

'Right. Well, let's see. You'll need to watch it.'

I certainly did not 'need' to watch it or any other game. Having just seen two people almost meet a tragic, wasted, death, I needed to do very little of a 'leisure', 'pleasure' nature, and Mgr Pàdraig's was certainly not my preferred location.

'I'm sure it will be fine, Colin,' Ruairidh said, 'I'll factor it all in – as far as possible. You on duty again for the priest?' he asked Ealasaid.

'No,' she replied flatly. 'Herself is back. Very quick after her father's death. I'll be here, though.' She glanced at the clock and made quick calculations, 'at 2.30pm with your dinner. Phone if you'll be late. One of my own chickens this one and what a pleasure to throttle it.'

Ealasaid's departure was welcome but being alone soon

felt oppressive. Yesterday's benign sun of reckless driving and a wreck of a car had been replaced by constant – seep to the skin then find the bones – drizzle.

On the next half-decent day, I'd head off early and at least reach the top of Ben More. As I'd only recently learnt, both Ìomhair and Mgr Pàdraig's forebears had lived out there – one lot eventually sailing deeper into the Catholic heartlands, the other choosing north and the reformed religion. Now descendants of both were back in South Uist in very different roles in a very different world.

Jane would have heard news of the car crash and surely understood my not visiting the *bodach*. No promise was made, and, given our parting circumstances, she may well not have expected me to appear. When next I did, I wondered what might happen.

Nothing! Nothing at all would happen! Jane was dangerous, or more likely damaged, and living in a volatile marital set-up with a thug. Safety, *stuamachd*,[139] propriety: these would be key if I were to continue recording Alasdair mac Sheumais Bhig and avoid trouble.

With fifteen hours of material on tape, was now, perhaps, the time to call it a day? How much more was necessary to validate my efforts or Alasdair's status as a *seanachie*? Ruairidh would be happy with what I'd collected; so too would The Scottish Archive. Then I saw my uncle's heroics on the Loch Aoineart road, plus his delight at depicting the *brà* for me, and duly opened my transcription notebook.

Before starting, I was overcome with a sudden need to speak to members of my immediate family. Life is so precious, Colin Quinn, I thought, so why do we take it all for granted? Why obsess about so many things, that in the end – the very end, without warning – don't matter a damn?

Dad's football chat was chirpy and helpfully distracting.

---

[139] controlled behaviour / temperance

'A telt you son that Holland wiz a force to be reckoned with. Wee Johann Cruyff'll be kickin' himsel, so he will.'

'*Seadh, a luaidh,*' Mum said, 'How are you all doing?'

'Fine,' I reassured her and that her older brother could now see the light at the end of the tunnel.

I said nothing about the car smash or our involvement. Inter-island-Glasgow-jungle-drums would deliver the news in a few days, followed a little after by the *Stornoway Gazette*. Would the nationals report it? I hoped not. One thing I did confirm with her – in English! – was this: 'Whatever your or Uncle Ruairidh's hopes for me were before coming to Uist, medicine is out the window. Okay! I will, though, sort myself out.'

'*Glè mhath, a ghaoil,*'[140] my mother's meek (perhaps reflective) reply. I hadn't brought my sisters' numbers so had to ask her for them. James and I never spoke on the phone, and this wasn't the time to start – however short our time on earth might be! Only Flora was at home, or willing to answer. '*Is that oor Colin I says to masel? He's gone awfy Gàidhealach oan us?*' Our chat was brief and factual. Uist was fine – it got a bit of a bad press in Barra. Certainly worth a visit. Nursing, she confirmed, was currently tiring and the matron a grim despot from Fife.

One number that did pop into my head – though never written down or previously rung – was Catrìona MacNeil's in Grìnn. Phone calls were cheap all-day Sunday – unlike life. I felt quite nervous dialling and my chest heaved while waiting for an answer. I'd almost given up when her stepfather's gruff voice came on the line.

'Are you well, Eòs?' I greeted him. 'It's Màiri Iagain Mhòir's son, Cailean. Is Catrìona there?'

'Just a minute,' he said, to my intense relief, and her warm, enthusiastic, voice blessed the moment.

'Are you back in Barra, *a Chailein?*' she asked.

---

[140] Very good, my love

'No, Uist.'
'*Seadh.*'
'*Seadh, ma-thà*. I just wanted to hear your voice.'
'And what do you think of it?' she pushed wickedly.
'As nice as you. You're a fantastic person, Catrìona, and I've been so lucky to have got to know you.'
'Are you alright?' she asked – no humour or mocking this time. 'Did something happen, *a luaidh*?'
'No. Nothing like that,' I said. 'Just sometimes, you have to stop and think about things – how important people are and if you don't ever tell them or show them, you might lose your chance.'
There was a longish pause at the other end, though I could hear her familiar breathing. 'I've always been fond of you Colin, but I thought you, eh... I've started seeing someone. What's the point of waiting around forever? Nothing serious, but I like him, and he's been asking me out for months.'
'That's great Catrìona.' I felt it was, though it hurt – more than I might have expected. Tears welled in my eyes, but I wouldn't let my voice betray them. 'You were right. I wasn't willing... no, I couldn't make a commitment. He'll be nice to you.'
'We'll see,' she said, ever the realist, 'how long it lasts. You'll be at university?'
'Should be, Catrìona. Come out for a weekend – a week, even!'
'As I said,' she replied, 'we'll see.'
I abandoned my books and went for a run; Eòrasdail's majestic soft machair bore the pain released in the beat of body and heart.

Mass in St Peter's was lightning fast, more typical of a six in the morning affair than an evening one. Mgr Pàdraig had asked his flock if he might start half an hour early. The World Cup Final, Allan explained (much as I'd rationalised with Ruairidh) came but once every four years. God – and more importantly the bishop – would surely understand. Some parishioners from further afield, Ruairidh said, felt the priest should have brought it forward the full hour, to let everyone home and settle with a cup of tea for the pre-match commentary.

The same crew (save the young lad with the vocation) were gathered awaiting Mgr Pàdraig's extrication. I wondered, and not for the first time, how much of what a priest performed was mandatory and what could be conflated, or skipped altogether, in extenuating circumstances?

"*I fhèin*"[141] – Maighread Bheag, showed us through to the sitting room where a sumptuous cold spread awaited. I could see why Ealasaid might not fully approve of this woman who seemed quietly confident and quite different to the stricken daughter we'd met, a fortnight previously, at her father's deathbed.

'I'll bring your tea and coffee in when Mgr Pàdraig comes,' she said. I detected something non-supplicant, non-deferential, in Maighread's reference to the priest without showing any lack of respect. Perhaps they'd known each other before he was ordained – cousins maybe? Or lovers? popped into my head as the priest popped into his sitting room. Is that what concerned Ealasaid? She might well have that level of inside knowledge.

'A vivid imagination, Colin!' my mother would have said at another time, in another place, a long, long way away.

Talking to her and Dad and Flora had made me realise how much I'd missed them. The last few years had been about acceleration, but this summer sojourn in Uist – with that weekend of fun in Barra – had made me yearn to slow the direction of travel so that we might share more, properly.

'Are they actually going to play?' Mgr Pàdraig's brother yelled. Was Calum now a permanent resident, I wondered? The Dutch players, having had to contend with a storm of

---

[141] Herself

ticker tape, were still waiting for Argentina to join them on the park with five minutes already on the clock.

'No wonder they're not impressed,' Murdo of the Two Ronnies remarked.

Ruairidh seemed particularly reserved, detached from us all; this was possibly the first quiet moment he'd had to sit down and take his mind off the previous day's events. He had made it back for Ealasaid's roast chicken but then the cousins' granny in Kilpheddar hauled him back out – the stress having re-triggered her funny turns. Mìcheal was much better – he had told her and me – but Eric Adams would continue to monitor him closely.

'*Mhoire Mhìn!*'[142] the priest yelped as captain, Ruud Krol, signalled for his team now to leave the field.

'Unbelievable,' echoed commentator Coleman. 'Are we actually going to have a final, I ask myself?'

'Did the trick though, David!' Bobby Charlton insisted a few minutes later, as both teams headed for the centre spot.

And the result of the actual football: one nil at half-time to Argentina but level again with only eight minutes left of the game to play. Holland had the wind in their sails and could have emerged victorious but an ugly Passarella punch on Neeskens broke their momentum.

Extra-time came, delaying *M*A*S*H*, the evening film, and it was Mario *Matador* Kempes who struck again before Bertoni sealed the fate of the Dutch – another World Cup Final defeat. This was Argentina's first-ever victory at this level and their chain-smoking, trench-coated, manager looked as if he'd just snuck through the gates of Paradise.

The crowd in Buenos Aires went 'absolutely mental' in the words of England captain, Kevin Keegan. Daliburgh was more subdued; we felt the Dutch desolation but also that they should have collected their runners-up medals – refusing was surely rather churlish?

---

[142] O Sweet Mary!

'Forty-eight free kick! Forty-eight!' their manager moaned. 'That's how much that idiot referee gives to Argentina!'

Maighread Bheag came and went efficiently. She did, though, watch a good bit of the match with us. Ealasaid wouldn't have done this, even if she were interested.

Thankfully Ìomhair stayed away and Mgr Pàdraig did not broach the subject of my recording work with Alasdair. Nor did he, in my uncle's presence – in wider company – encourage any conversation on the smash.

When Ruairidh received a call out to a dizzy chap with diabetes, the priest accompanied us to the door and thanked my uncle for his contribution to the future of the community.

'You are most welcome, Father,' his reply, 'and thank you for another very pleasant night.'

'Is this the last then?' Mgr Pàdraig tried to joke.

Ruairidh laughed heartily but didn't promise a future visit. His car spluttered a little before starting.

'Too much choke,' he sighed. 'I won't be here much longer, *a Chailein*. Less than a fortnight now.'

I didn't say anything.

'You don't have to stay: if you'd prefer to go,' he then half-shouted as the engine revved. 'Up to you, lad.'

'*A Ruairidh*,' I said. 'What did I tell you? I wouldn't want to be anywhere else.'

'Excellent,' his endorsement. 'I told her you'd be there tomorrow,' he kept his gaze on the road ahead, 'having missed the chance yesterday.'

Nothing escaped him. Nothing escaped anybody here. So, how would Jane be with me? Absolutely fine. She'd just have to be.

Chapter 19

If the journey out to Tìr nan Òg had been swift, the horse seemed to have even more energy as it raced back towards St Kilda and Skye. In no time they had reached the shores of the Gàidhealtachd. However, as Oisean rode through the lands he knew so well, he scarcely recognised anything. The vast plains, where the Fèinn practised for battle, were overgrown with briar and their splendid castles and fortresses now sad, dilapidated, ruins overrun with nettles.

THE PREVIOUS EVENING'S events in Argentina seemed to have had minimal impact on the atmosphere in Alasdair mac Sheumais Bhig's house in South Uist.

It did, though, strike me that while Jane's kids might be in school, was she not neglecting her crofting and domestic duties due to all this folkloric intrusion? Perhaps, at this time of year, most animal husbandry (the human version, too?) could be done at dawn and dusk – unless her parents did this for her too?

I knew that reports on Ìomhair would have been upsetting. Ealasaid relayed that his ranting last night was 'horrid – for a father of young children.' While he wouldn't have dared cross his 'holy' cousin again, she had heard he couldn't resist spoiling the residents' viewing in the island's new hotel. 'A bunch of pampered poofs' they were, and his advice as to what they might try after the game left nothing to the imagination. Ìomhair was now banned from there too.

Jane's placid demeanour gave nothing away. Had her husband got up for work today? Might he come looking for her at her uncle's? Her eyes bore no awkwardness or potential discomfort for me; the air was cleared, thanks to the car crash in Loch Aoineart.

'*Siuthadaibh, ma-thà, Alasdair,*' I began. 'Would you have a story today?'

'I'm not sure. Maybe I've given you all I've got.'

Did this reticence reflect tiredness – an understandable off-day for an old man – or because I'd failed to come on Saturday, as he had requested? He obviously needed a little coaxing.

'I bet there's plenty more where they came from, just take your time.'

'I told you about Oisean?' he asked.

'Yes, Alasdair,' I enthused, 'and you told it beautifully – how he was born and how he met his end.'

'Oisean was a very, very, gentle man, who didn't care for fighting at all, not like the others. There's too much fighting in this world.'

I hadn't heard him sound so down. Did he have deeper insight into Jane's home-life than one might give him credit, or was he talking in a wider context, starting in his case with WW1, the Boer War even?

Jane put more peat in his stove, stripped a piece of paper, quickly lit a cigarette and sat. Alasdair mac Sheumais Bhig gave a youthful, impish, smile and was off.

'At this time one of that lot they called 'Mac 'ic Ailein' was still in Ormacleit: they had this whole island, Clan Ranald, after MacNeil abandoned Boisedale.

'Now Mac 'ic Ailein had rent collectors, of course. And in those days, since there was no money in the place – nor now! – the people had to pay what they owed in grain.'

Jane gave a snorty chortle and emitted smoke through her nostrils; she really did resemble a dragon, with two little pointy teeth to add to her persona. What, then, were her sources of income beyond Ìomhair Dubh's conscience? Steafan's unsavoury allusion to other possible activities came and thankfully went. He had been keeping a low profile of late; it would be a treat to chat with Patricia again – watch and hear her sing beautifully. Alasdair was, though, deep in his story and I distracted; fortunately, the microphone remained focused.

'...but this particular year, two fellows came out to Loch Aoineart to pay their dues – to *Rubha an Taigh Mhàil*[143] yonder. You weren't so far from there yourself yesterday, *a Chailein*.'

Only Jane's lips smiled now – a wistful, compassionate, smile.

'Two full sacks of grain, they had, for Mac 'ic Ailein. And who were these men, but *Gille Padara Dubh*[144] and his son, Iain Dubh – *Iain Dubh mac Ghille Phàdraig*.[145] MacIntyres; you can still see the ruins of their house near Gèirinis, in a place they call An Geàrradh Fliuch.'

Alasdair came closer to the mic and raised his hand.

'"Tud, tud," one of the rent-men says when he has measured out the grain. "This bag is a 'peck' short."

'"That's strange," said Gille Pàdraig. "It was full when I left Gèirinis."

'"Well," the collector says. "It's not full now. So, how are you going to fill it?"

'"I'll just show you!" says Gille Pàdraig and he grabbed the cheat by the scruff of the neck then slit it with his knife until the sack was filled.

'And with that Gille Pàdraig and Iain Dubh headed home, but they both knew it wouldn't be long until the *tòrachd* [146] came.

'Nor were they far wrong, because when Mac 'ic Ailein heard what had happened he was furious. He wanted to slay the murderer of his rent-man, but he wouldn't dare, because he knew that Gille Pàdraig was as skilful as any man alive with the bow and arrow. It was said that he had no equal alive save perhaps

---
143 Rent-House Point
144 Black-haired Gille Pàdraig
145 Black-haired John son of Gille Padraig
146 pursuit, summons

his own son – Iain Dubh. Mac 'ic Ailein needed him badly, for his army, but I'll tell you, he also needed to show him, right there and then, who was the highest bird in the tree – the boss!

'If he could frighten Gille Pàdraig, that would do. And who should come *cèilidh*-ing on Mac 'ic Ailein shortly after this incident but MacLeod of Dunvegan.

'"Why" says MacLeod, "don't we pretend I have an archer in Skye who can shoot an egg off a person's head from, say, eighty yards, but that you said Gille Pàdraig could do the very same a hundred yards away. He'll be so full of himself that he'll try. But we'll get the egg placed on Iain Dubh's head and he'll surely injure him, in some way or another. Maybe he'll tear his son's skin, knock an eye out, or better!"'

Suddenly this rather jaunty tale of bravado and one-upmanship assumed a macabre air. Jane pulled her shrunken, knitted, cardigan over her large chest. I could see a hole yawning in her left armpit. This provoked a sudden, undesired, erection, which I tried my best to ignore. I'd pee in the byre when Gille Pàdraig had done what he had to do.

'Both men were sent for,' said Alasdair, 'and they rode up to Ormacleit Castle, each on his own horse.

'"Welcome to you and your son," Mac 'ic Ailein said.

'"*Seadh*," said Gille Pàdraig. "What do you want from us?"

'"Well," replied his landlord, "this gentleman here, MacLeod, says he has an archer in Skye who is so gifted he can shoot an egg off a man's head, with an arrow, from eighty yards away. However, I told him, "That's nothing. For I know a Uistman who can do the same but at a hundred measured yards from the target."

'"Really?" said Gille Pàdraig. "That Uistman is surely very good. Who is he?"'

This tightened the atmosphere. Alasdair scratched the outer edges of his two-day stubbled smile.

'"You!" said Mac 'ic Ailein.

'"Well, well," said Gille Pàdraig, "I've not a bad eye but I don't know if I'm quite that good."

'"Oh, but you are!" Mac 'ic Ailein said, and he then added his own lie, "I've bet my estate on it!"

'"Let me try," replied Gille Pàdraig. "But who will stand under the egg?" No one spoke. "As I said," Gille Pàdraig repeated, "I'm happy to try, but someone must stand under the egg." Not a soul moved. "Oh," he said, with a tighter grasp on things, "maybe that's why my son was invited too?"

'"Would he be willing?" Mac 'ic Ailein asked.

'Gille Pàdraig turned to Iain Dubh. "Will you stand underneath it, boy?"

'"If you want me to – that is my wish."

'"Oh, very good!" says the man from Ormacleit.

'The egg was attached to the top of Iain Dubh's head, and it was his own father, who measured the hundred yards and returned in the very same steps.'

All our focus was on Alasdair and on the fate of Gille Pàdraig and his loyal son: without any unwelcome distraction.

'Gille Pàdraig removed an arrow, took aim with the bow and was just going to shoot when he stopped, grabbing three more arrows from his bag and tucking them under his belt. He then raised his bow again and out flew an arrow – fluidly, elegantly– before it smashed the egg to smithereens, without raising a single hair on his son's head.

'"Congratulations!" Mac 'ic Ailein cried, "I knew I could trust you."'

'Sure thing!' Jane and I thought (though perhaps it was "*'S mi nach creid sin*,'[147] or something more idiomatic, she actually thought).

'"Right, *ma-thà*," said Gille Pàdraig, "I've done what I was asked to do, and I've also saved your land. Can we go now?"

---

147 I don't believe that for a minute

'"Of course, of course," says the laird. "But before you do that. Can I ask you a question?"

'"Ask away?"

'"I noticed," Mac 'ic Ailein says, "before you fired your arrow that you placed three other ones around you. Why was that?"

'"I'll tell you simply," Gille Padraig says, and he glares at them all in turn. "If I had drawn a mite's worth of blood from my son's brow, this arrow would have been for you, this one for your wife – The Mistress – and this last one would have pierced the heart of MacLeod of Dunvegan, who put you up to this!"

'"*Obh, òbh, òbh!*" says Mac 'ic Ailein. "Thanks goodness that didn't happen. Be going! Be gone! And don't let anyone stop you!"

'And with that, Gille Pàdraig and his son Iain Dubh returned to the Geàrradh Fliuch on their horses, and from that day forth, neither Mac 'ic Ailein nor anyone else gave them much bother at all.'

Jane and I both clapped. It was lovely. Simple, but so adeptly told it was of high art. I felt privileged to have felt it live in its natural setting.

Jane met me at the peat-stack on my return from the byre. The weather was hot and airless – Alasdair's house cooler and far more pleasant today.

'He used to always tell me that story, when I was wee,' she said. 'I didn't know if he'd tell you it though. You must be well in with us.'

'Must be,' I avoided eye contact, though I felt her gaze.

'The other one's back in two weeks, is he?'

I'd no idea what she was talking about.

'Dr Marr.'

'Is he? Yes.'

'You'll leave then; maybe before then,' she stated. I didn't reply. Ruairidh and I had still to discuss this properly, though Jane was right, of course.

'Well, laddie,' she said, giving me a playful prod in the belly, 'you'll just have to work harder in the days you have left!' With that, she headed in the direction of the byre, and I spotted the faded-pink toilet paper popping in and out of her cardigan pocket as her sturdy hips swung over the uneven ground.

'He was a real person, Gille Pàdraig,' Alasdair declared when we were back inside, 'who came here in the seventeenth century, from near Loch Awe. One of his descendants was a shepherd behind Corrodale. I met old Dòmhnall mac Eachainn a few times when he'd settled back in Tobh.'

Jane came in, replaced the toilet paper in its slot, which I'd never noticed before, and filled the kettle from the pail nearest the window and added fuel to the stove. She then began fuelling Alasdair's pipe. She never once looked at a clock, nor did she wear a watch.

'Iain Dubh had a daughter,' Alasdair began. 'Do you want to put that thing back on?' he asked, and I obliged by pressing the two buttons and re-checking my mic. There was no shortage of tape.

'This won't take a second,' he said. 'But best to catch it now in case the next world comes between us in my sleep, *a Chailein*. Iain Dubh mac Ghille Phàdraig – he had a daughter, and I don't know what all else of a family. By the time this daughter was getting on in years she was the only one left. Then she died. And they were carrying her coffin on the machair all the way down to Ìochdar when a terrible snowstorm caught them out. The weather got so bad that they had to abandon the coffin and rush home, best they could. No one could return for two or three days. And to this day, they say in Uist:

"*The day of the funeral
of the daughter of Iain Dubh mac Ghille Pàdraig,*

the worst day ever that came or will come."'

Jane offered me a lift home, which I accepted, gratefully. Our journey was relaxed, our conversation – though there was little need of much – unforced and comfortable. We agreed I'd be back tomorrow.

'But,' I said, 'I do fancy, heading up Ben More, one day soon. Might explore Corrodale too?'

'Make hay, Colin, while the sun shines!' she urged with a shrewd smile. Yes, well, indoors hay in the peat-warmed dim of Milton.

'Will the kids not have a Sports Day?' I asked. Ealasaid had said this was the last school week.

'Not sure,' she shrugged like an untrammelled teen. 'I'll check with my mother.'

Ruairidh was thrilled with the recording, especially the little postscript regarding Iain Dubh's daughter. 'I've heard countless references to that story, Colin' he said, 'but never recorded a complete version. The bit about their rent not being enough is also new to me, but it does give a stronger motive for Mac 'ic Ailein's dirty ruse.'

'And a "peck" of grain?' I asked.

'A Scots' dry gallon,' my uncle's knowledgeable reply.

'Take a bit of blood to replace that?'

'*Dearbha fhèine, a Chailein.*[148] About as much as those stupid fools lost on Saturday!!'

Young Mìcheal, was making steady progress; it was now unlikely he'd be transferred to Glasgow for further treatment; Eric Adam's skills had been up to the task. The boy's parents were much relieved and hugely grateful to the staff for the attention received. The Sacred Heart Hospital was now enjoying welcome respite – not even a potentially problematic maternity case simmering.

---

[148] Absolutely, Colin

My uncle too had enjoyed a straightforward day with modest surgeries and fewer house calls than was normal for a Monday. An on-call Saturday morning did though loom – his penultimate of this locum – so much could still happen.

Ruairidh told me he'd managed to visit Murchadh Caol and tee him up for a recording session the following evening. 'Good job we did get that extra box of tape, Colin,' he said with a slow smile.

'Might need some new batteries, actually,' I offered.

'The current ones will do your session tomorrow afternoon though.' He was keen I push on.

I reckoned they would. Ruairidh could, of course, record Murchadh Caol from the mains but he would wish to avoid imposing this cost on him.

Ealasaid had seemed a little subdued. I wondered if she was preparing for our imminent departure and her losing this key role. It would, though, give her a break; providing three meals a day, six days a week for two hungry men was no mean feat, or feast!

'Och, well,' she said, revealing little more. 'That's the World Cup all over for another four years. I'll miss it, you know. It gets you away from this place for a wee while. They certainly know how to enjoy themselves in Argentina. I never saw so many streamers in all my born days!'

Scotland's gallus over-confident claim to be champions now seemed like a distant memory – a myth akin to Alasdair's on Gille Pàdraig and Mac 'ic Ailein: containing real historical characters but placed in a highly fictional context. The major difference being that Gille Pàdraig's cockiness of the 'extraordinary' common man was founded on exceptional skill, unlike his modern counterpart.

An impromptu visit from Patricia and Steafan MacInnes provided much-needed relief from this anti-climactic musing.

Ruairidh immediately brightened and I could see 'method' in his twinkling smile; I had let him listen to our recording. He enjoyed Patricia's singing voice and style very much. 'How interesting, Colin, both the grandfather and her mother are there – in bucket-loads.'

Steafan seemed much more relaxed than previously. '*Seo, ma-thà!*' he said, extending an envelope to Ruairidh. 'If you can't manage the whole day, just come in the evening.'

Ruairidh opened a silver, gilt-edged, invitation with two names written on it.

'We're hoping you'll come too, *a Chailein*,' Patricia added with an excited giggle causing her to blush.

I was intrigued but could see some consternation on Ruairidh's face. Did he not know the couple who were getting married – their parents even?

'Oh, well, well,' my uncle began, 'this is most kind of you. We'll have to see... eh...'

'Sarah's a first cousin,' Patricia assured, 'Margaret's eldest. And Derrick's from Banff but really nice.'

'I'm sure he is. Sarah's the physio?'

''*S i, ma-thà!*'[149]

'In Elgin.'

'That's her.'

'Are you on-call on Saturday?' Patricia then asked – both of us it seemed.

'Yes and no,' replied Ruairidh. From mid-day he would be responsible for anaesthetic emergencies only; Eric would be the GP and surgeon.

'Well,' he looked over to me, 'we could think about it.'

'Your last full weekend,' Patricia stated. Yes, always a few steps ahead! We had decided to leave a week on Sunday, the ferry times being better for driving south, before my uncle then crossed to the Borders.

---

[149] She is!

'What are you going to sing at the wedding?' he asked Patricia.

She blushed again. 'I don't really sing in public.'

'Why ever not?' Ruairidh pushed. 'Your grandfather... there wasn't a do on this island without a turn from Crìsdean. You're every bit as good as him, in your own way.'

Pat glanced over at me. Had I broken her confidence? I didn't think so at the time but felt now perhaps I had.

Steafan looked at his sister encouragingly, 'What about a wee practice, then?'

Patricia sighed, then allowed herself to enjoy the attention, not something that came easily to her.

'Wait!' yelled Ruairidh, rising to get the Uher from the window ledge and switching it on.

'Go for it, dear,' he said. 'Any song you like – except the ones you gave Cailean!'

'Any other demands?' she asked, with a wicked grin.

'Two,' he said – trying his luck – 'You'll then have a choice on the day!'

This faux impudence brought a chortle, and without further preamble, Pat sang beautifully and with care:

'*A Mhic Iain 'ic Sheumais*'[150] – detailing a MacDonald v MacLeod feud, followed by an exquisite love song – its lightness being its depth – and not once did she fluff the high note of '*O my joyful brown-haired boy, you kept me wide awake last night.*'

'That was very good,' I said to Ruairidh, when they had gone. He had been far more effusive in his praise, almost making it a condition of his wedding acceptance that she sang. Steafan confirmed he'd act as minder: 'To make sure wee sister doesn't get steaming!' That got the laugh it deserved.

'She's excellent, though, Colin!' Ruairidh roared. 'Isn't Patricia a fine singer?'

---

[150] 'O, Son of John of James'

'Lovely of them to invite us to the wedding.'

'Yes, yes,' he agreed, 'very generous.'

I wondered to what extent Ruairidh's skilled management of the Loch Aoineart accident had contributed to this situation. Was he perhaps growing in stature just near the end of his stay here? Or was it the sudden realisation that he (or we?) wouldn't be in Uist much longer that prompted the late request for our company. If that were true, then who most desired it?

'Should be a damn good wedding!' my uncle enthused. 'Pipers in that family too, Colin, and St Peter's Hall is the best. Sarah's a sweet girl, her man must be okay.' I didn't say anything. 'You are coming? Cracking lassie, Patricia, so she is! Steafan's improving – *air a shocair fhèin*.'[151]

I told him of my plans to climb Ben More and to give myself a brief recording 'holiday'.

'You can leave that a few days, surely. There's good weather coming. Anyway, that hill's been there for thousands of years and there it shall remain. This might be the only *Uibhisteach* wedding you ever get invited to.'

'Cheers for that!' I joked.

'And what about Murchadh Caol's tomorrow evening? A splendid fellow. Do you know...?'

'*Leabhra thig*,'[152] I said, excitedly, 'and to the wedding. I've just got to try a bit harder for the rest of this week.'

Helped by the social deadline and the reality that time was running out for me too, I cracked on that morning with my studies. In the next four days, I also succeeded in recording an eclectic mix of treasures from Alasdair mac Sheumais Bhig:

A beautiful variant on MacCodrum and the seals – the beasts starting life as under-sea princesses before their jealous stepmother tricks them with her potions.

---

151 at his own relaxed pace
152 Of course, I'll come!

A ghostly priest who says Mass each year for Calum 'ac Fhionnlaigh's soul since he'd died without receiving the sacraments.

Eòlas an Dèididh – an incantation against toothache, which Fr Allan MacDonald collected in Eriskay.

Pìobairean Bhòrnais – a wizened *bodach* gives the youngest son fairy piping skills, then the lad breaks his promise and never plays again.

Jane was in and out. Her children did have a Sports Day and an end-of-year concert – both of which she attended, reluctantly it seemed. Mac Sheumais Bhig was quite comfortable alone with me and my *'machine'*. I kept the stove going and consumed less tea. He was quite lively and never complained once, except to voice his concern that I may no longer be interested: I was free to stop at any point.

'No, you can't!' ordered Jane. 'He's got more – much more. I'll remember some over the weekend and prompt him. You must come back on Monday!' I had learned from Alasdair that her kids were heading to their auntie's in North Uist for the first week of the holidays.

'But,' she said, dropping me off to walk through Eòrasdail, 'I'll see you tomorrow anyway.'

'Sorry Jane. Day off,' I protested. *This is terrible,* I thought, and getting far too intense. What exactly was Jane's game here?

'Not at my uncle's,' she laughed. 'Sarah and I were in the same class in school – a close friend at the time. We sort of went our separate ways, but I hoped I'd get an invite.'

Chapter 20

The people of the Gàidhealtachd looked very different too, in their attire, and none had heard of the Fèinn. Eventually Oisean was sent to the house of an old renowned seanachie. He remained on the white horse as he bent to knock the bodach's door. 'Well, well,' said the whiskery old man, when he understood the purpose of the visit. 'It must be about three hundred years since that lot were roaming around these parts. Wasn't there one among them they called Oisean – the bàrd?' 'Yes, there was,' said Oisean.

A NEW MONTH declared itself for Sarah and Derrick's wedding with a clear blue sky and a modestly elevated temperature. Just enough of a breeze was blowing to keep the heavily clad guests comfortable outside the church and all but the most tenacious of midges at bay.

For the Eòrasdail duo it had been a slowish morning. I had laid aside my course-books and the ever-growing mound for transcription; Ruairidh's late breakfast and initial lack of oomph were due to a 4.00am call to Frobost. 'A delightful old besom' he said, accepting an extra sausage; Ealasaid had sat waiting, a neighbour's new baby's cardigan taking shape between bionic needles.

When she was out of earshot, and without mentioning the patient's name, Ruairidh described an illness, he judged far less common here than in the cities. 'A real hypochondriac, Colin. Bill Marr warned she'd call regularly for a while, then just stop for months. I reckon we got off lightly!'

Being included in the team felt nice, though I'd hardly accompanied my uncle on calls over the last couple of weeks.

Not that this seemed to bother Ruairidh at all.

An deagh Dhotair MacIllIosa[153] – 'she's a funny one, Colin' – was able to convince the *cailleach* that her heaving chest, shortness of breath and crampy hand would not be heart-related – perhaps the result of a bad dream. She, in turn, was hugely, if not contritely, grateful and asked if he could eat a duck egg. Someone she had known – who'd breakfasted on two hens' eggs all his life – took a near-fatal reaction to his first-ever duck one.

Ruairidh assured the woman he had no known allergies and received six, which Ealasaid point-blank refused to boil, fry or scramble. 'Something about them I don't like,' she said. 'Was never really an eggy type!'

If we'd had this discussion six weeks ago our collective cholesterol profiles might have looked a tad healthier...

'Anyway,' Ealasaid added, 'I wouldn't put anything that Màiri Ruadh gave me near my mouth – shelled or fresh. Those cats do their everything everywhere.'

'Ha!' Ruairidh's acknowledgement of superior knowledge.

'She's related to the girl who's marrying today,' Ealasaid then stated. 'On her father's side – a half-sister of Calum Dhòmhnaill's she is.'

Ruairidh's face fell.

'Don't you be worrying yourself now, Good Doctor Gillies' – a great impersonation apparently – 'she won't be there. Màiri hasn't left that house in ten years.'

Ealasaid did eventually leave our house, and we left the duck-eggs well alone. Since the service wouldn't be until 3.00pm – to help guests flying from Aberdeen – Ruairidh and I made for the beach.

It occurred to me that this was the first time we had strolled in the village together, or anywhere bar the fifty yards over to Alasdair mac Sheumais Bhig's. We'd walked it twice only.

---

153 The good Doctor Gillies

It was grand to have the time to observe the early-summer normality of nature and man in Eòrasdail, and to see my uncle so relaxed and carefree, despite his disturbed night.

A wild-duck looked over from the loch south of the township road – Loch nan Nighean – then squealed as it tried to navigate the mesh of exquisite lilies floating all around. I wondered whether her eggs would be any safer to eat than Màiri Ruadh's.

'Now that flower there, *a Chailein* – no, that one over there!' Ruairidh pointed as we closed the gate to the machair, 'That's the Scottish Bluebell or *Currac Cuthaige*. Nothing to do with bells in Gaelic but with the cuckoo. The *currac* is her bonnet.' He bent down and placed two fingers around its slender stem: 'It wasn't only in the stories that we had our own vision of the world but in nature too.'

We walked in silence, as I considered the wider meaning of this information: that each culture has, or had, its own way of looking at and naming the elements within its environment – its own 'window' through which to see the world. Thus, shouldn't being bilingual – having access to two languages and their associated cultures – offer at least two windows; with the full view, hopefully, then greater or wider than the parts combined?

'And that one, *'ille?*' asked Ruairidh. I hadn't a clue – it was a tall, reddish-stemmed plant with creamy white flowers. 'That's *Crios Chù Chullainn* – Meadowsweet. Cù Chullainn, was another warrior hero,' my uncle said, 'who got bloody angry!'

'Unlike Oisean,' I added.

'Correct, but a sprig of this pretty flower under his belt could keep him calm.'

We'd met no one and were almost at the sand dune where I'd toppled down to my friend, Jane's, stern leather boots when, from just south of us, two Harrier Jets roared upwards, dipped, then headed east, low over Ben More and Corrodale.

Within minutes a rocket launched with an almighty bang.

'*A Bhochain a Mhìn!*'[154] Ruairidh screamed. 'Some of us were only in bed a short while last night.'

A rabbit darted out of a scraggy, sandy, burrow and another one with bleary eyes shot into it. 'Poor wee creatures,' said Ruairidh. 'If the myxomatosis doesn't do them in those damn rockets will put them apoplectic!'

We continued down to the shore and walked in a comfortable, sought-after, silence, between stones, shells, seaware and plenty of flotsam and jetsam – from planks of wood to plastic in all shapes and sizes and the ubiquitous estranged buoys. No further aircraft or explosive intrusions rattled our thoughts or the tranquil sighing of the waves.

'I'm enjoying your being here,' Ruairidh said without sentimentality.

'*Tapadh leibh*. It was great to get the chance.' It had been a unique opportunity. 'We'll do it again,' I added, and felt, at that moment, a repeat could be possible.

'Well,' began Ruairidh, 'Let's see what 1979 brings, or' he quickly added, 'maybe in a couple of years you'll be...'

The real question was would Ruairidh ever return here as the locum doctor? Until the last few days, I'd have said not. But the events of the car-crash and its aftermath had clearly given him a confidence boost. He was also delighted with the material I'd recorded and had spent one quiet night on-call listening for hours on end.

'You see, Colin, while the Edinburgh team – any professional folklorist – will possess skills we certainly don't have, people give us different information. It's the intimacy thing; just by being who we are and being here and interested.'

Certainly, witnessing my uncle's abilities with Murchadh Caol the other night had shown me that I still had much to learn. 'Maybe you've heard this one before, a Ruairidh,' he'd

---

[154] O my goodness

said. 'And if you have, too bad, because I'm now going to tell you what really happened…'

We were on the point of returning south, aware of time's capricious wiles and our being watch-less, when a different sound assailed our ploddy pondering.

Tormod Mòraig, in tractor and trailer, bumped and clattered out of what must have been a machair side-road and hailed us heartily. 'Thought you two had a wedding today?' he shouted above the din.

'We do that, *a Thormoid*,' Ruairidh replied.

'Leaving it a bit tight are you not?' our neighbour admonished, shutting off his engine.

'What time is it?' I asked. Tormod Mòraig always wore a wound watch.

'A quarter to two. I'll take you home now.'

Ruairidh looked at the set-up. We would be in the trailer. 'Thanks, *ma-thà*,' he said, 'but you've got too much to do. We'll be fine cutting over the wee hill. Let's go, though, *a Chailein*!'

I wondered – as we raced over Àrdan Beag – whether I would visit Tormod Mòraig again and what we might chat about without the World Cup. I had never seen Ruairidh move so quickly without actually running; his efforts showed the same focus as his much shorter dash to the Loch Aoineart *tubaist*.[155]

'Okay, *'ille*,' he said, looking up at the clock on our arrival home, 'we haven't even got twenty minutes. No baths, I'm afraid, but still time for a flannel scrub.'

My mother had made me bring 'good' Sunday clothes – which I'd worn only once to poor Norma's funeral. That light grey suit could take a green tie or perhaps the colourful patterned one. I'd have to polish my shoes – well, buff them with an old t-shirt. No need to shave: my growth wasn't

---

[155] accident

bad, and it might add a little something to the smart, but casual-at-heart, look.

I was ready very soon, before Ruairidh hailed me – to sort his sporran! I let out a shriek, more from surprise, because the kilt did suit his small, stouting, frame. 'You never know when the occasion will arise, *a Chailein*. Preparedness, that's been my approach; all my life.'

Rather than the various black-jacket options my uncle had brought a bottle-green tweed one and a darker-green tie – which was far too long and had to be tucked under his sweet-smelling leather belt with large buckle.

'I've a pair of brogues with those laces that tie up your leg,' he said, 'but they're a hassle, Colin. A small subtle garter in each stocking is just as effective. *Okay, ma-thà? Mach à seo!*'[156]

Unlike the island Sunday norm, where a group of males would gather outside the church before entering last to occupy the rear pews, St Peter's had a different, festive, feeling to it today. A piper greeted us as we approached the vestry.

We stood a minute to listen and Ruairidh shouted his name in my ear – or at least the family – MacKinnon's, he reckoned – 'other wonderful pipers, *a Chailein*!'

Two young men, one obviously local, the other much darker featured, led us in and asked on whose side we were, then pointed down to six or seven rows back on the left.

Patricia, Steafan, and their family were seated in the next but one row ahead of us. Both she and her brother turned round as did their father and mother – all of them reinforcing Patricia's open, alluring, smile.

Two sturdier, swarthier, men shuffled before a beautifully adorned altar as the sun streamed through the open windows, resting now and then with a rainbow splash on some of the

---

[156] Out we go!

ladies' wide-brimmed hats.

Other than the piper, Ruairidh was the only person sporting the kilt. The bridegroom and his best man had chosen light-coloured outfits with striking flares, but they had knotted their ties more modestly than many of the younger lads. For the most part, the older men wore dark, serge (or serge-like) suits often with a sprig of heather or an orchid fixed to a lapel.

At 1518 on my rarely worn digital watch, a hushed silence announced the imminent arrival of the bride.

A choir behind me started singing '*Reul Alainn a' Chuain*',[157] accompanied now by a much more enthusiastic organist as if jolted from a desultory dwam.

Sarah – led by her proud, nervous and elderly father – was radiant in her frilly white dress and veil.

Mgr Pàdraig also wore celebratory white vestments and his two young servers in soutanes were scrubbed spotless and scalped – very recently by the looks of their bristly necks. The priest swapped his customary Gaelic for English, that all understood and expected, to include the groom's side in the proceedings.

He welcomed everyone to the Isle of South Uist – and to St Peter's Parish Church – on such a joyous occasion and referred to the responsibilities marriage brought in addition to the 'fun'. Those from other faiths were encouraged to take part in the Mass, but 'to avoid any possible awkwardness,' he asked at a later stage, that only those who'd made their First Holy Communion came forward. Most of those who did, took the Host directly onto their tongues, although the rules allowing the use of hands had been in place for a few years.

After a brief personal prayer, Ruairidh rose from kneeling and squeezed past me to join the slow queue for 'The Body of Christ'. I'd not been a regular communicant for a while

---

157 'Sweet Star of the Sea'

– since before leaving home; to receive it today – while nice, participatory even – would still feel hypocritical.

All assembled, led by Mgr Pàdraig, gave a great round of applause when the couple completed their vows to be pronounced 'Man and Wife'. The priest did not then ask Banff Derrick – as happened in the films – to kiss his bride. 'All that stuff,' he said, 'can be left until later.'

Having spent all day in our own wee bubble, it was a release and a relief to chat outside with the family who had so generously requested our presence. I felt their deep respect for Ruairidh and a desire to include him in the bosom of the celebration. It wasn't difficult to bask in some of his reflected glory.

Sarah and Derrick seemed particularly chuffed that my uncle had come: 'I'm just loving Physio, Ruairidh,' she enthused, 'It's so logical.'

'Good for you, Sarah,' he supplied, as if he knew her very well and saw her on a regular basis. 'You'll be a great asset to the people of Elgin and this passionate prop-forward.'

'Second Row actually,' Derrick replied. 'Do these give the game away?' he asked, rubbing his lettuce lugs.

'No, no!' Ruairidh assured, 'Just the glint in your eye.'

I scanned Derrick's face and immediately focused on his obviously squint, knuckled, nose.

The piper continued to play throughout these exchanges – moving from marches to jigs and back. Patricia looked lovely in a short lime dress with a dropped but modest neckline. She cut a neat appearance and wore slightly daring, long, wedge-heeled boots. I reckoned she'd have to ditch those for dancing. Steafan had chosen a jacket and slacks, which looked too casual in this context when they would have been fine elsewhere. Quite a funny brother and sister duo, I reflected. Might they possibly be destined to live together like those of an older generation who'd forgone marriage or whom love had shunned? Could this in part be the motivation for Patricia's visits – to escape her fate? Perhaps it was now time for me to gently explore this theory, then do so more actively.

Just as we were heading back down to the hall, with the first hint of rain tinkling a corrugated-iron roof on the croft nearest St Peter's, Jane appeared at my side with Ìomhair right behind her. Their children stood mute to attention between them. Jane's outfit looked freshly *a la mode* and helped by generous makeup, it achieved quite a transformation.

'Were you not going to talk to me?' she said, in a way that should not have bothered Ìomhair – light, humorous, familiar-ish.

'He doesn't have to speak to the likes of us,' he spat, 'when there's better ones to talk to.' This jibe was unnecessary, and Jane ignored its poison.

'Isn't Sarah beautiful!' she said instead. 'How well that frock suits. You'd think it had been made for her alone.'

'Wasn't it?' I asked

'No. That's her mother's wedding dress. She was a very slim woman too in her day, Sìneag.'

My uncle had continued walking – subtly done too. 'Heading to the hall?' I asked Jane.

'Yes, yes,' she reassured me. 'Once I've checked on Alasdair. He wanted to see the rig-out. Keep me a dance,' she then shouted, and I felt her husband's mean sneer before he pulled her away abruptly. Could Jane have told Ìomhair that we'd kissed – to rile him or to try and keep me? It wasn't likely, but at the same time a most uncomfortable thought.

As we entered the Church Hall, we were directed away from the white-clothed and flower-decorated trestle tables to a smaller side-room where both Sarah and Derrick's fathers shook our hands and ordered the best man and ushers to pour drams.

I noticed small ones being put into the *Uibhisteach* glasses

– seasoned celebrators with a long night ahead – but the Banffshire boys were getting torn-in, including Derrick's ruddy-complexioned dad.

Having thrown back my drink in a oner, bar a few drops, I saw that the level in Ruairidh's glass had hardly gone down; Eric Adams was covering his GP duties, but a surgical or obstetric emergency might yet require anaesthetic skills. How much anaesthetic could *he* safely imbibe I wondered. 'Very little,' my uncle informed me, 'Especially on an empty stomach.'

'This man,' Sarah's dad was boasting, 'is a very good doctor. And he's a Barraman,' he added, without a hint of irony. 'And we here in Uist are very glad of him.'

To which Ruairidh gave an immediate, 'And we were both very glad to be asked to this special day, Calum.' He then shook cordially and efficiently with about ten others. 'I once worked on a fishing boat out of Macduff,' he enthused. 'Great part of the country – a hidden gem, really, and...'

'It's a peety then that the fowk there hae twa heids!' slurred the best man, with an ethanol burp. This provoked some mock offence from one of the ushers – a beast of a guy, whom I'd have dared tease only from the safety of an armour suit.

'Sarah's a lucky girl,' Ruairidh replied (most drolly, I felt). My second, slower, Famous Grouse urged a guffaw, but the Macduff bi-cranial kept my manners intact.

We then returned to the main hall where we stood around for a short time before sitting for the entrance of the special couple. Sarah and Derrick almost marched in behind the piper, beaming from ear to ear and scanning the clapping assembly, as they made their way up to the main table on the stage.

I searched the room and easily caught Patricia's eye, which she held comfortably before turning politely back to the woman who was tugging her sleeve.

There was no sign of Jane and Ìomhair. Were they, perhaps, evening guests who'd opted to attend the Mass of their own accord, or had something else delayed their return to the fold?

A stout, balding, gentleman, in a double-breasted suit – an almost accountant, I was told later – stood up and in a confident, booming, more lightly-accented, voice welcomed us all to the reception and invited Mgr Pàdraig to say Grace.

'*An ainm an Athar is a' Mhic is an Spioraid Naoimh, Amen,*'[158] he began, then gave a short prayer in Gaelic which he repeated in English.

The North Easterners seemed to be enjoying this experience and their 'Well dones!' and solid handshakes with the priest sealed their approval of religious and linguistic brevity.

Then came the women – a whole platoon of them – with trays of soup, followed by roast chicken and bowls of potatoes and bowls of carrots and of turnip and full jugs of dark gravy.

More whisky was laid at intervals on the tables and half a dozen little glasses in a circle round each bottle for future toasting. I noticed some of the Banffshire boys gleefully partaking despite the remonstrations of their disappointed wives and partners.

Ruairidh and I were seated close to young Mìcheal's parents, which I understood, but felt could prove a little awkward for my uncle. Mìcheal Mòr and Jean, however, showed almost undue tact: they made no mention whatsoever of the recent nightmare on the Loch Aoineart road. Instead, they let the lad opposite regale us with stories from a recent work-trip to Norway's stunning islands: amazing ferries too apparently!

'Great storyteller!' Ruairidh remarked, as we zipped in tandem at the urinals. 'Shame he never heard anything about the Fèinn!'

'He didn't?'

'Doubt it, Colin. You can tell. Somehow...'

That booming MC voice – this time in Gaelic – interrupted

---

[158] In the name of the Father and of the Son and of the Holy Spirit, Amen

my uncle's flow. 'It's yourself, *a Ruairidh*. The man who has yet to visit. And how's mac Sheumais Bhig pleasing you?'

'Very well, William,' Ruairidh replied oddly. 'Colin here has done most of the work.' I shook the man's large hand.

'Another one that could come and see me!' he barked, 'Or does he prefer lies?'

'Not my type at all,' Ruairidh confided back at the table, as the women now laid bowls of trifle before us. 'Quite a knowledgeable man too, William Campbell, but with a massive, fragile ego. A shame really.'

Only one more week remained. We would not be visiting him, hopefully; Ruairidh confirmed.

That same booming voice (one I was now acutely aware of) summoned Calum Dhòmhnaill, Sarah's father, to pay tribute to his daughter.

This he did almost inaudibly, directing his pride at his sparkling shoes. The relative extrovert, with dram in hand, in the back room with the boys, seemed subdued – by emotion or William Campbell's overbearing introduction. His sitting down won applause as strong, I'm sure, as his relief to be no longer speeching. It struck me as a little strange that the family hadn't asked Mgr Pàdraig, who was at the top table, to MC this part. Then again William Campbell evidently relished the role.

Next up was John – the best man. William didn't give us a surname, nor did he tell us what his issue with Macduff was. John scraped his chair to standing and launched into a series of bawdy stories that bore little relevance to the fact that today Derrick had wed the love of his life. He could have been at an awards night at the Buchan rugby club; and was it crucial the bemused *Uibhistich* learnt that the bridegroom had lost his virginity many years before meeting his bride-to-be? Sarah shook her head and threw back a clear liquid in her whisky tot – water perhaps?

The groom's speech saved the day, however. It was measured, discreet, generous, apologetic as regards his best man – 'He doesn't often get away for the weekend'– and sincerely appreciative of Calum and Mary-Anne's welcome into the Campbell family. Ah, I thought, hence Big William's unassailable role. On closer inspection, Ruairidh's nemesis was a rather filled-out 'ne'er-do-well' version of Calum Dhòmhnaill.

Derrick's final tribute to his new wife – a verse from Burns's 'Red, Red, Rose' – was brave (given his brawny pals) and poignantly delivered.

I felt a tear suggest itself in the corner of my eye – at a wedding of people I didn't know – and when I glanced over Ruairidh was dabbing with his dapper handkerchief to modest effect.

I'm sure he felt Aunt Emily's loss more sorely at times like these, but I also knew that she wouldn't have enjoyed this event: 'Too loose at the ends by far, Colin dear!' Emily valued a sense of order and formality that wasn't very *Gàidhealach*, it struck me then. In addition, my aunt held little tolerance for those who couldn't control their drinking, or themselves as a result.

When tables had been cleared – either away to the kitchen or pushed to the sides of the hall – The Wedding Reel was announced.

Derrick and Sarah faced best man, John, and Karen – the bride's oldest sister.

I feared the worst: John was now rubbernecked and legged. How much practice would he have had: a brief demo yesterday, perhaps, on arrival? Derrick gave him a stare and then consolidated this with a lengthy pep talk in his right ear – the slurring repentant nodding all the while.

The piper delicately executed his opening tune to guide the foursome with grace. I could see, from ten yards away, beads of sweat bursting onto John's concentrative brow – his hands swaying aloft like a hopeful Yoga novice. They were managing, though, to hold it together, aided, undoubtedly, by two former Highland Dance champions.

When all moved to the faster 'Reel' element, the piper did his best to maintain a steady, safe, pace. His attention was on the wobbly best man, as he birled Sarah before leaping to set to Derrick with a whoop from the crowd. Both pairs of laces had loosened, and I feared that if he didn't collapse first – his face drenched and grey – John would soon trip and clatter headfirst to his demise. Not yet! Derrick's will somehow kept his mate upright and then the piper's neat, if unorthodox, return to Strathspey (as groom found bride and her douce maid grabbed John) signalled a reprieve and that others might dance soon.

Proud Dad, Calum Dhòmhnaill, and Cousin William immediately presented themselves as suitable candidates and Sarah and Karen gratefully accepted. Derrick whipped his best man back to Banffshire safety.

While the chief wedding party had shown great effort and concentration and much luck on John's part, Calum and William turned the girls and enthralled the audience with poise, elegance and years of experience.

Just as the crowd gave a huge cry of appreciation, Ìomhair and Jane entered at the back of the hall. I could see by the way she was gripping her coat and her refusal of a drink – rammed almost in her face – that they were warring. Ìomhair soon wandered off towards some beer-swilling buddies.

I might have gone over to Jane at that point, but instead my attention and feelings were focused on Patricia. She was in deep contemplation with quite a serious faraway look on her pretty face. Some extended muttering suggested she was practising to sing. Her turn came after the fourth set of The Wedding Reel: which despite much cajoling, Derrick's father steadfastly refused to do.

Patricia chose neither of the two songs she'd sung for Ruairidh, nor the ones I had recorded that special afternoon. Instead, she gave a jaunty number about the trials of being a fishing-girl in Shetland and her poignant encore told of a woman's longing to marry despite her lover being at sea and others' criticism of his wayward ways.

One line '...*is nach bi stocainn nach bi bròg ort,*'[159] seemed suddenly apt, as I spotted exhausted John barefoot and conked out in the corner. Perhaps Patricia was singing it for his future wife.

Within minutes of her finishing this song, Ronald Lamont – the famous box player from North Uist – called us all on the floor for a Canadian Barn Dance. Steafan took Patricia up and I politely offered to take a cousin of young Mìcheal's. Ruairidh, whom I thought might have been tempted by The Wedding Reel, then raced onto the floor with an attractive blonde-haired woman in her thirties – early-forties at the most. My uncle was a great dancer, and his kilt swished rhythmically above his chubby knees.

My efforts sufficed, and I was relieved when Ronald announced a Dashing White Sergeant next. My beeline for the MacInnes duo secured contact with Patricia and her genuine acceptance of my compliments on her singing gave me pleasure.

The three of us were a good team and had a super time heuching and setting with many other guests as we progressed lithely. Patricia was a fit, elegant, twister and completed all her mid-round turns with ease. She held my hand – but not Steafan's – longer than was necessary at the end of this long, demanding, dance.

She then excused herself before heading towards the main door; I wondered when I could dance with her next. The second one after she returned? Hopefully it wouldn't be a waltz of any sort.

---

[159] ...and you won't have socks or shoes on

I turned to find myself facing Jane – now with her coat off and holding a tall glass. She looked nice and smiled without malice or resentment, but sadly, I felt.

'More like your type,' she stated, motioning her drink in the direction of Patricia's exit.

'Hello there, Jane,' I replied. Those strange feelings that stirred first in Barra, then caught me out in Milton after the accident were gone – spent, perhaps, in recording her great-uncle or spoilt by an ash-flavoured tongue and Ìomhair's cruel sneer. 'I bet Alasdair was impressed with you,' I tried.

She shrugged. 'He's not quite right today; not right at all. I can't put my finger on it.' Jane and her uncle's set-up was most precarious. I tried to show empathy by letting her continue.

'Ìomhair wasn't happy when I wouldn't leave him until my mother returned. Which she did eventually! Anyway, he'll be fine on Monday, surely.' A blank expression on my face prompted a, 'You are coming?'

If it were a nice day, I would be on Ben More. My head nodded all the same.

'He's got a special one for you,' she pushed. 'He told me it yesterday when he was in better form. Years since he's told that story, apparently.'

'I wonder...?' I began

'*Thugainn!*' she insisted, '*Schottische a th' ann.*[160] There's none under the sun better at it than Ronald Lamont.'

We were on the floor in seconds and Jane swiftly quashed any intentions I might have had of trying the Barra style.

She was an able, old-fashioned, dancer but with none of Patricia's athleticism; like a woman who'd been good in her youth but now had to conserve energy to reach the end without any loss in quality.

Jane's comment was true: Patricia was much more my type, but she was now dancing with quite a handsome guy

---

160 Come on!... it's a schottische.

in a snazzy jacket and safer trousers.

Ìomhair met us off the floor and offered me a swig of whisky, which I refused. 'Those young girls should watch out,' he said, pointing to Ruairidh. 'Him prancing about with *hee-haw* hiding his cock. Doesn't take much, Colin, does it?' He looked straight at me, bayed a dirty, mocking, laugh, then glanced back to where my uncle was having tremendous fun with one of Mìcheal Òg's lot. Ruairidh had earned their affection and was entitled to enjoy it – with all his modesty intact.

What a loathsome character Ìomhair was! I certainly would not miss him, though I'd have to remain vigilant and not carelessly provoke his temper in the meantime. This would mean giving him and Jane a wide berth tonight. I hoped she'd understand – poor oval-eyed Jane.

I also craved closeness to Patricia and a bright, melodic, Gay Gordons was about to help. We followed this with a rousing Strip the Willow, where I held her waist quite tightly and squeezed it on the twirls.

Soon after this, the band took their break and more food arrived. The now packed space and my desire for air – and to lose Ìomhair and Jane – drove me out and up behind the hall to a minute of contemplation in the mild starlit night. I must have dozed off, because next thing I heard was William Campbell's big voice announcing, as midnight approached, a repeat of The Wedding Reel. It would be great to try it with Patricia – the second staging was usually a less formal affair.

The bridal foursome was now, of course, down to a threesome, though Sarah's brother had taken sleeping John's place and danced well. I was getting ready to make my move, when Jane slipped her arm through mine – just as she had on that first strange day – and led us forward.

'I wonder will we manage it?' she asked with tobacco and hard liquor – Rum, I reckoned – on her breath.

'Don't know,' was my honest, deflated, reply. We did, as regarding the Reel. I'd never tried it before but had watched carefully at the start of the night. Jane was most able – as if she'd danced it frequently over the last seventy-odd years, her and Alasdair's steps completely in sync.

Her kiss at the end while 'safely' planted on my cheek, was too wet and the saliva slid down and behind my loosened collar.

Freeing myself casually from Jane proved challenging as the pulsing horde kept heaving us back together. When I did succeed, a changed, far colder stare from Ìomhair was my reward. If only I'd been able to read this properly – dig deeper into the disgust it awoke – much pain would have been averted.

Instead, Ruairidh approached and excitedly suggested that since we'd had a great night – and no one had called him away – we should leave now, to avoid the crowds and any *après-nuptial* scrapping. He had also offered, he said, to take Steafan and Patricia home; both had to be on the boat at six. My heart sank.

The journey back to Eòrasdail was full of polite chat, plus some discussion, led by Ruairidh, on Pat's songs, which would have been welcome any other night. I travelled in the front but kept twisting my neck to smile and make warm, encouraging, eye contact with her. It did, though, feel sorely like our moment had passed.

'See you,' she offered, at the gable-end and I wondered if I ever would and just how useless Colin Quinn could be.

'*Oidhche mhath, ma-thà*,'[161] said Steafan with practised neutrality. 'Thanks again for the lift.'

Ruairidh did get a call: at around 2.15am. One of the Banff boys had leapt off an old MacBrayne's bus and fractured his lower leg; Eric Adams set it under general anaesthetic just as the mid-summer sun was rising.

---
[161] Good night, then

Chapter 21

I am mere history, Oisean thought, understanding immediately what had happened. For every day he had spent on Tìr nan Òg he'd lost a year in the Gàidhealtachd. Having been almost a year on Tìr nan Òg, some three hundred years had passed at home.

With a heavy heart he pointed the white horse in a westerly direction. But before they had gone far, two lads stopped him and asked if he might help move a boulder from the middle of the road. Oisean, the son of Fionn MacCumhail, could not refuse.

THE WEATHER ON Sunday had been dry, but a long lie after the wedding exertions and Ruairidh's need to dissect (in lay terms!) every fibre of the bash, foiled any plans I might have had to climb Ben More.

Monday was foul, though my little rucksack was packed and the cheese sannies sat wrapped in the pantry. Ruairidh had agreed to take me to Stoneybridge road-end for 7.00am and rose to put the kettle on but didn't bother waking me.

'Maybe tomorrow, Colin?' he said. 'Or Wednesday? It's supposed to blow over. This is now July, after all. You can still come with me if you want, they're always asking after you: Theresa, Norma's daughters, *Caoimhin nam Pìob*.'

I had let him listen to some recent spoils but hadn't told him yet of Jane's request that I return today: Alasdair had something special to relate. Her children would be in Carinish for the week, so she could be in Milton to support her uncle. While Jane's presence was a definite plus early on, I was now proud of my solo achievements with the old man. Saturday night's strange intensity at the wedding had also made me less keen to spend time in a confined space with his grand-niece.

It was obviously irresponsibly fated – if not meant – that I should attend. Plausible excuses were found for Ruairidh, plus a promise of: 'I'll definitely come out with you by the end of the week, Alasdair's been asking…'

'Don't worry, *a Chailein*! If you are in a good furrow stay there. You're doing awfully well.'

Ruairidh anticipated a straightforward morning, so I should get a lift down with him after lunch. 'It is, though, Colin, the unexpected stuff that gets me still,' he said. 'One minute you're jogging along quite the thing, the next you're knee-deep in whatever.'

I tried to use the time to sort through some files and begin mentally to plan for packing at the weekend. I'd have to remember some eggs for Dad plus crowdie for Mum. Should I get some small presents for James and the sisters? I couldn't think of anything for sale in Uist they'd really want – the days of last-minute trinkets in Oban were surely over? Perhaps a few more eggs – though not Frobost duck ones! – and no crowdie for my brother!

I also reviewed my notes from last week's very productive few days with Alasdair. Full transcriptions were out of the question, but I wished to add detail from memory and re-listening to the more significant items. By doing so, I could prompt more usefully today when silence befell him or if he became a little tangential or repetitive, though for a man of 88 he was in fine mental shape.

Ealasaid's visit was brief – now the norm for Monday morning; her own chores and shopping demanded more of her attention than on the other days. In addition, she had a 'spring cleaning' to start today. Ealasaid did three 'spring cleanings' a year: commencing early July and building towards a final large one in spring.

On reaching a blank page in my notebook, rather than scribble the heading: 'Dòmhnall Dubh and The Canna Priest', I began a letter to Patricia.

My style, initially stilted, soon gave way to some lighter banter on our relative dancing abilities, and I did offer my apologies regarding the second Wedding Reel.

'Anyway,' I thought and wrote, perhaps it would be 'fun' to try out some dancing in Glasgow, though we could always start with a cup of coffee if she felt my feet were beyond hope. I wished her well in teacher training and was certain that with a voice like hers she'd have the kids mesmerised and eating out of her hand.

I'd post it from Oban or Greenock – allow her to get back to Uist soon after its arrival if not before. She hadn't said for how long she and her brother would be 'out', though Steafan's mention of previous sporting success at the Highland Games and this year's opposition suggested it wouldn't be more than a fortnight.

I slid the letter safely into a side pocket of my new, still chemical-smelling suitcase, and found a flat key there too. I'd hardly thought of my housemates for weeks: Rob was in France on the trail of some post-graduation contacts, while Jim was back working in his dad's farm in Auchterarder. Neither of the two ever had resits. We shared quite a driven domestic milieu; my problem was that I'd spent too much time elsewhere and paid the price.

I did, though, reckon that my 'concerned' tutors and 'patient' Advisor of Studies were going to get a pleasant surprise in early autumn: Uist had done the trick – donated its silence plus an acute lack of friends.

'Will you not come in a minute?' I asked Ruairidh as we drew in behind Jane's blue van in Milton. There was no sign that the weather was in any hurry to change: bucketing down, it was.

'No, no,' he said, 'I've got a young woman with a dirty throat. She pleaded with Eric not to send her off, as their kids are still small, so, we're injecting her with Penicillin four times a day – at home. Wouldn't get that in Glasgow, or in Duns! Or here for the first ten years of my career; it simply didn't exist, Colin. Every chance that young mother would have died. Good old Fleming. "Didn't we do well" – the Scots!'

'Ok, *ma-thà*, I'll get a lift home.'

'You'll have to,' my uncle said, peering through the windscreen. 'And tell Alasdair, I'll do a final check on his shingles before the end of the week.'

'What will I say to her?'

'Who? Jane? You'll thank her yourself, I'm sure. Where would you be without her?'

Further on in my relationship with Patricia, I thought. But where would Jane be without me? All this effort and time spent together had been important for her. I understood that and was glad of it.

Alasdair appeared unchanged: sitting prepared and ready to impart. Jane, though, was wearing much smarter clothes than normal, mirroring the *bodach's* trim attire. I wondered where she might be heading or where she had been. Why all the makeup again?

My chest gave a tight, painful, heave and I raised my hand to rub it; Jane knew I liked Patricia. A casual observer could have worked that out on Saturday night. Unless I was totally off track and that having dolled herself up for the wedding and then church yesterday, she simply wasn't ready to throw on the dungarees and those tough boots?

'Was at the lawyer this morning,' she clarified. 'Could easily have called for you.' She didn't add anything, but I inferred she wasn't sure I'd want to return to Milton today. How clearly had she felt my thoughts during The Wedding Reel?

'*Tha sgeul shònraichte agaibh dhomh an-diugh?*'[162] I asked Alasdair, having refused tea until later.

'Do I?' he turned to Jane.

'Of course you do. Just wait a second until I remember...' this was beginning to feel uncomfortable. Perhaps this should be my last visit.

'The old man, *an e*?' Alasdair said to save the day.

"*S e, s e!*' Jane exclaimed – genuinely, I judged.

'Who was this old man?' I asked himself.

'A *bodach* the Fèinn met, after spending a long, tiring, wet day on Beinn Ghulbainn and not a glimpse of a beast to be seen: a stag or roe deer, not even a hare.'

Our *bodach* was off, and Jane's relaxing back into her armchair and lighting a cigarette gave some comfort.

'And then,' said Alasdair mac Sheumais Bhig, 'when the gang were about heading for home, what did they see through the mist but a large stone building. As they got closer, they realised this was a castle – just as posh as their own in Almu.'

Jane met my smile appropriately and kindly; she really was an enigmatic character.

'Straight in they went because they were starving, but the whole place was in darkness, save the faintest glimmer from a corner right up at the back of the Great Hall.

'The Fèinn made for the light, where they met the *bodach* huddled over a fire with hardly a live ember in the hearth. That was the only light there was – the only heat – and this old bent man was blocking it.'

Alasdair stretched over and adjusted some strands of tobacco in his pipe before placing it slowly and carefully in his mouth. Jane did the honours with her lighter and steadied it while Bodach Gheàrraidh Bhailteis drew well with collapsed cheeks.

'"*Suidhibh!*"'[163] Alasdair barked, and I thought at first,

---

162 You've a special story for me today?
163 Sit [plural and with respect]!

he was referring – with mock respect – to Jane, but he was back in the lonely castle. 'So, they all sat on the floor in front of the fireplace. The mighty heroes of the Fèinn sitting on a cold, stone, floor at the command of an old, ragged fellow they had never met before.

'They were numb, and you could hear their bellies rumbling, but nothing more was said. They sat there as quiet as little mice just looking at each other and at the old man.'

Time was now gone, its relativity undisputed. The new spool of my recorder appeared sensitive to the relaxed telling and scene setting of this story, though I did have to make a quick grab, twist, turn and reel-on about three-quarters of the way through. Fortunately, Alasdair's pause was aptly generous – perhaps he'd had an eye on the machine too.

Sgeul shònraichte – a truly special story – and a most challenging night for the heroes of Scotland and Ireland:

A craggy wedder knocks Fionn flat on his back, but the old boy easily lifts the animal tying its feet as if it were a pet lamb.

After a fine supper Diarmad charms their stunning waitress, only for her to slap the handsome swordsman, then fiercely chide him. 'You didn't respect me when you had me and now you think you can just get me back. Get lost!' Diarmad swears he has never seen the woman in his life.

The Fèinn enjoy a good night's sleep in warm beds and a hearty breakfast. As they prepare to leave, MacCumhail thanks the *bodach* for his hospitality, but asks him if he might unravel the riddles of the night before.

Alasdair laid his pipe on the edge of the stove and cleared his lungs. Jane sat forward on her seat. The mascara accentuated her large, attractive, eyes and made them much more rounded.

'"The sheep," the *bodach* says to Fionn, "is life. And no matter how much you try to fight against her, your own life will always get the better of you."

'"Yes," replies MacCumhail, "I understand."

'"The beautiful maiden, she is youth. When you have her, you do not value her as you should. But as soon as you lose her, you will never, ever, get her back again!"

'"*Seadh dìreach*," said Fionn, "That's very clear."

'"And" said the *bodach*, rising,' Alasdair rose too, with a wobble, then firmly on his two smallish feet. '"I am Death. And you better watch out because I put my mark on everything!"'

'There you are,' he said, after a long pause. 'That's a story for you – a very special one.'

'Full of truthfulness,' Jane added.

'Packed-full,' her great-uncle agreed, as he sat back down and worked his tongue round his exercised lips. Jane took this as a signal to make the tea, to which she added pancakes to her mother's round scone. Alasdair had done his work for the day. Nothing more was offered nor demanded of him.

The rain had stopped by the time Jane and I ventured outside.

'No, never before,' she assured me, as we stood on the threshold opposite the peat-stack – the drain through the croft had flooded, I noticed. 'That's the first time I've heard it. He had some other *bodach* on Friday. What a cracker, though, eh?'

'The best, but maybe not one you'd immediately tell a little girl?'

'No,' she smiled, 'You're right there. I'll take you home, will I, *a Chailein*?' Jane made no attempt to go and kept her gaze firmly on my face, which then moved down to my lips. Her hands took mine in hers – gently stroking both palms. A full bladder of tea was now insisting I pay it attention – a useful way to break this tension, stop what was becoming hot, dangerous and frankly daft.

Twenty-year-olds, however, do not always do the right

thing, or at least the right thing at the right time. There may, on occasion, be a disconnect between logic and action.

Catrìona MacNeil had embarked on a new relationship in Barra and hadn't rushed to inform me of any problems. Patricia, of the beautiful voice and nimble feet, had embarked on an early ferry: no promises made, nor commitments discussed, my silly note apt to rot on reaching Oban's grim reality. There was no doubt that Jane and I had bonded strongly through our sharing in a unique culture, expressed sublimely; and she looked really quite different 'all dolled-up'.

Jane's lips were now pushing themselves on mine and my own parting to receive her mint-freshened tongue. Large firm breasts raised, and placed tightly against my thin shirt, were comforting and keenly arousing. Our lives were solely in the present, our youth intact.

I thought, at first, we had moved nearer the stack and that I was leaning against a particularly hard, tubular, lump of peat. Jane's sudden release of grip and backwards step told me otherwise.

'Hands-up fucker!' Ìomhair snarled in my ear, keeping the barrel of his shotgun in my right loin. I slowly raised them. 'You too, bitch!' he ordered his wife.

'*Na bi gòrach.*[164] Grow up!' she chided. 'Put that down, Ìomhair!'

The brute slapped Jane fiercely across the face – much harder than I had seen the gorgeous woman hit Diarmad in the story.

'What did I say?' he hissed, spittle spurting from his coarse mouth as he thrust the gun now in her direction. 'You fuckin too, whore!'

Jane raised her shaking hands and placed them behind her head. Ìomhair motioned for us to walk round and away from the far side of the stack – further from the house.

---

[164] Don't be stupid!

It was as if we had been caught, unwittingly, on the film-set of a low-budget Western. Ìomhair's ham-acting and stiff deportment would have been risible, were this not actually happening and the hateful clown aiming a double-barrel shotgun straight at us. Alasdair would presume his 'wee favourite' had driven me home. Ìomhair had kept the volume down and Jane's retorts were similarly muted.

Now we were standing well out of the 88-year-old's earshot, in a hollow I hadn't appreciated to be quite so deep. We were invisible, except to ourselves. My painful bladder threatened to burst and soak my clean cords. Might a neighbour just decide to call over to Alasdair's – see how he was keeping? That, surely, was about all it would take for Ìomhair to stop all this nonsense and behave himself. What time was it anyway? Where was the sun – far out west towards Tìr nan Òg?

I heard mac Sheumais Bhig's beautifully intoned respect of non-violence:

'There was a fellow in Uist at the time they called Oisean. *Oisean mac Fhinn ac Cumhail* – Ossian the son of Finn MacCool, but he didn't enjoy fighting and warring… and he never killed a man.'

'Right,' Ìomhair said in a much more controlled, darker, voice. 'Do it!' A sneer of a smile contorted his ugly face.

'Do what?' Jane's words were barely audible, from dry, tremulous, lips – which she couldn't stop touching with agitated fingers.

'What you would have done if I'd stayed just a bit longer at my sister's, because you're both so very clever. Or are you?'

I looked at her and could see terror in her eyes. Ìomhair meant this. Had he planned it all along; just biding his time – today's arrival the much dreamt of denouement? Catching us kissing must have given it to him on a sordid plate.

Of course, on another day with the sun high in the sky,

Gille Padara Dubh would simply have knocked the gun from the creep's hand with one deft blow, then speared a soaring bird: *'whose last shit creamed his head and filled his foul mouth!'* But plucky heroes like these – real or otherwise – were stuck back in the robust justice of fabled yore.

'Get your breeks down and do it,' Ìomhair barked.

'No, please!' She begged him, 'Please, please. No! I don't want to.' She extended her arms and began sobbing. 'This is Colin. He's nice. We're friends. Just let me be, Ìomhair, *a ghràidh.*'

'They are all nice; they are all friends; in the whore's den!' he shrieked, with a look of madness, as if preaching to a gathering of the depraved.

Steafan MacInnes's casual derision of Jane and her ways reverberated loudly in my head. This wouldn't be the first time. Had Ìomhair, though, chosen me – and my friendship with Jane – to push his vile game further?

'No! No more!' Jane screamed and I lunged at the bully.

'Now!' he roared, firing at my feet, before stepping back calmly. A fever raged through his eyes as his forefinger squeezed the trigger again. 'Now, *nice* Colin,' he menacingly stage whispered. 'Right now, I said.'

Jane rolled down her new bell-bottoms and then her pants. I tore at my belt and ripped open my buttoned fly before turning away to urinate with my back to them. When I was eventually empty, she passed me a clean tissue: the act terrified me, but I made sure to remove all traces from my penis before starting to pull my pants back on.

'Best get on with it,' Jane's flat voice uttered as she stood with her pale, plump, bottom towards me and her legs apart.

Why ever did my foolish mother make me join her grieving brother in Uist this summer? Where the hell was she now? *Where are you, Mum?* I shouted through my pained, palpitating, heart. *Mum, Mum! Where are you?*

But no one heard the feeblest bleat, and about twenty yards from where I had just received an elegant, mystical, story on the meaning of life and the futility of trying to outsmart one's own, I invaded Jane MacDonald.

I was first to climax – the toxic hurt surging into my groin – but Ìomhair waited until he witnessed his wife coming before spurting semen at her wretched, bereft, face.

I walked the four miles home – stopping twice to retch in the ditch and once to cry.

Ìomhair was a cunt. A total fucking bastard cunt!

Chapter 22

Oisean grips the saddle with one hand, and stretches the other down and under the boulder. 'One, two, three!' he shouts, and they move it a little towards the ditch. Oisean then gets his fingers fully underneath and they move the stone further. 'This time, friends!' he cries, taking his feet out of the stirrups and reaching with his arm as far as possible. The three of them push the huge weight and it begins to roll much more easily, when suddenly the straps under Oisean's saddle snap and he falls backwards onto the ground.

As soon as Oisean hits the earth that young, handsome, man turns into an old wizened bodach of three hundred years of age. The startled white horse howls in disgust and bolts west towards Tìr nan Òg.

THE VIEW FROM Ben More for miles around was amazing, but Ìomhair MacDonald remained a heinous beast: the most despicable 'fucking bastard cunt' that ever walked the planet.

This guy was a father of young children and an accepted member of the community, if a bit 'rough round the edges'. Sub-human vermin, he was!

Of course, I should have gone straight to the police – filed an accusatory report to get the pervert done, but I feared the repercussions for Jane.

Ìomhair would have insisted he'd arrived to find the two of us *in flagrante* and that this, understandably, had angered him. He'd have made sure she washed herself well and would have been able to give an account of all the time I'd spent alone with his wife and an elderly man: opportunities galore to get to know her better. He'd bribe witnesses who'd seen us dance The Wedding Reel; perhaps others knew of Jane's supposed reputation, it was unlikely Steafan found this buried in the sand of Eòrasdail beach.

Ìomhair would point to the same mental instability – his wife's difficulty controlling her urges and a lack of involvement with the children; he'd had no choice but to take them down to his sister in North Uist.

Ìomhair MacDonald was a foul thug but not an idiot. He knew how things worked. Having delayed my actions, I would then be far more likely to let them go when I left, which would be in four days' time.

He would also have judged, correctly, that such a story – no matter our innocence – would tarnish my uncle's standing in the community. He might never return.

So, I kept it all inside and later ate my steak pie, potatoes and peas listening as best I could to Ruairidh's account of his day. The woman with tonsillitis had improved though still needed to rest. Her husband was doing a great job with house and kids: *'duine ceart!'*[165]

Feigning tiredness, I had filled the bath near to the brim and allowed my corrupted flesh to sink below.

Gazing out, now, from Uist's highest hill, I could clearly see Eriskay and Barra sitting carefreely to the south and felt a painful urge to be with my own family in the safety of their love. Mum, though, was back in Greenock and the focus of the others would be elsewhere i.e. prodigal Aonghas's return. I couldn't bear the thought of meeting Catrìona – our youthful affection and respect defiled perhaps forever.

To the west stood St Kilda, Hirta. '*Oh nach tu bha an t-Hiort!*'[166] a popular rebuke. If only I were on St Kilda and

---
165 A fine chap
166 If you were only in St Kilda!

removed from this horrid reality.

A deer appeared and stared. Sabha, the mother of Oisean and lover of Fionn MacCumhail, inspected the sub-human species before her. 'You were cursed, Colin,' she said, 'by the inadequacy of your own life. You got involved with them, although you could tell from the start they were "touched".

'Think about it: the *bodach*, to whom his brother no longer speaks, a silent artist for decades? His quaint wee minder who, when not combing the beach for randy cattle, just loves sitting smoking and listening to her great-uncle's stories – in the modernity of 1978? Those lost, feral, kids who run amok somewhere far off physically and emotionally? Big, mean, anti-Peruvian Ìomhair – the twisted Hebridean male archetype – trying desperately to surpass his stereotype and succeeding with you anyway?

'Patricia and Steafan – is that all as it seems? And there's your own poor Uncle Ruairidh, hanging on for dear life to a past that held meaning and purpose for him: an important person in a small world; a provider within the defining safety of a loving, growing, departed, family?

'Take a good look at yourself, sonny!' the half-fairy beast reproached. 'I've seen it all, believe you me! But you need to get some perspective on your life, *"Before it completely defeats you!"'*

Bàrr na Beinne Mòire offered this and more and it shared the magnitude of my depravity with the Clisham, Skye's Cullins and Mull's own highest hill. Irrevocable it seemed too, but the splendour of Gleann Healasdail did seem to offer some possible clemency; so, I began running as best I could. Who wouldn't have in my position?

Less than an hour later, in the glen of the neighbouring giant, Corrodale, I was brought back down to earth with a sense of serenity – its stunning pristine cove and a few abandoned croft-houses huddled close to the river, *Abhainn Chorghadail*.

Alasdair had told me a brief anecdote on the death of an old woman out here, and how the efforts to carry her makeshift coffin were 'heard' months before she passed away.

I found two caves that might have sheltered The Young Pretender (a man also on the run from his conscience?) and left a message in a bottle in each.

In the first I wrote:

'Colin Quinn (20) visited Corrodale – Tuesday 4 July 1978. Good luck to all who find this. May America use her independence wisely!'

And in the second:

'*Bha Cailean Quinn – aois fichead – an seo air a' cheathramh latha de mhìos meadhanach an t-samhraidh sa bhliadhna naoi ceud deug trì fichead agus a h-ochd-deug. Cuin a thàinig sibhse?*'[167]

I then sat at the shore, ate my two-day-old sandwiches and downed a flask of tea. No ghosts of old – Bonnie Prince Charlie included – pursued me. After paddling for a few minutes in the freezing water, I ripped off my clothes and leapt into the sea to begin splashing myself from head to foot with salt water, screaming with the pain of the assault – screaming and screaming with the pain of the assault!

On dry land, the hairs stood shocked on my shrivelled scrotum as I rubbed with my cotton second layer, to get pants on. The sun warmed my spine and the backs of my legs, allowing this part of the process to proceed a little less frantically.

My toxic body felt much more alert. Was this what the deer of my conscience was alluding to – a deep, personal, rousing perspective?

The journey back out was a slog through the boggy moorland and took far longer than I'd expected; how did

---

[167] Cailean Quinn – aged twenty was here on the fourth day of the middle month of summer in the year nineteen hundred three twenties and eighteen. When did you (polite) come?

they ever manage to heave a coffin up and over there if not by the strength of purpose, necessity and faith?

I saw no further deer but spotted a pair of eagles and met a German naturalist with fortified banana loaf and robust Gaelic – which he spoke throughout our brief encounter at Loch Iarras. He also had a map. I had trusted my sense of east-to-west and the weather remaining fair. Neither, fortunately, let me down.

Ruairidh's accounts of those caught unaware in these hills belonged to another day, another time. Summer's gentleness had protected me, but would it or any other benign forces ever let me escape my rank carcass (like a rotten selkie!) to find it there on my return having been washed, hung out and folded neatly.

The following week I went to Confession, for the first time in ages, in a church near Glasgow's Mitchell Library. The hidden, unknown, priest listened without interruption and did not pass judgement. The cleansing activities, he advised, could continue if they were 'incrementally beneficial', but to stop them if they became a burden in themselves. His order that I say a Decade of the Rosary – 'with your full heart and mind' – hurt like no previous tokenistic penance. My efforts also earned frequent mental sighs and admonitions from Ealasaid. '*Nach tuirt mi riut, a Chailein!*'[168]

I never returned to thank Alasdair and wondered what knowledge he had of Ìomhair and Jane's odious mess. 'It is inauspicious,' I told Ruairidh 'to bid someone farewell a second time.' He visited him on the Thursday and was most satisfied with the recession of the shingles rash. They then talked about Highland courting customs. Jane was absent.

My uncle thanked mac Sheumais Bhig for what he had given so generously and asked him to sign documents allowing The Scottish Archive to care for his lore in Edinburgh.

---

[168] Did I not warn you, Colin?

'But Alasdair,' Ruairidh had said, 'this second form gives permission for your work to be kept here in Uist too. We must find the right place for it, and we will!'

With that, he handed over a bottle of Bell's at which the *bodach* shook his head, muttering disapproval, but never lost his grip. 'For the New Year,' Ruairidh pressed. 'Or if someone nice visits?'

I couldn't really see Alasdair giving Jane a dram. Sweets and cigarettes, yes, but not whisky; she had helped herself that time – the one and only time. For very different reasons he would not offer Ìomhair either.

Tormod Mòraig poured me a large glass, which I had to accept when I visited him later that same day. If he was surprised to see me it didn't show at all, and we both heard the news that Willie Johnston would face a lifetime international football ban. The rumour was that the SFA would approach Celtic's Jock Stein to take over at the helm.

Tormod Mòraig also made a point of telling me that Patricia had returned home alone and was apparently 'asking after me: when did I plan to leave?'

Her receiving a letter from me might suffice, but I wouldn't be sending it any time soon – if at all; the horror of what happened in Milton had consumed every other clean romantic thought.

On the Friday I accompanied Ruairidh on his last day of calls, stopping in at Murchadh Caol and Oighrig Thomais's to thank them also. Clearly, this hadn't been the most productive field trip for my uncle; too much getting in the way (my enjoyment in Uist included) but I knew, also, that he was thrilled by my success with Alasdair mac Sheumais Bhig. It wasn't just the material I'd collected, but that I had been sufficiently interested and motivated to do so, for him.

I wondered whether I'd ever try such work again. Mum's stories, while perhaps of a more domestic genre, merited retention for future generations. Dad certainly wouldn't do it, nor my sisters. James might.

On the Friday evening, we sat at a rather awkward table in The Lochboisedale Hotel with Eric Adams ('a taciturn man in company'), Mgr Pàdraig, a new district nurse and Ealasaid – attending under duress.

A bottle of Chianti helped ease the discourse and Mgr Pàdraig proved an engaging, inclusive, raconteur – when not trying to bully me off my chosen path. He knew how to help Ealasaid relax too, which she did, eventually, following an embarrassing, hilarious, mid-sentence burp. The Chicken in a Basket was very much to her liking and afterwards she couldn't resist rice-pudding. 'I never take anything I would make at home.'

'And you're saying you can't make that stuff, Ealasaid?' Ruairidh asked, with feigned or true incredulity.

'I can,' she admitted, 'but mine always has the taste of turned milk.'

It struck me then that for the first time in weeks – Anndra and Seonag's house in Barra, in fact – I was in the company of someone who mightn't follow Gaelic. Until that point, we had spoken only English.

Eric's inscrutable face did not confirm or refute this theory, but the chat swiftly switched 'spokes' – via a Mgr Pàdraig story on Seminary Semolina – and stayed there the rest of the night. No urgent case pulled either doctor away, which was a blessing, though had Eric received a call I'm sure the social effort would have eased. The stuffy, stiff-seated, dining room in the hotel probably played its part too. It wasn't a late night.

Loud, unfamiliar, ringing, however, woke me at around 4.30am and I immediately feared I'd overslept; fortunately, Ruairidh was able to offer some advice to the caller – from Fròbost! – which gave her and him a modicum of comfort.

Neither of us rose until after 10.00am. Ealasaid had made only toast and tea and was awaiting instructions on the rest.

We both pleaded very little appetite and buttered our toast carefully. She would be back at one *and* again for our evening meal! This being our last weekend in Eòrasdail, we accepted. 'But a light lunch, Ealasaid,' Ruairidh insisted. 'A wee sandwich, a salad even?' Nothing was promised.

After a walk through the village, the occasional car stopping – none containing Patricia – we both cracked on with our packing, stopping only briefly for Scotch Broth. Having someone to plan and cook meals was so helpful at this point, and Ealasaid's gathering various stray items meant little was forgotten. Ruairidh apparently did leave a *cromag*,[169] gifted by a grateful patient, but perhaps he meant to pass it on to the next locum, whoever that might be; just as it was my clear intention to donate *Thinking of Being a Doctor?* to him or her and their families.

Young Mìcheal MacLeod, of the *tubaist*, who'd got out of hospital on the Monday, then appeared with his mother bearing a massive salmon. 'It wasn't him that caught it!' his mum declared – her son wasn't a poacher! 'But he thought to give it to you.' The boy's freckly face reddened.

'*Tapadh leibhse*,' Ruairidh replied, 'I'll just have to run that bath; after all this time.' This got a laugh.

'No, you won't!' Ealasaid pushed. 'That one's swimming days are over. I'll put him into the new chest freezer. It will have de-frosted by the time you reach home tomorrow night.'

'And what do we do in the morning, *ma-thà*?' my uncle asked, after our tea of liver, kidney and onions. ('Without the onions,' I later joked to Dad, 'the meal would have been offal!')

'You'll get up at 5.15am. You'll then be in the queue on Lochboisedale pier before six.'

---

[169] a walking stick

'I know that,' he snapped. Ealasaid had reminded us twice when we needed to arrive and therefore when we should rise. 'About the fish?' he asked more gently.

'We'll both be there waiting for you,' she confirmed. 'I was coming anyway.'

Later when sorting my notes and folders, I tried giving Ruairidh back his *Ancient Celtic Tales*, to which he replied, 'You're the one who'll make best use of it.'

He also refused the slips of cardboard, on which he had scribbled the medical terms. 'So "Pathognomonic" means, Colin, that if this sign or symptom is present: bingo you've got the diagnosis. Whatever the heck "Pseudocyesis" is, or was, I have no idea. Obviously didn't need to either over the last 40-odd years. Keep the lot, lad – they might help keep this summer holiday for you.'

Oh dear, dear, if only such simple items, or my future listening back to the voice of Alasdair mac Sheumais Bhig, could do that for me: keep the summer. At one point last week they might have – after a little while at home to allow some of the strangeness of my experience to ebb gently.

Ìomhair's base violation had robbed me of this otherworldly and intellectual innocence. It had tainted my now close and cordial relationship with my uncle. My not telling him anything drove my guilt further, deeper, below my 'cheerful' demeanour.

A week or so ago I might have visited Patricia – as was expected. She wouldn't now make an unsolicited call; she could only do this when we were getting to know each other – before she'd sung and met my eyes and accepted a high polite percentage of dances.

Now that she'd returned by boat without Steafan, it was my place to call in and say goodbye; chat casually, clearly state no romantic interest in Jane, wish her a good summer and suggest a possible rendezvous in Glasgow in the autumn.

Ruairidh and I finished our preparations around 11.30pm and both set alarm clocks with booming ticks.

I woke half an hour before mine was due to sound and must have fallen back asleep – to a most vivid, jumbled, dream:

'It's okay,' Patricia was reassuring me, at the top of Ben More. 'It didn't happen. Jane swears it didn't, so does Ealasaid. It's just an Ìomhair Dubh ruse – he's not THAT bad! Let's do a schottische.'

'So?' I said, relieved and out of breath, 'Does that let us date, *ma-thà*?'

'Well...' she started.

'Well?' I asked her and myself as I leapt out of bed to silence the din; then the grim reality reasserted itself.

At Lochboisedale pier, I gave Ealasaid a brief kiss and then a longer hug – having stowed the salmon in a safe cool-box in the back seat of Ruairidh's packed wee sports car.

'Next year then, boys?' she asked.

'We'll see,' Ruairidh replied, 'what God brings us in the coming months. It was truly excellent though.'

I knew I should say something positive about the future, but I couldn't. Nor could I lie. I felt sure I would never be back in Uist – in any capacity.

'Yes,' I said, 'It was good and thanks very much, Ealasaid, for everything you did for us. I couldn't...'

The tears in her eyes stopped me from completing my sentence. Here was a sweet woman who thrived on caring for others – especially 'helpless or useless men'. Her type, at her age, wouldn't exist that much longer, ten to fifteen years maybe – three World Cups worth? How many males like us would tend to the needs of a house of 'useless' women? Very few, I reckoned. Women too deserved their turn of indulgence: the recording of tradition-bearers might be a good place to start.

It was when the ferry set sail that I spotted Jane. She was squatting – as she had been in Milton – on a slippery-looking ledge below the hotel. Its hardy black cannon had her head in its sights. Only this time Jane's arms were wrapped around her and her clothes were back to the drab variety.

I waved and she moved her head in response but kept her arms tightly round her body. Seeing her like this made me want to tell Ruairidh or call the police, do something of practical benefit, but the boat continued its seven-hour journey across the Minch and impotent anger gave way to paralysing shame.

'What a guy, *a Mhàiri*!' Ruairidh exclaimed, kissing his long-lost sister in Greenock. 'If you'd seen the amount of work Colin did. Unstoppable. He'll go far, this one.'

My mother hugged me close. 'A good time had by all then, *a Chailein*? You're terribly pale looking, son!'

'A great holiday,' I assured her. 'Where's Dad?'

'Backshift.'

'Of course.'

'Your tea's ready,' she pressed Ruairidh, 'and a bed made for you. What's the use in going all the way to Duns tonight?'

'Habit,' he replied and kept to it, leaving our house about quarter to ten.

Chapter 23

Now, I don't know how long Oisean spent back in the Gàidhealtachd; he may not even have survived the day. But one thing I know for certain is that he never set eyes on Niamh or Tìr nan Òg again... chan fhaca gu dearbha, riamh tuilleadh.[170]

A FEW DAYS after learning I had passed my exams, ('With aplomb' in Psychology, Big Ron told me in confidence) Ruairidh phoned. Alasdair mac Sheumais Bhig had died two days previously; Ealasaid thought we'd want to know. It had been a brief illness and Jane remained at his side 'the whole time'. His funeral would be the next morning – beyond the reach of any ferries or planes. *'Fois is sìth dhur n-anam'*,[171] I thought, and wondered had Ealasaid taken an executive decision regarding our attendance or had Ruairidh presumed I wouldn't want to go and not rushed to tell me.

I immediately set to work: listening back, transcribing word for word and editing my summaries of every item Alasdair had contributed – forty-seven in total.

I copied these pages on the swanky new university machine and drove them with the box of reel-to-reel tapes to my uncle's large house in Duns. Only one story did I pirate onto my own cassette recorder: *Oisean ann an Tìr nan Òg*. Despite its sad ending, I found it hopeful and imbued with true pathos, it was also told 'with aplomb' – Jane's interjection pure, unsullied. Could I carry this guilt much longer?

---

[170] No, never again
[171] May your soul rest in peace

'Time to downsize, *a Chailein*,' Ruairidh said, as he poured a cup of coffee from his percolator. 'Do you remember the old house in Eoligarry?'

I nodded. I'd spent two summers there before Gran agreed to something more modern.

'Ten of us lived there and now I'm rattling around in this place like some lost lord. It's ridiculous. I was thinking of Argyll – *Tìr na Fèinne*, by the Rest and Be Thankful – a two-bedroom cottage. Be in Oban or Glasgow in about an hour. You'd visit, wouldn't you?'

'Of course,' I assured him. But wouldn't his daughters prefer to return with their families to where they had grown up, in Duns? Could they all fit into a wee Hieland but and ben?

'Yes, well, you have a point there, Colin. Some compromise required obviously.'

We chatted easily – our Uist bond still strong – and listened to my first recording of Alasdair mac Sheumais Bhig, preceded, of course, by my practice run with Ruairidh.

'We didn't tape any more on your life,' I said. 'When shall I come to do it?'

'Don't worry, *a Chailein*. Compared to Alasdair, Nan, Murchadh Caol and these people I don't have much worth recording.'

'Rubbish!' I challenged. 'Right, *a Ruairidh*, give me that machine,' I started, microphone in hand. 'You were saying that it was through your aunt's help that you were able to attend St Andrews. What was it like for a young islander there in the '30s and '40s?'

My uncle's answers were full and considered and often wittily delivered. I learnt more factually about his life that afternoon than in six weeks in Uist. I had of course gleaned other things about Ruairidh during our time together: duty, tenacity, friendship – much more. What had he learned about me? What hadn't he learnt?

'First week back here,' he said, when we had finished, 'the other practice phoned and asked me to do a locum – Dr Julie's wee lad was sick. I agreed without giving it much thought. They're a nice bunch and always helped us if they could.' Buttoning my jacket, I scanned Ruairidh's tasteful, high-ceilinged, sitting room for a source of heating – a radiator perhaps. 'But that's it, *a Chailein*. I won't do another one – there or anywhere else. Uist was special: it has moved me on too, regarding Emily. I hoped it would and of course, you...'

'They'd have you back in a shot,' I pushed – why, I don't know, if only to prolong his or my own mortality. 'What about a shorter spell at Easter – fewer tourists about?'

My uncle laughed. His summer workload hadn't exactly been deluged by the demands of the hardy campers and caravaners.

'No,' he said, 'Enough's enough, but I am planning to spend time in Barra in the autumn – visiting and recording. There's a woman in Breivig...'

'And why not!' I half-shouted.

'Exactly, *a Chailein*. Why not, now?'

I enjoyed the cross-country drive back to Greenock and felt quite excited for Ruairidh. New freedoms meant new choices, some, perhaps, more honest than he'd ever previously allowed himself. I was also enthusiastic about being back in the big city with another year ahead of me as a student – one who would work consistently, this time. My energy levels certainly should be better now I was swallowing iron tablets three times a day.

'Really quite anaemic,' Mum's GP confirmed cheerily, the week after she'd first dragged me there. 'No wonder you've been tired. Cold also, Colin? Been on one of those new-fangled vegetarian diets over the summer, have you?'

'Hardly,' my brusque reply. I did though continue taking the pills for a good six months. Despite numerous tests, they never discovered the cause, and I never said a word to Ruairidh.

Nor had I uttered a word to him or anyone else (bar the Glasgow priest) about *Bodach-Bàis*[172] – the day Ìomhair put his vile mark of death on my carefree youth and dealt his wife such a heinous, debasing, blow. The letter I wrote on a pawnshop typewriter, and posted from Dundee, gave the Northern Constabulary more than enough information to start investigations. I trust they did, and that Jane was brave enough to comply.

Having still not sent that light-hearted, signed letter to Patricia, I considered cycling with it, one lovely crisp October morning, to Notre Dame's Halls of Residence; then a sudden darkening over Gilmorehill spire tempered my bravado and kept Uist and its secrets at bay.

Pat must have kept a low profile that year or else our circles just didn't overlap; I wasn't really one to frequent the Highland bars. By the time I'd transferred to Edinburgh for '79–80 we still hadn't met.

Five years later, a woman on a Stagecoach bus informed me that a Welshman had 'won her trust', and that they were living 'down there somewhere'. She made no mention of Jane MacDonald.

'Is Ruairidh Gillies,' she asked, as we grabbed our bags, 'your uncle?'

'Yes,' I replied.

'Well tell him the girl from the Crooked River, whose life he saved, is asking for him.'

I did, that night, and while most grateful, Ruairidh was unable to recall her: 'Kathleen, you said? It couldn't actually have happened **in** the Crooked River,' he said in his defence. 'You'd think I'd remember that!'

'You would,' I agreed and confirmed the time and place

---
[172] Old Man Death

of my dad's retirement do: 6.00pm at Oak's Tavern by Anderston Bus Depot on 30 August.

'Planning a speech?' Ruairidh probed.

'Absolutely,' I said. 'As good as you'd get from Alasdair mac Sheumais Bhig.'

May 2018

'Write about what you know': the workshop maxim often given to new aspirants. I had no wish to be a writer, or to trawl for fodder in the trough of a sealed-off past, but Kim was a positive, sensitive, facilitator and my attendance at her sessions – initially under (Ealasaid-esque!) duress – became crucial to healing.

My wife's sudden death had floored me; with no children of our own or delightful, little, Ozzie grandkids, to help ease the pain or make me try and crawl back up.

At Week 2 Kim produced a series of objects, asked us to select one and write for five minutes without stopping to think or edit. Those minutes felt like half an hour, and while nothing directly linked an old mortise key to Ovarian Cancer – the silent, wilful, slayer of beauty and spirit – I failed to stem its intrusive taunts. Rising and leaving would have meant disturbing the damp, voluble, scribbler beside me – so much more inspired, it seemed, by an Ace of Hearts.

So, I wrote:

'The right keys give access through entry points to past, present and future. If we wear them round our necks on lanyards, we will not lose them through carelessness, even when we should; even when the doors opened by them should long since have been torn from their hinges and piled on the blazing bonfire of...'

Kim called time before I could find the last word. 'Life' seemed insipid; 'existence' pretentious. And thus, it remained.

'Now,' Kim Hallington declared, 'I'd like you all to write for fifteen minutes.' The young dad opposite, recently fired from his Fitzroy employer, grimaced then groaned. The avid scribe, who'd alluded to 'another bloody breakdown', gave *her thumbs-up and a 'Good on ya, girl, ready when you are!'*

This time Kim chose our objects, handing me a fridge-magnet from the Spirit of Tasmania. *She and her partner had sailed over to spend Easter in Cradle Mountain before sampling some of Hobart's eateries – see if any approached Melbourne standards.*

I ventured no further than the ferry journey: my initial impressions of Colonsay pier; not recognising a single soul on board; wondering when and what to eat. Then the guitar duo appeared, plonked themselves down in the middle of my page, and sang as sweetly as any bona fide Beatle. I kept the demands for certain songs out of the piece but did mention a huddle of well-oiled crofters rocking home from a cattle-sale.

'Keenly observed,' Kim commented, when I'd translated the sentences, which had formed themselves, spontaneously and unapologetically.

'Do you often write Galick, Col?'

'Never.'

'A first; awesome! When roughly is it set?'

'May 1978,' my exact reply.

'The year my parents married,' she smiled. 'They chose to honeymoon in the UK, but in late October.'

By then I was back in Glasgow University doing as best I could to hide from my recent experience through earnest, regular, endeavour. It almost worked and no one came knocking on my door.

Kim's Write to Recover ran for eight weeks and my presence remained consistent, but by the end I'd had enough of mining the five senses and trying to 'show' the story rather than tell it in black and white. The discipline, though, did help lift me out of the doldrums and I was back at my desk within three months; an earlier attempt had failed badly – hence my engagement with this 'complementary' activity.

I'm telling you all this to give you some context as to

how the first seeds were planted of my attempt to broach this subject, recount my version of what happened – and it's only my version of that strange summer in Uist.

Afterwards, I let work as an Educational Psychologist, in a pushed department, curtail further delving despite Kim's enthusiasm: 'Ask yourself, Col, what is the real story I need to tell? Whose story is it?'

For years after – almost ten – the wide-ruled, eighty-page pad sat in my study, stuck between a tome on Australian flora and a tatty atlas; never opened, never thrown away. Then I saw you on stage at The Celtic Colours Festival.

In Melbourne we don't get too much trad on the terrestrials, but ABC ran a series last year on Canada and this show's focus was Cape Breton. When exactly were you there? It wasn't clear from the extract.

You have a beautiful voice and excellent Gaelic. I liked the way you introduced your songs bi-lingually. Tha do mhoit follaiseach, a nighean.[173] *My spoken fluency has atrophied since emigrating thirty years ago, though it did improve greatly, during and after that summer of 1978 – mostly just chatting and listening to Mum. I never did record her or do more with Ruairidh:* 'Ge b' e nach gabh nuair a gheibh, chan fhaigh nuair as àill!'[174] *he said, and he was dead right.*

My uncle lived longer than Alasdair mac Sheumais Bhig, but he couldn't tell you his name – never mind those of the mighty Fèinn – for the last few years. Perhaps you met him, at concerts or at The Mòd? He did quite a lot of that sort of thing and was well-respected, I believe.

It was definitely your mother's langan[175] *in your voice – that raw, natural, sound – I first recognised; you are, of course, much taller, fairer and finer-featured but, yes, with*

---
[173] Your pride is evident, young woman.
[174] He who doesn't take his chance when he has it won't get it later when he desires it.
[175] deer-sound

the same oval eyes. Apparently, my grandfather, Jim Quinn, was six-foot-two – unusual for a full-blooded Irishman, Dad reckoned – and also fair, though I only ever saw him in old black and white snaps.

You may have your own family, growing or grown-up and giving you time to sing and travel; if so, do they remember your mum? Would Jane tell them any of Alasdair's stories? I'm sorry that no one sent word of her death to me in Australia.

As I have detailed, I did write one anonymous letter, though, of course, I could and should have done much more. The guilt and shame have never gone away and probably never will.

I've resisted Googling you – though the temptation is great! – and Facebook is not my thing. I would much rather wait and learn your history face to face, heart to heart from you. I am so glad you replied to my email and have respected your request for the truth.

Being back here alone, after forty years, feels very strange! 'Eòrasdail House' ('a sumptuous, eco-friendly, dwelling for up to six sharing') has though given me time and space to write this as it should have been written and with you in mind.

So, the work is done, at least for now, and currently filed, rather old-fashionedly – but perhaps more safely – in a large manila envelope in my new, non-toxic smelling, travel bag.

I trust I will know when we have met and talked in Inverness, the most appropriate way to share my account of the summer of 1978 with you.

Perhaps I sent you a revised draft at some point in the future, that benefited from reflection and distance and a deeper knowledge of you and your life. You could even be reading (or listening to) this short accompanying note after my passing: an event for which I have no immediate plans I must say!

We'll see what's best. What is important right now is that I came to Uist and finished the story that asked to be told; and that after all those years we are in touch. I'll stop there and finish packing.

Sin agad thu, a Niamh. Thoir an aire ort fhèin.[176]
Mise le spèis,[177]
Cailean.

---

[176] There you go, Niamh. Look after yourself.
[177] Respectfully,

Acknowledgements

MANY GENEROUS PEOPLE have directly helped me or offered advice over the last few years while working on this novel, firstly in Gaelic and now in English.

I would like to express my gratitude to the following, who read earlier drafts, gave interviews or provided specific insights: Audrey Robertson and her daughter, Lesley Harley; Cailean MacLean; Jan Patience; Douglas Watt; Stuart Kelly; Johan Smith; Joan MacDonald; Michel Byrne; John Shaw; Sophy Dale and Marion Sinclair.

I would also like to record my appreciation to the following who assisted with my research in Uist and Barra: Angela MacKinnon; Iain Stephen Morrison; Ronald MacInnes; John Joseph MacDonald; David MacPherson; Murdo MacRury; Gillebride MacMillan and my late parents-in-law, Calum and Peigi MacRury.

I am most grateful to Gavin MacDougall and the whole team at Luath, especially to my editor, Kira Dowie, and to Jennie Renton, for their meticulous work, and to Amy Turnbull for creating such an attractive cover.

Taing mhòr to Alison Lang, John Storey and the team at the Gaelic Books Council who first believed in the novel and nurtured its development, and to Book Trust Scotland who further assisted this process.

Huge thanks to my wife and family for their love and ongoing support of my writing over the years – mo mhòr-bheannachd oirbh!

And finally, thank you for buying and reading the novel. I hope you enjoyed travelling to South Uist in 1978 to experience this Summer Like No Other.

Martin MacIntyre,
May 2025

Luath Press Limited

committed to publishing well written books worth reading

LUATH PRESS takes its name from Robert Burns, whose little collie Luath (*Gael.*, swift or nimble) tripped up Jean Armour at a wedding and gave him the chance to speak to the woman who was to be his wife and the abiding love of his life. Burns called one of the 'Twa Dogs' Luath after Cuchullin's hunting dog in Ossian's *Fingal*. Luath Press was established in 1981 in the heart of Burns country, and is now based a few steps up the road from Burns' first lodgings on Edinburgh's Royal Mile. Luath offers you distinctive writing with a hint of unexpected pleasures.

Most bookshops in the UK, the US, Canada, Australia, New Zealand and parts of Europe, either carry our books in stock or can order them for you. To order direct from us, please send a £sterling cheque, postal order, international money order or your credit card details (number, address of cardholder and expiry date) to us at the address below. Please add post and packing as follows: UK – £1.00 per delivery address; overseas surface mail – £2.50 per delivery address; overseas airmail – £3.50 for the first book to each delivery address, plus £1.00 for each additional book by airmail to the same address. If your order is a gift, we will happily enclose your card or message at no extra charge.

Luath Press Limited
543/2 Castlehill
The Royal Mile
Edinburgh EH1 2ND
Scotland
Telephone: 0131 225 4326 (24 hours)
Email: sales@luath.co.uk
Website: www.luath.co.uk